She Danced Anyway

by

J. J. Ranson

The Wild Rose Press, Inc.
PO Box 708
Adams Basin, NY 14410-0708
Visit us at www.thewildrosepress.com

Publishing History
First Edition, 2024
Trade Paperback ISBN 978-1-5092-5449-1
Digital ISBN 978-1-5092-5450-7

Published in the United States of America

Dedication

To Bob,
thank you for saying,
"Whatever you do, never stop writing."
It was the best encouragement from the best of men.

Acknowledgements

She Danced Anyway is a miracle. In between me snatching the story idea and this book appearing in your hands, many people worked special miracles in my life and, hence, this book.

To Bob, my darling husband, I offer the deepest gratitude. You were the first to help me make time and space for my writing, even while I was caregiving. This book is for you.

To Amy, my neighbor, friend, COVID walking buddy, and terrific story coach: those lunchtime walks were therapy for me and fuel for this story. Your inspiration is everywhere here!

To Mom: thank you for the decades of encouragement to keep pushing forward.

To my children, Sarah, Victoria, and Brandon: I appreciate your listening ears. You seemed to be paying some attention when I chatted on about my book. To Victoria, my voracious reader, thank you for reading the early drafts.

To all the other superb people in my life (hikers, wine lovers, neighbors, and church friends): Thank you for telling me you couldn't wait to read this story!

To the editors who made this better every round: Lara Zielinsky of LZ Edits, and the amazingly positive Nan Swanson at The Wild Rose Press. We wouldn't be here without your guidance.

To every book lover, librarian, and teacher out there: please keep putting your favorite books into other people's hands. I'm a writer today because of people like you in my own life.

Prologue

March 1923

Elizabeth Alter looked both ways down the alley before turning the knob on the garage's side door. Once inside, she stood still to give her eyes a minute to adjust. She hadn't appreciated the moon's brightness until she stepped out of its silver glow and into this musty darkness. Elizabeth blinked, and her father's Model T loomed in shadow to the right.

Boxes stacked against the wall on her left tilted like the Tower of Pisa. She wondered what was in them. If a box contained a blanket, all the better. Otherwise, Elizabeth needed to decide where she'd sleep tonight. It must be nearly midnight.

Elizabeth had to be out of here before Father left for his job at the bank. Her stomach lurched at the thought of being discovered here, hiding like a tramp.

She blinked into the darkness again, considering the car as a bed. Did she have another choice? *I'm definitely not sleeping on the packed earth floor!*

She sniffed the frigid air. Dirt. Oil. Leather. Maybe she'd remember these one day as the scents of her shame.

The car door groaned. Her hand slid along the tufted leather of the back seat and settled on a rough wool blanket. *Thank goodness something's on my side tonight.* Her knees hit the floorboard hard.

"Oof," she muttered as her cheek grazed the seat.

Shivering, Elizabeth huddled inside her navy-blue coat, uncomfortable. The wool lap blanket barely covered her feet and shins. The tufted leather wouldn't yield to any part of her. Her mother might say her hard head had met its match.

Through the tiny garage window, Elizabeth watched the moon slip behind the giant oak in the back yard. Tears threatened.

"I will not cry. I will not cry."

What had she been thinking? Blurring the lines between dance partner and romantic partner wouldn't bring the life she craved. She shook her head at her foolishness.

She just needed time to sort through everything—Mother. James. George.

These problems were temporary. She'd fix everything. Wouldn't she?

Not if tonight was any sign. For hours, Elizabeth had wandered the city streets and lurked on subway platforms, waiting for the right time to sneak back home. Though Elizabeth was exhausted to the bone, the emotional strain of the last week still fizzed within her veins.

She took a deep breath, and her eyes fluttered closed.

A rustling noise jolted Elizabeth awake. How had she fallen asleep in this awful position? Not a trace of silver moonlight glittered on the window now.

What if a mouse had been the noisemaker? She jerked her feet back onto the seat and readjusted the blanket.

A bird chirped outside, the high pitch bursting

through Elizabeth's sleepy fog.

"Oh, no!"

Elizabeth bounded out of the car, cramped limbs protesting her swift movements. She shrugged out of her coat to examine yesterday's dress.

A peek out the window told nothing of the hour. A fuchsia haze skimmed the treetops. Deep purple above would melt into that same floral hue when the sun rose to kiss the morning sky.

What a lovely day it might be. For someone else, perhaps.

Her suitcase stood right inside the door, but it held no wardrobe fix this morning. Behind an old mop bucket on the back wall, she hid the evidence of her sneaky return.

Now to get out before Father found her in this distressed state. Elizabeth's mind was in such a jumble she'd never be able to defend this hideout to him. Why she'd slept in the garage was the least of the questions she would be required to answer. She didn't expect a triumphant entry when she walked through the front door tonight.

She fingered her tangled brown hair and grumbled at the idea of entering the library so disheveled, at the jokes to be made. Was it possible to avoid the staff all day? Hardly.

After disappearing for a week, she had some explaining to do.

Chapter One

Five months earlier—October 1922

These in-between days were hard on girls in pretty dresses. Elizabeth huddled with her best friend against the cold, rough brick of the dance hall. She ran her hands up and down her arms to warm them. The sheer gold gossamer sleeves of her silk dress were hardly a covering. The pale October sun had gone down while they were inside, and now she wished she'd brought a coat.

Voices of policemen carried through the crowd of dancers, so they stopped their furious whispering to listen, hoping to find out why they were there tonight. Were the police looking for alcohol? Or had New York's moral superiors convinced officials to make an example of this dance hall?

"They couldn't have been searching for alcohol, could they? I didn't see any," Elizabeth whispered into Jocelyn's ear. The white feather on Jocelyn's headpiece tickled Elizabeth's cheek.

A few dancers milled about on the sidewalk, voices rising and falling with open curiosity. Many of the dancers had quickly left the block, refusing to linger.

Elizabeth noticed several young men casting glances in Jocelyn's direction. Now they were out of college, Elizabeth no longer envied the male attention her blonde friend garnered. She didn't mind her own dark looks, though admittedly her brown eyes were boring compared to Jocelyn's startling green peepers.

Jocelyn stared at her friend with sympathy. "For a researcher, your observational powers are embarrassing. Let's skedaddle."

Elizabeth grabbed her friend's wrist.

"Wait. We still don't know why they're here."

"Don't bring attention to yourself, girlie. Asking questions is risky."

Elizabeth quirked an eyebrow at the timidity of her usually brave friend. Jocelyn was almost famous for her daring ways. Maybe she should listen to Jocelyn's surprising warning.

"Oh, look. Your date, what's-his-name, is talking to a policeman. Wave him over."

"Mark," Jocelyn said firmly. "If you had a fellow, he could look out for you like that."

Elizabeth rolled her eyes and said nothing. This wasn't the time to discuss her lack of male companionship. Or more precisely, her lack of interest in male companionship. She was glad Jocelyn's cousin, Charles, had come along tonight. Dancing alone or with other women wasn't nearly as fun.

Ten minutes later, Elizabeth stood with Charles, Mark, and Jocelyn by the corner of the dance hall. The one remaining policeman wasn't looking their way, but he was bound to run them off soon enough. After the police found no hooch in the dance hall, they'd sent the dancers home.

There would be no punishments for dancing this night, other than being denied more time with the thrumming jazz she loved so much. Elizabeth wondered how much longer the city would hold out against the complaints emanating from churches. "Evil dancing" had become the targeted sin of the times. Elizabeth didn't care about alcohol bans.

"It's late and I'm cold. Time to go home." The tension of the police raid had taken something out of Elizabeth. "And we're all agreed, no word about this raid?"

Everyone nodded in agreement. She pecked Jocelyn on the cheek and waved at Mark.

"Thanks for giving me a whirl, Charles."

"Charles to the rescue, as always." He sighed and gave her a silly salute. The red embers of his cigarette danced in an arc above his head.

She would have no problem getting home on her own. The lamplights continued to flicker, and the occasional car rumbling by would light her way.

Elizabeth thought about Jocelyn's date for the night. He had been friendly enough to their little group. Jocelyn didn't seem to mind that he touched her a lot and held her tightly when they danced. Elizabeth wouldn't have tolerated that behavior.

It was a new decade, and women were feeling their oats. Everyone wanted to have their cake and eat it too, but she was far more practical. Elizabeth would keep her heart and body under lock and key until the right person came along, certain she'd recognize when that time came.

She didn't want it to happen too soon, though. There were things to do, experiences to enjoy before she settled down. Honestly, settling down sounded terribly dull.

Arriving home, she leaned against the front door in the front hall and breathed in the clean scent of polish and the lingering notes of her mother's floral soap. She made her way quietly up the dark staircase. Her room was to the left. Her younger sister Anna's room was down the hall to the right. The third floor housed their parents' rooms, and the stairs to that floor stood opposite Elizabeth's bedroom door. Those stairs had often felt like an invasion of her younger self's privacy, though she'd had nothing to hide.

The dark wood banister curved to the right and created a railing where she could spy on the front hall. As a curious teen, she'd sat cross-legged on the landing and eavesdropped on conversations that drifted up from the front parlor. Rarely had she learned anything useful. Now, she'd put away such childish things and sought the information she wanted more directly. Her college studies had helped her develop those skills.

Elizabeth pushed her bedroom door closed and removed her shoes. They thudded one by one onto the smooth sky-blue carpet that covered most of her floor. She pulled the brass chain on her vanity lamp; a soft glow spread like gold vapor on the dark wood. She moved across the room to close the white lace curtains, then the heavier blue ones, shutting out the starry night.

Her dress came off next, then a silky cream slip. She left them neatly on the back of a chair. Tomorrow, she would inspect everything for stains and loose threads.

She caught sight of herself in the vanity mirror. Her stomach would be completely flat if not for protruding hipbones. She stared at her back, where her ribs showed faintly under pale, unfreckled skin. Her dancing kept her slim. She wasn't concerned about the tree-like silhouette her height and weight offered. Willowy was nice, wasn't it? Elizabeth's five-foot-eight-inch frame made her a head taller than most, and nearly eye-to-eye with many young men.

She dug around in a vanity drawer for the jar of cold cream hidden there. Elizabeth rubbed impatiently at the soft pink rouge she'd applied before entering the dance hall. She wished she didn't have to hide something nearly all her peers were trying out these days. Her mother needed to get with the times. But she wasn't ready to say that out loud. Not just yet.

Elizabeth put on a nightdress and slid under the heavy blue coverlet. Cool sheets settled around her legs. She was asleep in minutes, the rhythms of the evening's jazz left behind on the streets patrolled by police.

Chapter Two

Elizabeth took the subway to the other side of Central Park the next day. With only Sunday foot traffic, she could enjoy the unhurried pace and weekend quiet within the tunnels.

The Weber Butcher Shop sat in the middle of 2nd Avenue between 84th and 85th Streets. Its gold-and-green-striped awning made it easy to spot. She rang the bell marked "Weber" and waited for Jocelyn to run down the steep, dark stairs to let her in. They lived in an apartment above the butcher shop Jocelyn's father had inherited from his German immigrant parents.

The Webers' apartment was the perfect size for Jocelyn and her "Pops." The kitchen and living area were open to each other but separated by a small dining table and four chairs. They each had a bedroom of their own, and a third tiny room served as Mr. Weber's business office. Jocelyn's chief complaint was the butcher shop smell that seeped up through the floors.

Jocelyn's Pops greeted Elizabeth with a warm, beefy hug, saying, "You have been a stranger, Little Miss Elizabeth."

He laughed, then patted his daughter's back.

"What am I saying? There's no little girl here! You two are growing up before my eyes. What your parents must think of your independence, right?"

Elizabeth smiled and shrugged one shoulder. She

found herself at a loss for words, since he clearly thought Minnie and Henry knew about her dreams. She looked at Jocelyn for help.

"Pops, let's have that ham. Hungry, Elizabeth?"

"Starved! It smells divine."

The smoky scent of baked ham had started her mouth watering the moment she walked in. She'd only had toast for breakfast, hours ago.

As she pushed her plate away, groaning in ecstasy, Elizabeth put her hand on Mr. Weber's. "You are quite the cook. I've missed eating here. It's so calm. And easy."

"Ah, not like your mother's big dinners? Eh?"

Elizabeth shook her head and gave him a rueful grin.

"Your mother ordered a roast for next week. I'm grateful she orders from my shop each month. She passes at least two butchers to come here."

Surprised to hear this, Elizabeth said, "That is good of her. But she knows you have the best beef in town, too."

"Psshhh. I do my best."

Elizabeth enjoyed talking with Mr. Weber, who still had a lot of the Old World in him. His parents had brought him from Germany to New York when he was a little boy. His English was sprinkled with old-country colloquialisms, no doubt influenced by the many Germans living around his shop.

Elizabeth looked over at her friend. "Okay, so what are we doing this afternoon?"

"Thought we could visit the boardinghouse and talk about how I'm going to fit all my clothes in my room."

"Well, have fun. I don't want to think about my little girl moving. I must keep pretending she stays."

"You've been a twosome for so long."

"Your parents must be sad, too."

Elizabeth bit her lip. It took all she had not to put her hands together and shamelessly beg.

"Oh, Mr. Weber. Um, please don't mention this to my mother when you see her. I've, uh, not broached the subject yet."

"Don't wait too long, little miss."

She nodded as Jocelyn guided her to the bedroom. They plopped together on the bed. Elizabeth groaned again as she folded an arm across her stomach. "Your father stuffed me like I'm a bird or something. I won't eat for the rest of the day."

"Well, you'll need your energy. This house is a bit of a walk from here. At least we can cut through Central Park. Your favorite place!"

Elizabeth opened one glaring eye.

"You lie there and let me show you this wardrobe of mine. It's busting at the seams, and the one in my future room is so much smaller. Really, it's tiny, like a miniature from a dollhouse." Jocelyn covered her face with her hands. "How will I decide which things to leave behind?"

"Maybe your Pops will let you leave your summer things here in the winter and vice versa."

"Aren't you brilliant?" Jocelyn smacked her friend's foot hanging off the bed. "Let's get on with it, lazybones. Looks like rain out there, but let's wait to go underground until after a walk through the park."

On the way over to Mrs. Nesbitt's boardinghouse, they discussed rent prices and roommates and what Jocelyn expected out of her landlady. Elizabeth mostly listened, expressing occasional disbelief at what she was hearing. Jocelyn was bubbling over like a hot pot.

Elizabeth could not understand how this had all been negotiated. Jocelyn's stock was quickly rising in Elizabeth's mind. Jocelyn was stepping bravely into the mysterious world known as independence. It was beyond her imagination how she'd manage all this herself one day.

Seeing the little room that would be Jocelyn's new home, Elizabeth privately questioned the wisdom of the move. The room was smaller than the one Jocelyn already had, and only her father, the dearest man, to deal with while living at home. Why move at all?

But she said nothing, just nodded and made agreeable noises as they looked around. As an only child, Jocelyn was ready for a sisterhood bonded by a shared bathroom. This became clear to Elizabeth as her friend giggled with her future housemates.

Elizabeth studied the movements of the young women. The girls slipped in and out of each other's rooms like sisters, borrowing clothes and makeup. Jocelyn would fit in well here, far better than Elizabeth would. It was quite crowded and noisy—so different from home.

Was she ready to share a space with someone who wasn't a family member? Could she stand sharing a bathroom with four other girls? Where would she eat? Would she cook her own meals?

Elizabeth crushed down these personal concerns. These questions made her head buzz with serious doubts about starting a life on her own. It all looked so difficult.

****

Elizabeth and two coworkers occasionally met up with Jocelyn to have dinner. Tonight, they gathered at a diner nestled in the blocks between the library and the bank where Jocelyn worked.

Discussing men, dancing, sex, films, and drinking occupied most of their conversations. Jocelyn always had at least one young man on the line. Elizabeth expected to be regaled by her dear friend's stories of romance and the occasional heartbreak—the men more likely to be heartbroken by Jocelyn. Matilda and Jean were far more serious in their pursuit of men—they wanted husbands.

"Have you met the Circulation supervisor?" Matilda asked Elizabeth, while Jean watched a black-haired fellow walk by their table. Desperation floated off Jean like the steam rising above her coffee. Elizabeth wondered if men could sense it and how it might make them feel. She suspected it made them run off in the other direction.

"He's a looker, James is."

Jean stirred a spoon through her soup. The black-haired fellow's lack of interest made her shoulders slump under her powder-blue sweater.

"I've no idea who you're talking about. Who's James?" Elizabeth asked.

"I'm surprised you haven't seen him. He sometimes ventures on the public floor, helping patrons find books when everyone else is busy."

"Well, I'll know where to find you next time you disappear," Elizabeth said as she wiggled her eyebrows at Matilda.

"Nothing's going on there. That's why we thought you'd make a good match for him. He might be interested in someone more, you know, more…" Matilda stammered as she searched for the right word to describe

Elizabeth's type. Matilda's face went red. She picked up a spoon and started slurping her soup.

Elizabeth knew what her friend was implying. Someone upper-class, educated. She couldn't help how she'd been born, so she worked hard to fit in as much as possible. That meant never talking about going shopping or mentioning anything about the Alter home.

Neither of her coworkers had gone to college, but they were smart. And funny, which was the best part about working with them. It helped to laugh at work sometimes.

Right after college in June, Elizabeth had begun her job at the Fifth Avenue branch of the New York City Public Library. Her experiences at Barnard landed her in the research department on the fifth floor. Very few days were the same as she fielded questions from staff, patrons, other libraries, and academic institutions. Overwhelmed by the library's massive collection that topped a million volumes, Elizabeth quickly settled into a few areas of expertise and handed over divergent questions to Matilda or Jean. Some days, she felt the same pressure as when she'd prepared a paper in college. She couldn't help but love the job.

She'd been encased in a tiny office—a former storage room converted when the public library grew quickly. Walnut file cabinets were her backdrop as she worked at a small table. While she pondered a patron's question, she'd rub her fingers absently over the scratches on the walnut-stained surface. Years of cleaning and waxing had rendered the raw scratches a darker brown. Sometimes she'd stare at them until her vision blurred and they took on the shape of a person, a dog, a box. She once decided the Little Dipper had fallen from the sky and etched itself into her worktable.

She kept piles of books and papers there, and on the rare occasions she needed to type something, she used the typewriter pushed up against the wall outside her office. When she sat there, Matilda and Jean had to squeeze by. Her coworkers usually had a giggle about gaining weight or being pregnant as one of them tiptoed past with her back grazing along the opposite wall.

Elizabeth took for granted that she had plenty, while others struggled to make ends meet. Under the diner's table, she brushed her hands down her fine wool skirt. Its deep gray perfectly matched her sweater. Her white blouse, in its flawlessly laundered form, announced her family's economic status.

Jocelyn worked at a bank a few blocks from their library. She had a similar wardrobe but wore her clothes and jewelry with more panache, and she always sported a bright lipstick. It was Jocelyn who'd convinced Elizabeth that her parents would not kill her if she wore a little makeup now and then. Elizabeth still hadn't walked past her parents in the parlor wearing more than a pale shade of lipstick, though.

Back in college, Jocelyn hadn't been afraid to compare her wardrobe with Elizabeth's, admitting that half her wardrobe came from either a neighbor or a secondhand shop. Her father was of little help when it came to fashion. Jocelyn's mother had died of pneumonia when Jocelyn was ten years old. She counted herself fortunate that her Aunt Tilly and several mothers on their street kept an eye on things requiring a feminine touch.

Elizabeth looked across the table to where Jean and Matilda were in a whispered conversation with a striking woman standing over them, her hands rested on the back of their wooden chairs. Her purple satin dress was tight and lowcut.

"Do you know her?" Jocelyn interrupted Elizabeth's thoughts with a whisper.

"No, but isn't she beautiful?"

She could barely tear her eyes away.

Jocelyn shrugged. "Probably a gangster's moll."

Elizabeth's mouth dropped open. With two fingers, Jocelyn lifted Elizabeth's chin to close it. They began giggling.

"She isn't, is she? How can you tell?"

"Honestly, you're so naïve."

"What would I know about gangsters? And surely they wouldn't be around here."

Elizabeth had long relied on her friend to educate her on more worldly things. She stared at the mysterious woman and pondered how she'd met a gangster. The woman pulled herself up straight, brushing over her platinum-blonde hair with her right hand. She nodded at something Matilda said and turned away toward the door.

"Who was that?" Elizabeth almost pounced on her friends.

"My cousin," Matilda said as she reached for the bread.

"She's related to you?"

"Well, by marriage, actually. Her father married my aunt last year."

"Oh, I thought, well—"

"You mean, she's gorgeous. And we look nothing alike."

Elizabeth ignored that and said, "She's stunning, all

that hair. She must have men falling over her."

Matilda rolled her eyes and finished chewing before she answered.

"Did you notice how tall she is? Not a lot of fellas seem interested in a giant."

Elizabeth raised her eyebrows at Jocelyn.

"Oh, but she had one guy. Last year. He was shorter than her, came up to her chest. Lots of family jokes about that one."

It was Elizabeth's turn to roll her eyes.

"Don't you ladies grow weary of all the rules? Tall women can't date short men. Women can't stay single and make their own living. No public dancing. On and on it goes. Do this, don't do that. It's tiresome."

She thrummed her fingers on the table. Her lips pressed together. Her friends had stopped chewing and stared at her.

"Why don't we do what we wish?"

Jean started laughing, her cheeks bright pink. Then Matilda joined in, her ample chest bouncing above the table.

Elizabeth looked at her friend sitting beside her, but Jocelyn hadn't joined in.

Jocelyn dabbed her mouth with a napkin and shrugged.

"When're you gonna start your revolution, my friend?"

"Why must we have a revolution to become independent women?"

Elizabeth shook her head in dismay.

Later that night, as she got ready for bed, Elizabeth thought about Jocelyn's call for revolution.

She didn't want to get married on her mother's

timetable. She didn't want to live in this blue room, beautiful though it was, until she left for a new home with a man.

Was she willing to declare war to get what she wanted?

Chapter Three

A burst of laughter jarred Elizabeth's attention. The unwelcome noise came from behind the nearby shelves. Leaning forward in her chair, her ribs touching the paper with her notes, she peered down an aisle and saw a man's back. He was quite tall, over six feet. His white shirt and gray trousers were nicely pressed, from what she could see. His head shook back and forth as though in disagreement.

She heard the higher pitch of a woman's voice and glimpsed a pale green skirt. She watched the fine movements of his back as he waved a hand around while he talked. Elizabeth strained to hear what they were saying, but could only make out a few words. Hardly enough to understand what they were chatting about, but she kept watching and listening.

The man turned and headed toward her table. He smiled in her direction before she could put herself back in her seat. Pink climbed up her cheeks.

A thick mop of sandy blond hair hung over his forehead. She thought his gait was uneven at first, then attributed it to his having to maneuver between the long wooden tables and high-backed chairs. He was good-looking. Features in all the right places. A smooth, broad forehead and neat eyebrows above glacier-blue eyes. His nose was perfectly straight. Nicely shaped lips broke easily into a smile.

"Hello. You've got some work there." He nodded at the materials spread out in front of her. Surprising her, he put down the gigantic stack of books he carried with a loud thump. Was he going to sit down too? She hoped not.

"Yes, a research project for a patron. It's been going on a while."

"You work here?"

"In research, yes."

His eyes lit up. "Oh, you must be the Elizabeth."

"The?" Her cheeks flamed. Matilda! She'd blabbered about her, probably when she should have been working.

He laughed again. It was a warm, melodious sound, so natural it was clearly something he did often.

"I'm James, by the way. Circulation."

"Oh, right. I've…" She stopped herself, not wishing to let on that she'd heard of him.

James smiled, his eyebrows slightly arched as he studied her. Embarrassed by his steady gaze, she glanced down at her papers and back up at him.

"A pleasure to meet you, Elizabeth." He bent at the waist, arm sweeping down gallantly as she imagined Sir Walter Raleigh would have done. She couldn't help but squirm. Heat rushed across her cheeks again.

"Right. Good to meet you too." Embarrassed by her business-like tone, Elizabeth fingered the edges of her notepad.

Grabbing the stack of books, he nodded at her and walked off. The uncomfortable silence threatened to break the spell that had just been cast.

"Until we meet again, James." She tried a light tone but feared she might have sounded like her grandmother instead.

"See ya around, Elizabeth. The Elizabeth." He chuckled, forcing her to smile at hearing that laugh again.

She watched him walk nearly a block's length of the room. He did have a slight limp. Was he trying harder to hide it, in case she was watching? He might be a proud man. She thought about the Great War. So many men hadn't survived.

Sadness swept in and enveloped her like the bathwater when she dipped her head beneath its surface to wet her hair. The first boy she ever kissed, Billy Schutts, had died after fighting only weeks in France. Several other schoolmates met similar fates. Her first year in college had been a jumble of emotions. Excitement about her education and new experiences had made a sloppy stew with the tears and pain of terrifying war news. After years of death, the war ended in the middle of her first term at Barnard. What celebrations they had! But the happiness those young women felt paled in comparison with the joy of families whose sons were finally coming home alive.

The Alters, with two daughters, spared the tragedies of the war, celebrated with neighbors whose sons returned home from England or France. Every house on the block had displayed flags or patriotic bunting. In 1918, on a chilly Saturday in late November, car horns sounded off in a messy harmony of joy. Even Henry pulled his car from the garage facing the alley and laid both of his hands on the horn. The Alter women, that day, stood on the sidewalk, waving at the passing cars. Minnie fluttered a white linen handkerchief for mere seconds before she dabbed at the happy tears on her cheeks.

Mrs. Lovejoy from next door hugged Minnie and threw back her head and let out a surprising, "Whoop!" Johnny Lovejoy had arrived home weeks earlier, moving gingerly with a cane, white cotton wrapped around his head. Elizabeth and Anna had shuddered in unison when he climbed out of a taxi in front of his boyhood home. Yet on that special November day, Johnny was nowhere to be seen. There'd been whisperings along the street that he was depressed. Minnie had tut-tutted about it one night over dinner and her daughters had listened quietly without remark. What did they know about feebleness (as their mother put it) and coming home from war?

Still, by early December 1918, not all the war's survivors had returned home. Logistical problems and hospitalizations kept some young men in Europe for months after the armistice declared the month before. No more fighting. That they were guaranteed. The families merely had to wait.

So, in every borough of New York, celebrations continued almost weekly into the new year as their native sons returned home, some still whole, others mangled for life. It was in her sophomore year that Elizabeth stood on Fifth Avenue with her family and Jocelyn and her father for the big parade with the 1st Division in full gear. It was both exciting and unsettling to Elizabeth to see the combat armaments and uniforms of war on display. By now, reality had set in. The war was truly over, and some young men she had known were dancing in heaven instead of with her.

The silence of the space was broken by the cough of an elderly patron walking by. Weariness overcame her. Thinking about death and war did that. Energy leaching out like the life of a dying soldier. God, she was morose all of a sudden.

Remembering the woman's voice she'd heard earlier, Elizabeth peered down the long row of shelves, but all she saw were dust motes twirling in the fading afternoon sunbeams. She studied her surroundings and allowed a smile to wipe away her sadness. She hugged herself for her great fortune to work in this place.

Elizabeth sat in the loveliest spot in the library. On the third floor, the Reading Room glistened and beckoned to all who might linger in this iconic building. November sunbeams dove into the enormous space and got trapped in the prisms of the chandeliers that decked the enormous space. Just walking from end to end could tire a less fit person, as it spanned two city blocks.

Elizabeth breathed in the familiar scents that reminded her of Barnard's Milbank Hall: books, dust, wood, and wax. They warmed her as much as the sun's rays did. When she stretched and arched backward, her view took in the fifty-two-foot ceiling's mural of sky and clouds painted far above the chandeliers. This room inspired awe; a place she had been privileged to work for the last six months. Here, she'd found a home for her mind.

Several days a week, Elizabeth took her research materials there rather than return with them to her tiny hole in the research wing. Her boss, Mr. Gerold, had called that office "cozy" when he introduced it to her, but everyone else laughed. It didn't matter to her. She loved her work and would do it anywhere. And in the Reading Room, she could spread out the books, maps, or other materials she was perusing for research patrons.

It was also the perfect place to meet with patrons to

discuss their questions and sometimes review archived materials with them. The room itself lent authority to the materials and the researcher. Elizabeth liked the gravity the space offered, given her youth and inexperience.

And now, in this room, she'd met the famous James. His smile dazzled in her memory. She had no idea why she was thinking about him.

Packing her research took a few minutes, giving her time to pull herself together. Matilda and Jean had asked her to go to a movie after work. She thought it was by Cecil DeMille, but she wasn't certain. Elizabeth didn't follow movies and actors as closely as her friends did. She much preferred books. Still, any chance to stay out and avoid listening to her mother was always welcome.

By the time she returned to her little cubbyhole of an office, her friends were chatting together, clearly lollygagging rather than working. It was not yet five, according to the clock above Mr. Gerold's office door, so she set about organizing her work to be ready on her desk in the morning. Her white cotton gloves lay like praying hands over the papers.

"So, Elizabeth, do you mind if we go to Garrison's Deli for a quick dinner first? Matilda says—"

"Yes, fine." She distractedly interrupted Jean and reached for her coat.

"Oh, you're ready, then. That's a first. You ready for quitting time a bare minute early!" Jean hooted so loudly, Mr. Gerold looked up with a scowl. The lamp's golden shimmer shone like a lighthouse beacon from his balding head.

"Let's scoot, girls."

Jean shepherded them out into the hallway as they giggled and carried on like fun-loving girls, their three dark heads passing by the glass of their supervisor's window.

As they walked down the library's broad stone steps, Elizabeth almost told them about meeting James. But she didn't want his boyfriend potential to become the focal point of their quick dinner. Her friends' imaginations would head that direction so fast her head would spin.

He might be friendly and fun, but unless he was a skilled dancer, she couldn't be interested.

Chapter Four

Anna, Jocelyn, and a few others accompanied Elizabeth to a dance at a nearby community center. They usually traveled in packs of four or six, an even number, so they could dance together and not leave someone sitting or dancing alone.

Elizabeth had started coming here last summer, and the doorman, John, had taken a shine to her. He teasingly called her "Norma" because he thought she resembled the actress Norma Talmadge. The comparison flattered her, but she struggled to see the resemblance beyond her long, dark bob. Maybe her nose turned up like Norma's? Eventually, she stopped looking in the mirror for any proof of the star qualities John saw in her. Resembling a movie star was intriguing at first. Then she decided it didn't matter.

As she gained her footing in adult life, her view of herself as a modern woman was far more important. Her mother's constant pressure to surrender to a traditional life wore on her. Logically, she knew it was probably the easier, safer way. For most women, anyway, she'd remind herself. If she remained in her parents' home too long, she feared she would give in and settle for marriage to someone. Who would that possibly be? She had yet to meet a young man who could hold her attention.

The autumn days were shortening. It quickly turned cold after the sun disappeared behind New York's stone facades. The six of them had been standing outside the dance hall at least a half an hour before John strolled up the sidewalk, checking out the group and ensuring the hopeful patrons were behaving themselves.

Elizabeth had watched John contend with a lot over the past months: police, preachers, and the church ladies with their silly signs. Any patrons who wanted to start trouble with the unwelcome visitors could go somewhere else, and she'd seen John, in his green doorman's suit and hat, make that very clear on his sidewalk strolls.

"Hey, hey, Norma!"

"Now, John," she whispered, "you know it's Elizabeth."

"Yah, yah. Come along with your chickadees. Not sure you can find a table, but…" His words disappeared into a fierce bite of chilly wind as he strode ahead of them. Elizabeth and her friends squealed at half volume and followed him swiftly to the entrance. His hatted head bounced along the top of the crowd. Elizabeth had nicknamed him "Big John" to her friends, given his towering height, but she'd never tell him.

None of them dared look at the poor frozen ones left in the jagged line, though Elizabeth noted a tiny blonde girl with her back against the wall and her fellow standing close to shield her from the bitter chill. Thank goodness for chivalry, thought Elizabeth, as the girl's flapper dress was merely scraps of fabric held together with skimpy lace and costume jewelry. It looked a lot like a slip. Her dingy brown coat was threadbare and missing all its buttons. The girl puffed on a cigarette in a long Bakelite holder, standing in her beau's protective cover.

Elizabeth happily joined the herds on the dance floor

for a bouncy foxtrot and the Lindy Hop, but she hadn't adopted the flapper fashion embraced by many of the women on the dance floor. One of the best things about being born in 1900 was escaping the restraint of a corset. By the time a woman her age would have been required to wear one, the corset had gone the way of the musket. She and her friends laughed at pictures of the old-fashioned garment, hoping it remained a relic of a confining past.

She adored pretty dresses. Tonight, she wore a silk tunic dress colored to resemble a Singapore orchid. The white bodice slowly merged into purple, the deepest hue on the last few inches of the hem. Her dress covered her shoulders and dipped modestly below her collarbones.

Flapper styles were so revealing that many young women changed into their party clothes at a friend's house or in a dance hall's toilet. Their parents wouldn't have let them out of the house dressed so skimpily. Anna always had an eye out for adventure, but Elizabeth never witnessed her sister change dresses when they were out together.

Together, the sisters had crafted a tentative peace with their mother around their dance outings. She didn't like the "wildness" that surrounded jazz and dance halls. Minnie had so many opinions about the ills of the world. The girls tiptoed around her just in case Minnie found something new to oppose.

Anna was light and bubbly where Elizabeth was dark and serious. Anna was fairer of skin, and her hair shone a sandy blonde that she longed to color a glossy platinum. Knowing their parents would vehemently object, Anna wisely accepted the shade God had given her. Still in college, she was lucky to have time to curl her bob before going out on Friday nights. With her curls and waves, she appeared playful, while Elizabeth's straight hair only emphasized her seriousness.

Elizabeth admired a lot about her sister—her forthrightness, and her love of spontaneity and fun. But deep thinking and imagination were equally important gifts, so she'd decided long ago not to fight her constant reflection and daydreaming habits.

Tonight, though, she was most serious about dancing. She didn't have a date, and she didn't want one. Jocelyn had a new beau, and Anna had met a young man from college. Barnard women had their pick of fellows across the street at Columbia. But when Elizabeth had been a student, the schoolwork had mattered more.

Jocelyn's cousin Charles had come, and Elizabeth knew he was good for a few twirls around the dance floor. Her friends also moved to the music with Elizabeth. They counted on her to teach them all the new dance steps.

Elizabeth studied the dancers while she sat and bounced her feet to the jazz music. The rhythm of jazz was a pure celebration to any devoted dancer. A live band's vibrations could still strum through her bones a day later. Sometimes, she'd see a man who had a natural rhythm and picture him as a long-standing dance partner. A brilliant dancer who wasn't also keen on her would be a windfall.

"What's going on in there?" Anna tapped her sister on the top of her head. Elizabeth leaned closer to hear her over the band.

"Pfft. Nothing. I'm tired, though. Think I'll walk home."

"Shall I come with you?" Anna asked sweetly, but

her sister saw the way she looked over at her date.

"Oh, no. It's only three blocks. You stay and have fun."

"If you'd had a date, you might've wanted to stay longer."

Elizabeth rolled her eyes at her sister. She stood and swung her coat around her shoulders.

"I'm not looking for a fellow to fill my nights."

"Mmm, yes, we've all noticed. Minnie, in particular." Lips pursed, Anna folded her arms across her chest.

Elizabeth laughed at Anna's mimicry of their mother.

"I'm managing just fine, as you can see." Elizabeth leaned in to give her sister's cheek a peck. "Toodle-loo, dear sister."

She gave Jocelyn a quick hug, promising to get together the next day to start her packing. Elizabeth couldn't help but be envious of her friend's newly won freedom. Well, she was almost free, and so far, Mr. Weber hadn't threatened to change his mind.

When she stepped outside the hall with its overly warm, stale atmosphere, Elizabeth gulped eagerly for fresh air. The chill burned her lungs, and a shiver ran down her spine. She tugged the thin, purple woven hairband over her ears in a useless attempt to warm them, then tucked her hands into her coat pockets.

She made a quick study of the stars wandering across a shimmery black sky. She could identify the moon, of course, but was never sure if she'd correctly picked out the two dippers. Stars twisted and revolved through space, but without the right knowledge, one never knew where constellations would be found.

"Here a star, there a star. Some lose their way." She quoted Emily Dickinson quietly as she continued to stare upward.

Just like the stars that were constantly changing places, she thought about how her parents would respond to her proposed change of place. A dramatic shift for them to consider. And object to.

Elizabeth sighed into the night. The uncertainty excited and troubled her at the same time. Her stomach did a quick flip.

Yet she'd relied on the status quo long enough. Nearly twenty-three years old, she believed moving out into an independent life was a natural "first." She was ready to shake things up a little. If she didn't, she might lose her way.

Where this sudden initiative had come from, she didn't know, but she liked the hopeful feeling it gave her.

She stopped in front of her home's front door and turned to stargaze a little more. Those specks of light were signs of hope to her. Winking in camaraderie.

She went inside and found the parlor dark. Elizabeth breathed a sigh of relief and headed upstairs. She didn't have to be brave tonight.

Chapter Five

"People should dance at home, that's all," Minnie
said as she signaled Mary to remove some platters from
the table. "It's unseemly for women to dance with men
they don't know."

Minnie liked to use these dinner discussions to pass
along repeated wisdom to her daughters, with the bonus
of having others as allies against the many social ills she
wished her daughters would avoid.

Elizabeth sighed a little too loudly, but kept her eyes
down while she cut through a slice of warm roast beef.
The clicking of forks on china faded away as aunts and
cousins glanced around the table for some unexpected
entertainment.

Elizabeth was certain Minnie wouldn't be calling
attention to her own daughters' dancing amongst this
group. Family opinions mattered far too much. Minnie
enjoyed entertaining her two sisters and their families.
Everyone dressed up in their Sunday best. It was
accepted family dogma, though, that Minnie was the
favored daughter. Her home was the largest, her
daughters the most accomplished, as the only college
attendees, and her dinners—cooked by the talented
Mary—were not to be missed. You might get talked
about if you had other plans.

Truthfully, each of the Finnegan sisters had married
well. The three sisters had grown up well-fed and

sheltered, but there'd been nothing left over for college or any extras like party dresses and new shoes every season.

Preparing for Sunday dinners was tense—that is, until the family began crossing the threshold. Minnie barked orders at her daughters while she hovered in the kitchen, supervising their part-time cook, Mary. Elizabeth and Anna were assigned hostess duties to greet and settle the aunts and cousins who came once a month. Henry huddled in his study, joining the family only at the chime of Minnie's crystal dinner bell. "Much like a Pavlovian dog," Anna had whispered once to her sister.

This Sunday, Minnie developed quite a head of steam over a recent dance hall story from one of the city's newspapers. Around the ten-seat dining table, nearly everyone had an opinion about these controversial places, particularly since public dancing remained socially unacceptable.

After nearly a decade of fervent objections, politicians, pastors, and even dance masters were aligning closer and closer to minimize the scandalous dancing that had emerged with jazz music. The dancing, in their collected opinions, was too fast, too close, and would inevitably lead to the worst kinds of promiscuity and many disreputable social outcomes.

Their parents accepted that she and Anna continued to go out dancing with friends, because the girls promised to avoid the more troubling parts of the city. There were many places to find musical entertainment and dancing. Community centers held dances, as did city parks. In the parks, sometimes two bands would play and hundreds of adults, from college-aged to those in their forties, would gather for dancing and food. Dances in the park were Elizabeth's favorite, where she could disappear into the crowds if trouble ever arose. And, though trouble, like occasional fist fights or church lady protests, sometimes found these dances, they continued weekend after weekend.

The sisters would not give up on their fun. Not after the flu epidemic and the Great War had stripped them of so much and opened them up to grievous pain and loss.

Aunt Amelia, who lived five blocks away, informed the family that her neighbor's church ladies' group had stood outside a dance hall in Manhattan for five hours. They'd carried placards and waved the signs in the faces of the young people entering the hall. The young women's dresses were appalling, with bare legs and arms shimmering in the moonlight. Young men with slicked-back hair ground their cigarettes into the sidewalks. The police would surely arrive during the evening, so these outraged ladies had assumed. Yet, the police had not come. Elizabeth was relieved to hear this resolution to her aunt's story.

As the oldest, Amelia ensured that she sat beside Minnie at these dinners so they could share the occasional whispered gossip. Their dark heads bent together were largely ignored by the rest of the clan. Though she lived mere blocks away and was now a widow, Amelia rarely visited her sister outside these monthly dinners.

For years, Elizabeth and Anna had been fixtures in Amelia's house, playing with their oldest cousin, Judith. Two years older than Elizabeth, Judith had ordered their play. While Elizabeth wanted to play "school," Judith wanted to play the more appealing game of "house." Anna was happy just to be included, even though it meant being bossed about by the older girls. Judith sat across from the sisters now, but they hadn't spent time much together since Judith finished school and started working.

Judith was twenty-five and engaged to a man she'd met after the war, when he came into the pharmacy where she worked to get a medication for his mother. To hear Judith tell it, love at first sight was undeniable. Elizabeth and Anna liked their only female cousin, but one Sunday dinner a month was enough to have Judith go on about her fiancé, Desmond. No doubt after the wedding, next summer, another chair would join the already crowded Alter dinner table.

The rest of the Sunday dinner crowd was composed of Minnie's younger sister, Janice, Janice's husband, Tom Miller, and their two sons, Thomas Junior and John. They were the quietest bunch of people Elizabeth had ever met, though they seemed to absorb everything going on at these events. Janice and Tom lived with their boys in Tom's family home in Queens. Her sisters acted as though she lived in Maine, often leaving her out of shopping expeditions and lunches in their early years of marriage.

"Lovely to see you," was the most Janice ever said to her niece, her soft moist cheek pressed against hers. During that brief monthly hug, Elizabeth looked forward to the scent of gardenias wafting from Janice's thin body. Though Janice was reserved, Elizabeth liked her, and she sensed a strength hidden behind her soft brown eyes. The boys had been rambunctious as toddlers. "Hellions" according to Minnie, making for noisy, calamitous Christmases at the Finnegan grandparents' home in Stamford, Connecticut. Now the boys would soon finish high school, one right behind the other.

"Thomas, are you excited about leaving high school next year?" Elizabeth decided to ferret out a conversation with a Miller boy, no matter how tricky. She and her sister hadn't had the same relationship with the Millers as they'd had with Judith's family.

His fork paused on its way to his mouth. Then, a smile cracked open his serious pale face. "I can hardly wait."

"What're you going to do after?" Elizabeth noticed the movement of Janice's hand on her husband's arm, as though bracing herself for something.

"I'm going to drive a truck!" He exclaimed with the excitement of a six-year-old.

Minnie put down her fork and looked at Janice and Tom, questions dancing. Janice started shaking her head.

"We're not sure what he's going to do yet," his mother offered quietly.

"I am!" Thomas' voice raised slightly. Janice dropped her eyes and smoothed the white linen napkin on her lap. Her lips pressed tightly together.

Elizabeth regretted poking the silent bear of the Miller family. She bit her lip and looked around the table. Except for Anna, everyone was playing with their food, the soft scraping and clicking of silver on plates the only sound in the room. Anna looked about ready to burst out laughing.

Having caused this surprising ruckus, Elizabeth was tempted to smooth things over. But how? What could she say? Junior had finally spoken at a family dinner, and the tension sidled around the table… No, this wasn't tension, it was shock. The stunned silence continued for more excruciating seconds.

The opening door brought welcome relief. Elizabeth's exhale drew a glare from Judith.

"Ahh, the baked custard is ready! Thank you, Mary," beamed Minnie as the cook entered the dining room and placed a tray of custard cups on the buffet table.

The festive scent of milk and nutmeg filled the room. Mary carefully served each of them the individual desserts. Elizabeth didn't want one, but she didn't dare draw attention to herself by saying, "None for me, Mary."

With another Sunday dinner nearly over, Elizabeth and her sister would have to listen to their mother's mumblings about dancing and family issues for at least the next week. Minnie was predictable. If only Elizabeth had been her usual quiet self and hadn't asked her cousin about his future. She couldn't help herself, since thoughts of the future occupied her from morning to night.

When she was younger, Elizabeth would sneak a book to the table, and she'd read a page whenever she was unobserved. Books, she always believed, might save her long into the future. She was a thinker. The way she drifted off, deep in thought about a book she was reading, drove her mother batty. Minnie hated repeating herself, unless, of course, it was a favorite quip or life lesson she was born to relay repeatedly: "Waste not want not," "Mind your manners," "That's not very ladylike," and "Don't look at me like that," to name a few.

The negativity of her mother's words seeped into Elizabeth's soul, and she feared the day she'd repeat them to her own children. If she had any, that is. She mused that repeating "helpful" words of wisdom is a curse that flows through the matriarchal line, generation after generation.

Elizabeth wanted to do things differently. She wasn't even sure what she wanted out of her life ten years from now, but she bucked against the ridiculous notion that a woman would go to college to find a husband and then pretend she knew nothing. Kisses and more for the husband, bottles for the babies. What was there for the woman in that? Oh, she knew all right. She watched her mother, happy in her homemaking, directing others, lunching with ladies once her girls were old enough to be left alone. The endless lunches. Elizabeth craved those like a fork in her eye.

She spoke none of this to her parents. They both maintained a traditional view of the world where women made the home and men made the money. She always hoped her father might be more open-minded, given his place in the world, seeing women succeed in his workplace. Perhaps his thinking was evolving, but she'd never asked him. At least two women she knew of had moved into supervisory positions at his bank. When he'd shared this news at dinner last year, Minnie had clammed up and looked swiftly at her daughters. Her antenna perked up, seeking any note of interest. She didn't want her girls to get any ideas. That quick swivel of her head might have been a warning to Henry to not put such rebellious ideas in his daughters' impressionable heads.

Minnie acted mortified and desperate, clearly wondering how to explain how her intelligent and beautiful daughter had not had a single date since she left college. To Elizabeth's way of thinking, if her mother quit focusing on it, stopped muttering about it behind her teacup, perhaps her club friends would be uninterested in

Elizabeth's mysterious, rebellious ways. Surely there were women of her mother's generation who had also balked at the Victorian mores that stymied women and still threatened to keep them from reaching higher planes in business and intellectual pursuits.

Elizabeth shouldn't have to defend herself. But she was still working it out in her head.

She didn't need a man to be happy, of that she was certain. And here began her internal debate about what she wanted versus what she needed. She needed a full life defined by her. That life would include a meaningful career, good friends, and dancing. She wanted a dance partner—to dance the night away, then bid "farewell" under the stars.

She thought such a life was appetizing, full of a flavor delivered by friends and music. Concocting this soup meant she needed a kitchen of her own, didn't it? She desperately needed to get out of her childhood home and start creating a delicious life.

But right now, Elizabeth needed to get out of this dining room. She patted her mouth with her white linen napkin and said, "Mother, I'll help Mary clean up."

She stood without looking at anyone and left her speechless mother watching her exit.

Chapter Six

Elizabeth brushed off her co-workers' lunch invitation, preferring the courtyard's sunny shelter. December days were still bright, and the sun offered a thin warm shell, so she wanted to eat lunch outside until New York winter temperatures forbade it.

Walking down the back stairs, Elizabeth was startled by James entering the stairwell. She hadn't seen him since their brief introduction in the Reading Room weeks ago. They exchanged an awkward hello as they stopped on the landing.

"Lunch." Elizabeth said, lifting a lavender fabric bag and turning toward the steps. After a long morning in the dark archives, she was eager to breathe pine-scented air.

"Me too." James held up a paper bag and shook it. The crinkling paper sound echoed against the cement walls.

He hesitated, then plunged forward with a question. "I'm walking to the park to eat. Wanna join me?"

Elizabeth thought for a moment.

"Would you like to try a better place?"

"Oh-ho! Sounds enticing." James laughed.

Elizabeth rolled her eyes. Then beckoned with her index finger.

"This way."

They walked without speaking down two flights of

stairs. Thoughts darted around her brain, but she couldn't settle on a conversation topic. She willed the silence to cover her noisy mind like a fire blanket. Exiting the stairwell, Elizabeth led James on a weaving trail through empty gray halls, their footsteps leaving a musical echo behind them. Elizabeth leaned into a heavy-looking door sporting a sign reading, "Secret Garden." Someone at the library had a sense of humor.

"My, my, where are you taking me?" James asked as the door opened, winter blue sky and tree tops suddenly exposed.

The skinny December sunlight cast a pale glow over the cozy spot. Granite walls matching the library's facade encased the bricked courtyard on two sides. Heavy black iron tables and chairs, definitely throwbacks to the Victorian era, dotted the brick-paved expanse. Farthest from the door, a three-foot black fence finished the enclosure. Tall trees rose on the other side, shielding the courtyard from passersby.

"I like to sit here. It gets the most sun." She set her lunch on a table nearest the fence.

Like kids in school, they each surreptitiously reviewed the contents of the other's lunch. Both had sandwiches, but that's where the similarity ended. James had a shiny red apple, while Elizabeth had an apple strudel, baked by Mary. As she unwrapped the folds of waxed paper around it, she told James about Mary and her fabulous cooking.

"Mm, I'd be fat as a house. And look at you, so slim."

"Ah, well, we have a dog, so I walk a lot. I don't skip many of Mary's desserts, I promise you."

"Never had a dog." James shook his head, and the

sun glinted like sparks off the top of his sandy-haired head.

"Here." She handed over half of the strudel. "You must try it after I've bragged about it."

Flaky bits of golden pastry fell onto the table when James took his first bite. He rolled his eyes back into his head. "Oh. Oh. Oh," he exclaimed in pleasure.

Elizabeth smiled, nodding. "What'd I tell you?"

They continued to talk about the strudel while they finished it together.

"So, tell me about your sad life without a dog." She poked out her bottom lip in a mocking pout.

James waved off the question. "Nothing to tell. Enough mouths to feed without a four-legged one."

He described his crowded household while the noonday sun moved across the sky and behind him. He lived at home with his parents, his Uncle Abe, and a sister named Katherine. And they had a boarder, he added. Everyone went to work each day, including his mother, who worked for two families on the Upper East Side.

He paused his story and asked, "What about you?"

Elizabeth hesitated. Her life was a fairytale compared to his. Why had she invited him to invade her quiet lunch time, anyway? She was not spontaneous on her most vibrant days. Seeing him headed to lunch, she'd felt compelled to ask him to join her. She reminded herself he'd invited her first. Should she have said, "No, thank you," and walked away? Being polite came naturally, so here she was, worrying over a simple conversation.

James seemed like a fine person, but this garden intimacy overwhelmed her. What could she tell him?

Could she be interesting and funny? Was her life interesting? Did she know how to be funny?

Elizabeth pondered so long about what to share that James cleared his throat. She wouldn't talk about her mother. Not here. This special garden where she'd thought about how she was growing into her work life and her next steps to independence. She didn't think about Minnie much during the day, and she liked that her work was absorbing enough to crowd out her doubts about the future.

So Elizabeth talked about her father working at the bank, her mother always being at home when they grew up. She told him about Anna's mischievous ways, leaving out a few salacious details.

"I'm afraid we've overstayed our lunch time," Elizabeth said as she gathered her lunch things.

"Well, I've enjoyed this. I'd welcome trouble from my supervisor and do it again."

Elizabeth raised an eyebrow. "Next Friday? Same place, same time? If the sunshine holds."

"It's a date. Uh, a deal."

"Let's go. I better guide you back through the maze, so you're not lost in the basement all weekend."

James twisted his face into a mock grimace as they meandered between the tables back to the garden door.

On the third floor, Elizabeth gave James a wave and continued up the stairs. She wasn't sure if she was warm from the sunshine or because of how nice James was.

She pursed her lips and wondered again if he could dance.

****

Butterflies tumbled around her stomach when she imagined her second lunch with James on Friday.

43

She hadn't had a man interested in her since…when? Nicholas Pendleton, her third year, perhaps. That was two years ago. Where did the time go? She was a little, no, a lot out of practice. But what did she have to practice? She was always herself.

Yet she held back her opinions often. Especially at home. Particularly the ideas she didn't believe men and her mother wanted to hear…about marriage, men and women in relationships, working women, the women's vote. Still, she thought about so much more. Most men were uncomfortable or intimidated by a woman who spoke her mind too emphatically. But her mother spoke her mind, and that was all that counted.

Elizabeth bit her bottom lip and shook her head. She was putting the cart before the horse. It didn't matter if James was interested in her anyway.

Elizabeth brushed her hands down the sides of her gunmetal gray dress and fingered the pale gray piping around her hips. Then she retied the pale gray bow at the base of the shallow V-neck and fastened the silver buttons at the cuffs. The hem brushed just below her knees, and soft gray stockings completed the look.

Satisfied she looked pretty but still willing to work all day, Elizabeth left her bedroom and went downstairs to get her navy wool coat. It had gotten colder since last Friday. She prayed she wouldn't have to eat lunch in her coat. Foolishly, she wanted James to see her dress while they sat in the sun.

She stared at the sky from the top porch step to make sure it was showing up for work today. She was depending on it. The biting air made her rush to the nearest subway station. It was too chilly to walk extra blocks aboveground.

At noon, Elizabeth waited for James at the same stairwell landing, in case he missed a turn in the labyrinth of dim, gray passageways.

He began their walk by describing his weekend as a handyman's helper for his father. His family's old house required so much work all the time, and he wasn't sure if he was ready for the responsibility of his own home.

"At least you're honest!" Elizabeth exclaimed as she rummaged through her lavender bag containing the lunch Mary had packed for her. She held up a sandwich wrapped in paper.

"See this? I'll be honest and say I could not assemble this every day. I suppose I'm accustomed to being spoiled."

James had a mouthful and began shaking his head.

"You're right. When I joined the Army, I realized how spoiled even I was."

Elizabeth leaned forward. "Really? How was it?"

"Of course, the war was practically over by the time I got to England." He took another bite of sandwich. Elizabeth watched him decide which parts of his story to tell.

"You can tell me anything. I'm not squeamish."

He cackled, "Oh, there are no gory bits in my tale."

"Thank goodness!" She held up her sandwich in salute.

And so he leaned back in the black iron seat and told her how he ended up in England with the Army.

When the country passed the Selective Service Act in 1917, James knew they would draft him. He volunteered to get his choice of assignment in the intelligence ranks. He modestly described himself as a quiet thinker and trusted his observation talents could be put to good use. While he ended up working in intelligence gathering, it was nothing like he had expected.

He received new assignments as the needs and the technology changed. First, he assisted with deploying tethered balloons, which were the most dependable, stable information gatherers at that moment of the war effort. James and the Army discovered he possessed a keen mechanical insight. As the war wound down, he repaired the radios and cameras mounted in observation planes, which supplemented the work of the tethered balloons. He was incredibly fortunate to be on the front lines of that work and to use his skill to defend what was right.

It hadn't been all work all the time. There were moments of levity and joy, even while climbing mountains of bad news. Working for a year on the southern coast of England, he experienced the best and worst of the climate. The surf pounding the shore's rocks was beautiful and angry at the same time. A man could be killed in those waters, but since James never learned how to swim, he left that to his friends, and he remained an observer on the cliffs. The winds were so high and the surf so fierce, he got bathed in the mist and splash from the English Channel. He'd return to his barracks with a soaked and frozen uniform but happy to be safe and unharmed.

"May I ask you something?" Elizabeth asked.

"Ask me anything."

"When we first met…in the Reading Room?" He nodded while she struggled with how to ask a personal question.

"I thought you had a slight limp?" She ended her

statement as a question, unsure how he might respond to her imposition.

"A war wound, yes." And then he laughed. "Brits can't drive."

Elizabeth tilted her head and frowned.

"A British soldier clipped me with an armored car." James rubbed his thumb down his nose and shook his head in amusement. "Such foolishness. Nowhere near the action, and yet I get a star for being injured at camp."

"A boy I went to school with, Billy…he died in France. He was there hardly any time, for a few weeks. I don't know what happened to him. He's just gone."

James laid his hand over hers for only a moment. "I'm so sorry, Elizabeth."

"There were so many lost. All around our neighborhood. The war, the flu, I… We all just lost count." Survivor's guilt had consumed them all.

She shook her head and studied her hands in her lap. "The war's over four years, and we're still wrapped up like old women in this maddening despair. It's unbearable."

He looked up from his apple, sympathy in his eyes. The sun was behind him. Its beams warmed her cheeks.

"Do you dance?" she asked, studying him as thoughts played across his face.

"Dance? Me? Not really."

"I love dancing. Would you come with me next Saturday? Give it a try?" Elizabeth pushed her cake wrapping away. "I can teach you…"

"I have two left feet, dear girl. Make that three left feet! You don't want me on any dance floor."

Elizabeth was disappointed, but she refused to let it show. He'd spoken with such certainty.

"Look at the time!"

Elizabeth rushed to gather her things while James did the same. They walked through the library's basement labyrinth, while Elizabeth's mind bounced around about how to talk to him. Should she bring up a new subject or try to convince him further what fun he'd have dancing? How strongly would she argue for his participation? She glanced over when they turned each hallway corner. He looked straight ahead, apparently lost in thought.

When they arrived at the third-floor landing, she realized her brow had been furrowed in concentration. A headache had formed where the lines striped her forehead. On the top step, James blew out his breath and reached for the doorknob.

"Well, I'll see you again sometime, I'm sure." He lifted a shoulder in a quick shrug.

"Of course." She smiled and turned to the stairs to continue her upward journey. On the second step, she looked over her shoulder to find James staring after her.

"I think I'll be fine going up here on my own." She pointed up the stairs.

"I imagine you'll do anything just fine on your own, won't you?"

She nodded once and started up the stairs. The doorknob squeaked, and then the door shut with a soft click.

Surprised to find she was holding her breath, she let it out forcefully.

She sat at her desk, thinking about her conversation with James. He was intelligent and fun to lunch with. By the end of the day, though, she was relieved he'd turned down her dancing invitation. Maybe Jocelyn could help her out with a dance partner again.

If James wouldn't dance, then that was that. Did she want to teach a novice how to dance? Honestly…what was she thinking?

Chapter Seven

"Teddy's back in town." Minnie's cup rattled as she poured more coffee.

"What? Oh, I hadn't noticed visitors across the street." Elizabeth put the newspaper down.

While eating breakfast, she'd feigned intense interest in the newspaper to avoid conversing with her mother. Minnie was undeterred by a bit of ink and paper, of course.

"He rode the train in from Washington. Arrived Thursday, I think. Teddy may be here through Christmas. You could see him."

Her mother beamed like she'd offered a brilliant solution on a silver platter. For a nonexistent problem, thought Elizabeth.

"What? Why? That's over."

She waved away the idea. The last thing Elizabeth wanted was a rekindled "romance" with Teddy. They went dancing a few times during her last year of high school. She couldn't recall the last time she'd seen him.

Minnie interrupted her thoughts. "Well…"

"No, Mother. Ancient history." Elizabeth licked a finger and turned a page of the newspaper. She hoped her determined concentration would end this unnecessary conversation. Elizabeth's focus was finding a new dress.

"His mother…um, Sarah says his engagement ended."

Minnie smiled primly over the silver rim of her coffee cup.

"Don't look so pleased. Poor Teddy might be heartbroken."

"Or ready for a new romance—" Minnie said, her voice rising at the end, excited by the possibilities.

"Oh no, you don't! If you try to get me near him, I'll quit speaking to you."

"You hardly speak to me now."

"Because most of our conversations are about marriage. And my failings on the subject."

"It's no mystery how your father and I feel about you girls and your future. We want you respectable and cared for."

Elizabeth's nostrils flared as she put her hands flat on the table.

"Why must we have these nonsensical discussions? I don't want to be cared for! I can take care of myself!"

"Can you?" Minnie stared back at her oldest daughter.

Elizabeth's stomach tightened.

Was it true she could take care of herself? What evidence did she have to offer right now?

Elizabeth curled her fingers around the newspaper, folded it, and started out of the dining room. As soon as she realized she'd left her dishes on the table, she spun on her heels to move them to the sink. She'd be cursed if she left evidence of being incapable of the basics of living.

Minnie was focused on stirring cream into her coffee. Elizabeth thought she saw a smirk playing on her mother's lips.

Back in her bedroom, she took in her surroundings.

She was spoiled, she'd concede that. What did she know about living on her own? Or taking care of herself? A false claim if ever there was one, and her mother knew it.

"Grrr…" she growled and threw the paper on the floor, its pages scattering across the carpet. An advertisement for Lord & Taylor popped out at her, and a shopping plan emerged.

Elizabeth wasted no time getting ready. She needed to get out of the house before her mother pointed out more flaws in her reasoning.

She tried to recruit Anna, who'd been out late last night and refused to be roused from bed.

Elizabeth spent a few moments playing with Maisie.

"Businesses don't let pets in stores…yet. How can I try on a dress with a dog in tow? Good question, huh?" Maisie's tail wagged with obvious understanding.

"Dear sweet doggie, I'll walk you when I get home. I promise."

****

Lord & Taylor's dress racks proved a grand disappointment. Back out on the sidewalk, Elizabeth considered her next move. She took two steps one way, then spun around to go back the way she'd come.

"Is that a new dance you're trying there?" She turned to see James leaning against the store's stone facade, smoking a cigarette. Wisps of white smoke swirled up and away from his right hand.

Incapable of a witty comeback, Elizabeth blinked and smiled nervously. "Hello, James. What are you doing here? Shopping?"

"Ha! No. I'm helping my uncle."

"Oh?" She looked around for the missing uncle.

"He's inside, dear girl. He does repairs in the jewelry department. I try to help on Saturday when he's busy."

Elizabeth summoned a bit of bravado. "Three left feet, but you're good with your hands. Is that right?"

"So now you're a flirt, Elizabeth. I should take you dancing. You think?" James stubbed out his cigarette on the stone wall, his gaze fixed on her. Warmth spread through her. He was actually flirting.

"I like the way you blush. It's sweet."

Elizabeth's face got hotter. "Um…I don't know what to say."

"Say you'll go dancing with me. You said you like dancing, didn't you?"

"I love dancing. But…I thought you said you didn't want to dance. Why would you—"

He waved her words away. "We should go, you and me. I need to make something up to you. I laughed the other day and I think hurt your feelings."

She took a deep breath and words tumbled out. "Tonight? Jasper Hall, eight o'clock?"

James pushed off the wall and nodded. "See you there."

He walked up to the department store's glass door, turned, and bowed with a sweep of his hand toward the pavement. He grinned and went inside. She giggled.

She ran her hands down the front of her navy coat as she thought. Next steps. Get home and call Jocelyn. They had an evening to plan!

Chapter Eight

Elizabeth and Jocelyn arrived at Jasper Hall at seven-thirty to find a place to sit. By the time James showed up, Jocelyn and her latest boyfriend, William, were doing the Lindy Hop in the hot pulsing dance crowd. Clearly, some dancers had been scratching the wood floors for hours. Red-faced men with loosened ties tightly held women whose errant strands of hair stuck to damp and glistening necks.

Elizabeth glanced at her shoes as she smoothed her hands down the pale blue silk of her full skirt. After an exhausting search, she had finally found this dress in the fourth store she visited. James was studying, with some skepticism, the dancers in front of him. He appeared to be looking for a dance step he could manage.

They hadn't stepped foot on the gritty dance floor yet. Based on the frown on his face, Elizabeth was certain she'd made a mistake. James was most decidedly not the dancer in her dreams.

"All right, let's give this a whirl," James pulled a surprised Elizabeth to her feet. She stepped in front and led him to a corner of the floor. She didn't want other dancers to bump into him while they tried to get into their own rhythm. Elizabeth had helped friends in college with dance steps, so she confidently led James through the basic waltz steps, tapping on his right shoulder to signal stepping right, pressing the ball of her palm against his shoulder to have him step backward. Though wooden in his movements, he was a fast learner. Not that the waltz was difficult.

They continued their waltz as Fanny Brice's "My Man" played. James hummed near her ear. His pleasant tone surprised her.

James leaned back to read Elizabeth's expression and grinned through the lyrics, "I don't know why I should. He don't treat me good. Ha!" He laughed as he pulled her back to him. He knew song lyrics? What a surprise this James was. He clearly had a sense of rhythm never discovered or used. And she'd been worried about his limp; shame on her doubting instincts.

As they headed for the main doors to enjoy a few seconds of fresh air, a short man in a brown tweed suit startled Elizabeth when he emerged from a dark corner near the entrance. She noticed his mustache first, then his hair—with a coating of Brilliantine so thick it gave the appearance of a helmet of black patent leather. She couldn't imagine a woman kissing him, not with that slimy mustache. He stuck out his right hand to shake James' hand and introduced himself. "I'm Jim Bellamy, the manager here. I want to ask you two something."

"Ohh…kay." James said slowly, with a quick glance at Elizabeth.

"I noticed you teaching him dance steps, is that right?" Two fingers holding a matchbook pointed at her. He stared straight into her eyes without blinking.

Elizabeth blinked at him. "Yes, I was. Why do you ask?"

"You looked really good at it, ya know? I think people here would like to learn the correct dance steps."

She cut her eyes over to James, who was staring at

the stained beige ceiling.

"I don't understand."

"Well, I'm askin' if you two young people would do a dance demonstration here next Saturday night. Say, at six o'clock."

James let out a whistling breath toward the ceiling.

"Can we talk about it first?" Elizabeth smiled at Mr. Bellamy and pulled on James' arm. They moved toward the door.

"No, absolutely not." James pulled his arm gently out of her grasp.

"Wait. Let me ask you something."

"What?"

"Am I a good teacher?" She cocked her head sideways and looked at him.

"Yes. Actually, you surprised me. And you were very kind."

"Oh. Well, then. All we would have to do next week is what we did tonight."

"In front of people."

"True. The dance floor is full of people now. But I understand. We weren't performing."

"I don't know, Elizabeth." James ran a hand across his face. "I don't do that kind of thing."

"I understand. I could always ask Mr. Bellamy if he'll let me use a different partner."

"No. Um, wait. Give me a minute." James took a deep breath and walked in a circle in front of her. He shoved his hands in his pockets and searched the ceiling for an answer, as if he'd found an oracle.

Elizabeth glanced around for her friends, but the lobby had the look of a platform when a train was coming. Everyone moved in one direction, toward the dance floor. She could hear a popular song starting up, and then "A Pretty Girl Is Like A Melody" drifted into the lobby.

"All right. Let's do it." He held up a hand to squash her excitement. "First, I have questions for the man."

They turned back to where they'd spoken to Mr. Bellamy, but he was gone. Of course, a busy manager couldn't loiter around waiting for two dancers to make a simple decision. Elizabeth scanned the lobby, then started in the direction of the dance floor.

"Whoa, I see him. Over there." James pointed to a spot in the lobby where the overhead lighting was out.

As they headed his way, Mr. Bellamy broke away from the man he was talking to and smiled. "So, you decided?"

"We'll do it." Elizabeth exclaimed and clasped her hands together.

"I've got some questions, Mr. Bellamy."

"Very well."

James got his answers about the time and location of the dance demonstration. They learned he wanted the foxtrot as their featured dance. Mr. Bellamy would provide refreshments for them and their guests. Only one table, he advised. Judging from the condition of this building, they knew he could ill afford to refresh the masses.

"We'll be here early, at 5:30, next Saturday, promise!" Elizabeth shook hands with the surprised Mr. Bellamy.

James and Elizabeth returned to the dance floor to start their practice sessions.

"I can't believe you!" squealed a clapping Jocelyn when she heard the news. "Can we come? Please, oh, please?"

"Of course. We. I, that is, need support. You just have to promise not to laugh." James looked at the ceiling and whistled out a breath again.

"Come on, let's practice." Elizabeth held out a hand to him.

Later, during a slow waltz, they debated how they'd prepare James on such short notice. He offered to meet her to practice in the library's courtyard at lunchtime.

Elizabeth couldn't remember ever having such a marvelous time out dancing. The four of them laughed, swapped dance partners, and told funny stories from their childhoods. Elizabeth thought she might like William more than Jocelyn's previous dates. James certainly got along with him. But he got along with most people, it seemed to her. Still, William was a step above the last fellow Jocelyn brought dancing—Mark, with the roaming hands.

William's family owned an automotive repair shop in Queens, where he'd worked since he was thirteen. He looked at Jocelyn like she hung the moon. They'd met at a dance hall that summer, but for several months he'd been shy about asking her to go dancing. Once he'd gotten up the nerve, Jocelyn hadn't been dancing with anyone else. Elizabeth wondered whether her friend was considering an exclusive arrangement with William. Jocelyn had avoided romantic commitments over the four years she and Elizabeth had been friends. During college, they'd discussed their imaginary futures as unmarried, childless women—having fun and living their own dreams, not those of others.

Bone-tired and silky-hot, the girls headed home in the same direction, leaving their dates talking in front of the hall. The men planned to walk to the same subway station and part there. James lived in Brooklyn and William in Queens. A streetlamp flickered, a sure sign it was creeping past midnight.

Making James her dance partner was an interesting turn of events. She wondered about his transformation. He wasn't a great dancer, but now he was eager to go what seemed like an extra mile. For her.

Chapter Nine

A frigid, cloudy day greeted Elizabeth and James when they entered the courtyard for lunch on Monday. Elizabeth had begun worrying about their chance for dance practice when she woke to a lumpy white-and-gray sky that promised snow, not sun. Now giggles erupted from their throats simultaneously when they stepped out into the sunless courtyard.

"Well, let's just eat our lunch," Elizabeth offered, as she tossed her lunch bag onto the table. She sat in a chair with her coat on.

"We could dance with our coats on."

"Let's eat and see how cold we feel." Disappointment clouded her words, along with her frothy breath.

Alone in the courtyard, Elizabeth and James nibbled on their sandwiches and talked about Jasper Hall. Dancing to jazz in a public dance hall had been a unique experience for James. He fumbled his words as he talked about the dancers and the music, which made Elizabeth want to correct him. So she changed the subject.

"How did you come to work at the library?"

"I like books. I'm a curious person. When I heard about the job, I dropped in and talked to someone. They're not here anymore."

"What kind of books?"

"Oh, anything. Though I prefer autobiographies and

history. I suppose you read a lot?"

"I do. I think I'd rather read than do anything else. Maybe even more than dancing." She winked at him.

"Hmm."

"Hmm?"

"You're an excellent dancer. Well…to me, you are. I haven't danced enough to judge."

Elizabeth smiled and started to clean up her lunch things.

James frowned as he asked, "What are we going to do about practicing? It's winter! I don't think we can expect warmer weather this week."

"Did you get a look at the stage in the Jasper?"

"Uh, no. Why?"

"Come with me." She walked to the door while James followed in confusion.

Once inside the basement hallway, she found what she was looking for.

"Here. Let's hang our coats on this doorknob."

"We're going to dance in here?"

"Why not? It's almost as wide as the stage."

They slipped off their coats and settled their lunch bags on the floor underneath them.

Elizabeth held her right hand up. James moved into her stance.

"Now, James, you have the musical voice, so you get to hum for us."

"Wha…?"

She laughed and began to count beats in four-four time. "We're doing the foxtrot, remember. One and two and three and four."

James stepped back as Elizabeth stepped backward as well. "Sorry."

"The man steps forward first. Two steps, then left, and dip slightly."

"Got it. I think." He laughed and shook his arms like they were rubber.

"All right, we're a bit nervous. That's natural. Let's dance a few repetitions."

She held up her right hand. James took it. His other arm went around her back. Elizabeth rested her left hand on his shoulder and nodded.

"One and two and…"

James took a deep breath and stepped forward. They drifted in a diagonal between the gray walls.

"You need to breathe," Elizabeth whispered.

James lost the rhythm and stepped on her right foot. They separated and bent over, laughing.

'Arghh, I'm so sorry. I'm no good at this."

"We'll try something different. Stand two feet away from me."

"You're afraid I'll crush your other foot?" He stared at the ceiling and let out a breath.

"No, focus on the movements, not on me. Just hold your arms where you would if you were holding me."

"I like holding you."

"Stop it. And one and two and…"

She backed up two steps, and he followed her. He stepped left, and she stepped to her right.

"Quarter turn."

"You're a taskmaster."

"James!"

"I'm still moving, aren't I?"

They stepped and dipped slightly by bending their knees in the narrow hall until James stopped to ask a question.

"Am I doing this right?"

Elizabeth pivoted a quarter turn, her black skirt billowing slightly as she faced him. "I'd have stopped you, if you weren't."

"Good. Let's do it together now."

She walked down the hall toward their coats.

"We can do that tomorrow."

Disappointment crossed his brow. She gave him an indulgent smile. "Can you practice tonight?"

"Where would we do that?"

"I meant tonight at your home. You, on your own."

"Oh, right. Well, um, I can try. Are you really sure about this?"

"You will be fine, James. Saturday will be here and gone before you know it."

He scooped up his lunch bag, and they returned to the stairwell. As they climbed the stairs to his floor, he asked about her current projects. "Are you working in the Reading Room today?"

Because the Reading Room occupied the same floor as his department, James had developed the habit of strolling past her if she was working in there. James took advantage of her proximity when he could. Mostly, they spoke of work—the project in front of her or some mishap in Circulation.

She shook her head. "I've a pile of ancient documents in my office to review. I shouldn't move them."

"Till tomorrow then." He gave her a salute and opened the third-floor door. He disappeared and the heavy wooden door closed with a thud.

She stared trancelike at the closed door, remembering James singing "My Man" two nights ago.

A little shiver passed through her. The stairwell was unheated, she reminded herself as she pulled her coat tighter around her waist. To clear her mind, Elizabeth sprinted up the stairs to her floor.

****

"I'd get these steps down better if we had music."

"Unfortunately, humming and beat counting are the best I can muster, James."

She patted his shoulder, and he took a step toward her as she backed away.

Wednesday was no warmer than Monday, so they'd retreated again to the hallway after quickly eating in the sun-splashed cold. This section of the library's basement was used mostly for storage, so there'd been no traffic to impede their dance practice.

"I'm sorry my hand is so sweaty, Elizabeth." He rubbed his right hand on his shirt.

"One day, you won't be nervous at all. Can you imagine that?"

"No, honestly, I can't. You've been doing this, what, since you were four?"

"But…notice what you just did! You talked while you danced. It's sinking in and you don't have to concentrate as much."

He grinned. And stepped on her foot.

"Ow!"

"Argh. See? I'm clumsy no matter how much you try to convince me otherwise."

"All right, let's try something different. You're going to hold me more tightly, and I want you to concentrate only on the way my hips and shoulders move. Feel the rhythm."

"This should be interesting." He wiggled his

eyebrows.

Elizabeth scowled at him. "Never mind."

"No, let's try that. I'll behave."

"Yes, be a grownup, why don't you?" One corner of her mouth tilted up, so he'd know she was teasing.

"Here goes." James placed his left arm around her waist and pulled her close. He took her hand in his still sweaty one.

"Let me lead. I'm still stepping back, though, okay?"

"Got it."

"And…one and two and…"

They danced down the hall and pivoted to return to where they started.

"That was good. Let's do it again, but close your eyes this time."

James frowned.

"Trust me?"

"Well, I hardly know you."

She giggled and slapped his shoulder. "You just held me closer than any man ever has, so trust me."

"Lucky me." He wiggled his eyebrows again.

"Oh, heavens."

"I can behave, I can. I promise." He chuckled.

"And…one and two and…"

They kept up the practice for several turns down the hallway. Elizabeth watched James' focused expression. With his eyes closed and his lips slightly parted, she found herself imagining him kissing her.

"Oof!" Distracted by that thought, she forgot to pivot and bumped into the wall. Still in motion, James' weight pressed into her and she was pinned there. James' eyes flew open, and looked into hers. Elizabeth swallowed.

"All right. End of lesson. We should get back to work."

James backed away, still focused on her face.

"How'd I do?"

"You're getting better."

"That's it?"

'You'll be fabulous on Saturday."

"Why do I get the feeling you're humoring me?"

They were quiet on the walk back to the third floor. Elizabeth pondered their growing closeness and the wisdom of letting this friendship flourish. James was much like an open book about his feelings on the subject of them together, unless she was misreading the situation entirely. It was up to her to ensure things didn't get out of hand.

"You want to practice more, or have you got it?"

"I need to work on it more. Tomorrow?"

"See you at lunchtime, then." Elizabeth swiveled, and sensing James was watching, she walked rather than sprinted up the stairs. She listened for his door to open and close, but it didn't. What was he thinking about right now?

Oh dear, she thought. Whatever was she thinking? Or was she thinking at all? Her strong mind and sense of the future were missing in this moment, lost in the memory of James' lovely lips so near hers.

Having James in her life would be nothing but trouble.

****

Elizabeth had a surprise waiting for her when she returned to the Research Department offices.

Mr. Gerold informed her that Jean had announced

her engagement while she was away at lunch. He held her gaze briefly, as if he thought she should have informed him.

"Well, this is news to me! Hm. I'll get back to my work."

Elizabeth didn't see Jean on her way back to her desk. She hadn't heard of a serious boyfriend in Jean's life. It was a puzzle. She'd find out soon enough from Jean or Matilda before the workday ended.

"A baby?"

"Shhhh!!" Jean looked cautiously over her shoulder. She had pulled her chair into the doorway of Elizabeth's cramped office. She was brimming with the news of a baby coming and her wedding, both just months away.

Elizabeth couldn't help but glance at Jean's stomach. It was as flat as a pancake, of course. She wouldn't be showing this soon, and hopefully not by March either. The plan was to keep the cat in the bag as long as possible, then announce in May, "Surprise! A baby is coming!"

"Tell me about the baby's father."

"Oh, he is just fabulous about everything! He can't wait to get married."

Elizabeth tilted her head, suspicious about such exuberance. That wasn't how she imagined most of these conversations going between frightened couples, suddenly expecting a baby after knowing each other only months. In Jean's case, it had to be a weeks-long romance.

Jean must have read her mind because she piped up with an answer: "I met Billy in high school. We saw each other at a dance in October and started a thing."

Ah, a thing. The famous "thing" that made babies.

Elizabeth was worried for Jean, afraid for her future. She assumed Jean would not be working after her wedding, and she would be missed in the research department. Jean, for all her chatter in the office, was a hard worker. She thought research problems through, while Matilda usually jumped into a project without a plan.

Mr. Gerold had sighed in frustration over Matilda's desk many a day. Pages of documents from the archive floated around her desk, often unused and unnecessarily exposed to air, soil, and oils from ungloved hands. The risk to these old documents was considerable each time they were removed from their safe storage.

Elizabeth stayed late that day to finish a project. Looking around the darkened offices, she mulled over the changes that would come to their department in the coming months. Jean was about to go through something life-altering, and Elizabeth hoped her friend wasn't relegated to wife and mother forever. That was too much to ask of a woman these days, in her opinion.

She, too, had some life changes to consider, like finding a place to live. Having done no research on that front, she wondered if she'd ever leave her family home.

Surely she'd escape, she thought, as she slipped into her navy wool coat. Adjusting her hair under her lovely navy hat, Elizabeth smiled at the idea of living on her own, coming and going, no questions asked.

Chapter Ten

"Aren't you dapper?"

James wore a black serge suit and a white shirt. His tie sported a black-and-white diamond pattern.

"Yeah, but look at you." James' eyes drank her in. She twirled once, causing the pleated black hem to flare. Her dress was a narrow sheath of wine-hued silk. Black piping ran down from the high neck to the hem every few inches, creating the impression of a fluted column. Jet earrings dangled from her ears. Anna had helped her iron her dark brown hair into Marlene Dietrich waves.

Mr. Bellamy had even gone to some extra effort in the ballroom. The stage was decked with a Christmas tree, shimmering with red and gold ornaments. Elizabeth and James walked up the stage steps together.

"Let's go behind that piano and practice a moment. I want you to feel how the stage floor gives a little."

"Elizabeth, I…"

"Shhh. Come with me."

They moved quietly at the back of the stage and, quickly, James got his confidence back.

"You're marvelous. You know that? I could not do this with anyone else." James ran a sweaty hand down the front of his jacket.

"Tell me what you'll do if I make a wrong step."

"I'll keep dancing."

"Perfect. All right, we're ready. Let's find the band

manager. What do you think of our dancing to 'Margie'?" Elizabeth glanced back at him.

"Good choice. I know the words."

"No, you must not sing. Focus, James."

James sighed. "I bring so little to your little play, and you won't let me sing."

"My little play?"

"Ignore me. Let's find the band manager, shall we?" He grabbed her hand and helped her off the stage.

While they'd practiced, their table had begun to fill. Elizabeth waved at Anna, Jocelyn, and William, already seated there.

"When will they feed me?" James whined dramatically, then grinned at her.

Elizabeth waved the band manager down to ask about the music. She drifted off with the fellow, and James sauntered over to Elizabeth's friends. Anna introduced herself, but James wasn't paying attention. Elizabeth watched her dance partner watching her while she talked about the music for the demo. She saw his body relax when she started back to the table.

"We got our song." She clasped her hands in front of her chest.

"Where's Bellamy? Isn't he here to tell us when to do this?"

"Stop worrying."

James loosened his tie at his neck and unbuttoned his top shirt button. Elizabeth glanced his way but said nothing. She chatted with Anna and Jocelyn. William had wandered off. Charles, Jocelyn's cousin, hadn't arrived yet. The band warmed up, sending tuneless notes tumbling around the room.

"William's back again? That's a good sign."

"Time will tell." Jocelyn shrugged.

The girls laughed. Poor fellow, mused Elizabeth. A loud noise stopped their laughter and their attention turned to the stage. Mr. Bellamy stood uncomfortably on stage at a microphone. He introduced the dance demonstration and beckoned to Elizabeth and James. They mounted the stage stairs and stood beside him. James refused to glance at the audience. The ballroom was not full, but well-dressed dancers steadily filed in while Mr. Bellamy talked. He stretched out an arm dramatically in their direction and the band started to play "Margie."

The couple faced each other, held up their arms, and moved into each other's stance. Elizabeth nodded, and they were dancing. James was naturally tempted to study his feet, but Elizabeth kept smiling at him to maintain his attention. He got too close a few times, his breath warm on her cheek. She whispered to him as the song ended, "Look at you!"

They held hands and bowed to applause and whistles. Anna squealed, "That's my sister!" She twirled and whooped and made a lot of noise.

James pulled Elizabeth to him and hugged her. Her heart sent a sizzle up to her brain and a momentary lightheadedness blurred her vision. The applause grew louder. James beamed at her. They turned again to the audience and bowed in unison.

Mr. Bellamy was good on his word and kept their table satisfied with refreshments all evening. The group danced merrily until nearly midnight.

During a brief break from dancing, Mr. Bellamy gestured to James, who tapped the chatting Elizabeth on the shoulder and thumbed at the manager. They left the table and joined the man near the dance floor.

"I want you to do this after Christmas too."

James pursed his lips and avoided Elizabeth's gaze.

"Do you have a featured dance in mind, Mr. Bellamy?" Elizabeth asked, avoiding James' eyes as well.

"How's about the Shimmy?"

Elizabeth's mouth dropped open, but she closed it quickly.

"Um, don't you think that's easy for everyone already?"

"Maybe, but can you class it up a little? Make it look better? People wanna ban it, ya know?"

"We'll be back." She took James' hand and walked him to the lobby. His eyes went to the ceiling immediately. He exhaled a whistling breath between his teeth.

"Geez, Elizabeth."

"Right, but…the Shimmy is very easy. I mean, anyone can do it."

"Ahh."

She shook her shoulders back and forth, then leaned to each side. "That's the Shimmy."

"I've seen people do that. Sure."

"Listen, if we can get free admission and refreshments, why not do it? It'll be a new year, too. Our 1923 will start with dancing!"

"I don't know what that's got to do with the price of tea in China, but if you say so."

"Happy birthday to me!" Elizabeth exclaimed as she clapped her hands and headed back to Mr. Bellamy. James trailed glumly behind her.

"Same deal? Admission and refreshments for our

table?" Elizabeth asked.

"Deal." He reached to shake James' hand, but Elizabeth put hers forward.

"Thank you, Mr. B. We'll be here in three weeks." His brow furrowed. He shook her hand while looking at James.

Elizabeth smoothed her hands down the front of her dress and beamed at James.

All he could do was shrug. He didn't look terribly happy about it. She knew he'd come around.

As they returned to the table, she thought about spending more lunches with James, practicing their dancing. He was growing on her, she admitted to herself.

She kept reminding James to focus when they danced. What was happening to her own focus?

Chapter Eleven

Henry Alter seldom spent evenings after work in the small library off the parlor. But it became his Saturday home when his daughters no longer demanded his special attendance at tea parties upstairs, private dance recitals, playing dress-up, or crawling around their small backyard talking about insects. He had been brilliant at the backyard business, being very knowledgeable about bugs. His college studies had been in biology, yet he ended up in banking and finance. Henry excelled at that, too, and had become an investment house manager before turning forty.

The girls had been young, and in grade school, when he started working late and missed dinner sometimes. That was the part the girls hated most. Father made dinners fun. He encouraged them to shine and kept Minnie from fussing about spoons, spills, and slurps. If she wasn't already in bed on his late nights, Elizabeth would visit him while he ate alone in the kitchen. It never occurred to her at age eight that Mother should share that time with Father.

He always welcomed his family of women into the dark-paneled library. Elizabeth especially, because she usually entered to take something off a bookshelf. To the left of his desk was a wall of shelves that climbed almost to the ceiling. Henry carried her on his shoulders for long stretches of time while she asked about books and read the first pages, still up in the air, breathing in dust, polish, and the manly scent of the special man carrying her.

Henry removed his reading glasses when she entered. It was Friday night, and Elizabeth had elected to stay home, away from the dance halls. She was tired too after a busy week. Projects in her specialties created a mountain of expectation, and Mr. Gerold had remarked that her reputation was the reason such a list of research requests tumbled across her desk. Some people thought she could discover anything from the "Annals of Time," her unimaginative nickname for the library's vast archive rooms.

Henry Alter had a frank gaze—the look of an accountant—and he leaned back in his chair, a signal he was free to talk. Arranged like a business office, two deep green chairs faced his desk. To avoid the feeling of an awkward interview, she pulled a chair beside his desk and sat. She examined her nails while she gathered her thoughts.

"In summer, I will be out of college a year."

He nodded. She studied his face, wondering if he knew where she was going with this.

"I want to live on my own. I need to be independent before I get married or anything."

"Or anything?" He was always like this. Exasperating! One couldn't get away with flippant words around Father. Everything needed meaning, or a framework.

"I don't know what that means, maybe moving away for a different job. Maybe not getting married."

"You just turned twenty-three last week."

Henry picked up a gold pen and tapped it on his desk. "I remember the morning you were born. Your

75

mother wanted to end 1899 with her first baby. For some silly reason I don't remember. But you refused to come until 1900."

"I've never heard that story. You're not implying I'm stubborn, are you?"

She grinned at her father.

"Not at all. You're a determined young woman, as you should be. And I agree with you. Your desire to move out of your family's home is understandable. But…"

"Will Mother agree with you?"

"Ahh, so that's why you're here."

She shook her head fiercely.

"No. That's not why. If you cautioned me or suggested I wait, I would listen to you. You're reasonable."

"And your mother's not." Statement and question blended in one.

"I don't think she's going to like my moving away at all."

"Elizabeth." Henry captured her gaze.

"Yes, Father?" She sat up straight, sweaty palms resting on her knees.

"I agree with your mother in certain respects. Both of us, of course, have always imagined you leaving this home. When you got married."

"Oh, no. I didn't expect that you'd be on that bandwagon too." Tears threatened, clogging her throat.

Henry sighed and shook his head.

"Where do you think you would live, my dear?"

"I'm not certain. Jocelyn just moved into a house with other young women. A rooming house. It doesn't sound optimal."

"Optimal." Henry chuckled. "That's your kind of word."

She bit her lip. Tears pricked the corners of her eyes again.

"I've got no ideas. Not sure how to start."

Henry patted her hand resting on his desk.

"How did Jocelyn find her rooming house?"

Elizabeth pursed her lips in thought. She shook her head.

"Maybe she told me a customer of the shop gave her an idea. I'll ask her."

Henry nodded. He slipped his glasses back on, the lamp's light blinked across the disks of glass covering his eyes.

"Tell me about this house."

"Jocelyn's? Well, it's around 45th. Yes, near the Tenderloin District. Her Pops isn't too pleased about that. Or any of it, really. But…"

She smiled tentatively at her father before she continued.

"The house is quite nice. And clean. All women, of course. And Mrs. Nesbitt, she's the owner. She might be a bit strict."

Henry sat silent. She imagined the wheels turning in his head. Elizabeth resisted the temptation to fill the silence. Her grandfather's mantel clock pushed its soft ticking into the void.

"Let me give this some consideration. I may have an idea or two. Don't get your hopes up."

She leaped up and hugged him tightly. "Oh, thank you, Father!"

"There's one other thing."

Elizabeth clasped her hands in front of her and

leveled her gaze at her father.

"This young man. James, is it? What are your thoughts about him?"

"Well, he's very nice."

"He was in the war?"

"Briefly, in England. He's only twenty-seven, Father. Not much older than me."

"I wasn't worried about that."

"You're worried about James?"

"Not especially, no. Your mother might—"

"Oh, I can imagine. Not quite the perfect match since he's from Brooklyn?"

Henry removed his glasses and wiped them with a white handkerchief.

"If things get serious, be prepared for it to come up."

Elizabeth stood beside his desk.

"Thank you for the warning. I'm glad we can speak like this. Not all my friends have a father like you."

Henry nodded as he put his glasses back on.

"Well, my dear, you're a delightful young woman. I enjoy your company, too."

Elizabeth moved around his desk again and kissed him on the top of his head. His dark hair was thinning a little near the crown. She hated to think of him getting older.

"And Father…"

"Yes?"

"We won't get serious."

Up in her room, Elizabeth looked out her window into the rainy darkness. She wished she could see the stars and moon. Instead, droplets on the glass sparkled in the light of a streetlamp. Leaning her forehead against the cool glass, she closed her eyes and replayed tonight's conversation.

Was Father on her side? About an apartment, at least?

James was a more troublesome issue. But was he really a problem for her? Hadn't she just told the truth?

Elizabeth sighed, her breath creating a foggy circle on the glass. If only she could wipe away the fog of doubt from her mind as easily as clearing fog from a window.

Chapter Twelve

The Shimmy had been banned in some cities, but younger people loved the dance. Elizabeth didn't tell James she'd seen a couple tossed out of a dance hall for dancing a too-risqué version of the scandalous dance.

Elizabeth had concocted a string of moves to make the Shimmy a classier dance, as Mr. Bellamy had requested. Her ideas allowed for the shimmy motion to occur when the couple was not touching, since the movement while they were together was considered overtly sensual and therefore the main reason for objections to the dance. Waltzing steps brought the couple together, but then he released her into a spin. The dancers shook their shoulders left and right while facing each other. They came together to repeat the waltz steps.

They performed to the song "The Sheik of Araby." Its two-beat time was perfect for their new version of the dance. If the Jasper audience was disappointed in the slower, less physical version of the Shimmy, the couple never knew it. Again, like the last one, this demonstration was met with thunderous applause. Mr. Bellamy sidled up to them later that night to thank them for exceeding his expectations.

"I really thought you might do something shocking. Thank God, you didn't! Jasper Hall has to stay open. Ya know?" His hair sparkled in the dim light of the chandeliers overhead.

"Indeed, Mr. Bellamy. We're glad you're pleased." James reached out to shake the man's hand.

"You wouldn't do another one, would you? You're good for business!"

"Uh, no. I'm sorry, but we can't." James avoided Elizabeth's glance. She stood tensely beside him, waiting for the manager to leave them. Mr. Bellamy accepted the answer with a sad shake of his head.

"Let me know if you change your mind." He offered as he backed away with a slight bow.

"We could've discussed it."

"No, Elizabeth, a discussion would have led to another demonstration. You're determined. You're used to getting your way, aren't you?"

"I'm not! You think I'm bossy?"

James quirked an eyebrow at her, and she slapped him lightly on the arm.

"Shall I ask Anna? What would she say?"

"Go ahead. I can beat her into submission tomorrow." She laughed. "I'm joking."

"Let's get something to eat. All that shimmying made me hungry and thirsty."

James and William spent some of the evening talking quietly together. Elizabeth suspected they were talking about women. One of them would glance over their way, and heads would nod.

Anna wasn't yet aware that her sister had set her sights on an apartment. Elizabeth cornered her sister and begged for secrecy while they were in the ladies' room.

"I want to tell you something, but I don't have to tell you at all. I need you to swear your silence."

"All right. I can keep a secret."

Elizabeth raised her perfectly shaped eyebrows at

her younger sibling.

"I can! Now, tell me."

"I talked to Father last Saturday about wanting to find my own place." Elizabeth grabbed her sister's forearms and beamed.

"No! Why's it a secret?"

"Mother, of course.

"When are you moving?"

"Well, I need to find a place first. You're not getting rid of me that fast. But I hope I can get everything worked out before summer comes."

""My, my. Aren't you independent? You've started getting on with your life."

A girl coming into the ladies' room interrupted them. Both sisters nodded at her. Elizabeth grabbed the open door and said, "Come on. We're missing dancing time."

"Wait. Does James know?"

"James? No. It's fresh news, a week old."

"Shouldn't you tell him? He really likes you, oh boy."

"You think so?"

"Oh, Elizabeth. Don't be thick. You like him, too. We all can tell."

Elizabeth whirled toward Anna.

"You're talking about us? That's not fair."

"It's silly prattle. Just a little speculation." Anna fluttered her eyelashes at her sister.

"Arghh." Elizabeth stormed to their table and stood in front of James.

"Dance?" he asked.

"That would be lovely." She smiled at James, then glared at Anna.

She didn't feel like dancing right now. The idea of romantic speculation about her and James made her panic. She did like James, a lot. But she didn't need a man muddying up her plans to become an independent woman. She wasn't getting serious about anyone, not even a man as lovely as James. These days, married and independent didn't go together in any sentence describing a woman. Nor any sentence her mother might utter.

Anna had asked her about telling James, as though Elizabeth were keeping a secret from him. She wasn't! She respected her mother, no matter how annoying Minnie might be. Elizabeth owed it to her parents to discuss such an enormous change with them first. Her stomach tightened at the thought of that conversation with Minnie.

Out on the dance floor, James struggled to get Elizabeth to talk. The slow waltz was the perfect dance for having a private conversation. Her lips remained tightly closed and her mind seemed far away.

When the tune ended, she stood stiffly, while dancers moved around them.

"What's the matter, Elizabeth? You came back with Anna all out of sorts."

"Can we talk?"

"Of course. Maybe out of the ballroom." He gestured to the door leading to the lobby.

They found a quiet, dark corner. Leaning against the wall, she folded her arms over her chest. James' eyebrows furrowed together.

"I'll ask again. What's going on?"

"Did you know they're talking about us?"

She nodded impatiently toward the ballroom. She

didn't tell him she hated being speculated about. Particularly about things she had little confidence in. Were they a couple or were they dance partners? She had only wanted a dance partner when all this started.

What did she want now?

Anna's comments had made her angry and confused. What was she missing? Or was she intentionally avoiding the subject of romance and its necessary entanglements?

"Who?"

"Our friends. They're wondering about us together."

"Oh dear. That's horrible." James put a hand against his cheek in mock horror.

It was her turn to knit her brows together. She struggled to detect his meaning.

He chuckled. "Elizabeth. My, my."

"What are—"

"I…like…you."

"I like you too. You're funny and easy to…what?" He was shaking his head. He took her hands in his.

"I like you and want to date you. Actually date you. Not just dance for peanuts."

She blushed.

"There's that sweet blushing again. I hope I'm the only one who gets that reaction."

"They're not standing in line, if that's what you mean."

"I doubt you'd have to try hard to change that."

She snorted a laugh. "Honestly, James."

"Honest James is telling you the truth. You're lovely and frighteningly smart."

They were standing toe to toe in the dimly lit corner of the lobby. They quietly studied each other.

Embarrassed, Elizabeth broke the staring exercise first. She rubbed her bare arms.

"You want to date me?" She looked at him with wide eyes.

Hands in his pockets, he rocked back on his heels, threw back his head, and laughed.

"Would you go?"

She shook her head to clear her thoughts. She looked away, into the ballroom.

"Elizabeth?" James' voice reached into her. It sounded like a plea.

"James," she sighed, "I…I'm not sure I want to date anyone. Not seriously. I want to be on my own. Oh…never mind. You don't understand."

"What don't I understand?"

"All right. I don't want to sound presumptuous, but I've no genuine interest in getting married anytime soon. And…"

James leaned forward, listening, his hands in the pockets of his black pants.

"Yes? Keep goin'." He grinned at her, and she wanted to bolt. She was serious about her life and here he was, grinning like a hyena.

"You're embarrassing me." She rubbed her arms again and looked away.

"Look, I said 'date' not 'marry,' okay?"

Elizabeth frowned.

"Elizabeth, dear girl, can we just go out to dinner or something? No strings."

"Promise?"

"This will be the strangest thing I have ever said. I will not ask you to marry me. Satisfied?"

"So, we're just friends. Dinner, not a date? Right?"

"Well, hallelujah, that's settled. If that's what we call it." James shook his head and stuck out a hand toward her.

"Shall we?" he asked, pointing to the ballroom. The band was playing a waltz, James' favorite.

"I suppose I should tell you. I'm thinking of moving to an apartment."

"Really? Hmm."

"I haven't started looking yet, but—"

"I bet there are great places in Brooklyn. I'll start looking." James wiggled his eyebrows.

"That's awfully kind of you."

"Really. You'd leave Manhattan and live in Brooklyn?" He frowned at her.

"What? No, I don't suppose I would. Look in Manhattan, will you?" She moved into his arms for a waltz.

"I suppose it's a mistake to tell you I'd do anything for you."

Elizabeth stepped back and stuck a finger in his chest. "You can't say things like that to someone you're not dating."

James looked at the ceiling and blew out his breath.

She didn't know what he was thinking, but she suspected he liked her too much to keep his promise. Elizabeth also suspected they were making a mistake. She was definitely making a mistake, but dinner sounded nice.

Chapter Thirteen

Elizabeth bounced out of bed on that late January morning and threw open her thick blue drapes. The sun screamed "good morning" in the winter sky. Touching the cold window, she decided it was a sweater day. She found thick tights to wear with a basic black skirt and a heavy cream sweater.

James had seen her nearly every workday for the past two months. She doubted he studied a woman's wardrobe. She smiled at herself in the mirror. That motion reminded her to check her teeth. She grimaced to display her bottom row and then pulled at her cheeks to see inside her mouth. Her mouth was fine, but she breathed into her hand. Maybe she'd spend some extra minutes with her mother's special tooth powder this morning.

When James arrived, she was ready in her navy coat and her favorite hat. James had turned up in a black double-breasted coat over his usual work clothes. He'd tried, she could tell.

"Hello," he said as she pulled the heavy black door closed.

"Good morning, James." She hurried down the steps to meet him on the sidewalk. She looked up at him and smiled.

"I am a little earlier than noon. Did you know the Sunday train from Brooklyn practically comes straight to your house?"

"Does it really?" She frowned, doubt in her tone.

"Ah, you're too smart for me. No, it does not. I got off on the opposite side of Central Park. My mistake. I'll take the right train next time."

"Ever the optimist."

"Elizabeth, you are positively horrible to me."

"Lunch then? I'm famished."

"It's your turn to lead on, I suppose. Where are we going?"

"What about Garrison's Deli, near work?" She readjusted her hat and tucked a strand of hair behind her ear.

He nodded as they started up the sidewalk. Someone laughed, and it sounded awfully familiar.

"James?" The high-pitched voice of Lillie reached her ears. She and another young woman were walking toward them.

Elizabeth glanced over at James who was still looking over his shoulder for the location of that voice.

"I didn't know you lived around here, James."

"I don't. Elizabeth lives here." He pointed his thumb over his shoulder toward the Alter home.

"Oh." Lillie looked at James, then at Elizabeth, her expression perplexed.

"See you at work tomorrow, Lillie." James smiled at his young coworker.

Lillie's friend pulled at her still form and they moved slowly away. Lillie gave Elizabeth and James a last puzzled glance and walked on down the sidewalk.

"Interesting," James muttered as they walked in the opposite direction.

"She must live around here. Ugh."

"Elizabeth. What's wrong with Lillie? She's a kid."

"A kid who has a crush on you."

Elizabeth laid a hand over her heart in a mocking gesture.

"Women. Honestly."

"Pay attention. You'll see what I am saying is true."

"Right. I'll pay more attention to Lillie and see—" James turned around to face her, walking backward. His wide grin mocking her.

Elizabeth interrupted, "That's not at all what I meant, and you know it."

James snickered.

They chatted amiably all the way to the subway ticket window. James bought their tickets, only pennies each, but a wave of guilt washed over her. His family was not well off, and he lived at home to help out.

Standing on the platform, James turned to face her. "About your moving-out plan. Have you made any progress since last week?"

"None. I've only circled a few advertisements in the newspaper." Elizabeth sighed.

"When I got out of the Army, my buddy Andy asked me to live in a rooming house he'd found. Thought we'd be two happy palookas chasing dames." He shook his head and laughed.

"Why didn't you?"

"Nah. I needed to stay with the family and help out Pop."

As the train rushed into the tunnel, she held her hat so it wouldn't blow off. Her coat flapped at the hem. The thick air was like a hug, and she slid closer to James as the train stopped. His hand brushed the small of her back as he maneuvered them onto the train before the doors closed.

The rattle and jostle of the train kept their arms touching the entire ride. Neither one attempted to pull away. They rode quietly, each in their own thoughts.

Elizabeth looked at their window reflections that brightened and darkened as the train shifted through tunnels and lit platforms. She pondered their conversation at Jasper Hall, and wondered if two people of the opposite sex could remain only friends. She couldn't conjure up a living example. Elizabeth was determined to live on her own and focus on a profession—in what, she didn't know. The library wasn't her final workplace, but it was far too early to consider a different job now.

"This is our stop." James' voice broke through her reverie. He was standing with a hand open to her. She waited for the train to stop before getting up. He held her hand as they slipped through the crowd of people exiting and boarding, then let it go to point out the stairs they needed to take. Her arm felt heavy without his touch.

Garrison's Deli was busy. They entered the warm restaurant filled with customer voices and the clinking of dishes and silverware. A voice from the kitchen announced their arrival. Quickly, a waitress in a blue-and-white-striped uniform dress slipped a ticket pad in the white apron's pocket and sashayed toward them. She took the longest strides, and the result was a full sway of her hips. As she walked by, a few men watched over their coffee cups.

She was pretty once. Her red hair was fading—a bottle rinse had been applied too long ago. She greeted them brightly, through red-stained lips, and led them to a table in the front corner by the window.

"Thank you." James set his hat on the table, then pulled out a chair for Elizabeth and nodded at the waitress.

"Coffee?" They both nodded at Yvonne, her name announced by the tag she wore.

"You been here before?" asked James.

"Jean, Matilda, and I came here a few months ago before going to a movie."

"What movie?"

She put her hand over her mouth and pondered. "I don't remember. Isn't that terrible?"

James shrugged. "Didn't make an impression, sounds like."

"I prefer books. But I told you that already."

"Same reason I love the library."

She nodded and looked at the menu. "I'm having a club sandwich."

"I was thinking that, too."

"I'm not terribly hungry. Want to share one?"

"My mother is making a Sunday dinner tonight, so that may be best. My brother and his family are coming." James placed his menu on top of hers.

"You have a little nephew, right?"

"Danny." James' eyes lit up as he described the toddler's antics.

"He sounds like a sweet, funny boy."

Yvonne interrupted their conversation with the sandwich platter.

They ate quietly for a few minutes, satiating the hunger pangs roused by the deli's mouthwatering smells of frying meat and baking bread. It didn't take them long to polish off the shared sandwich.

James helped Elizabeth into her coat, and they left

the deli to wander aimlessly for a little while, moving between warm sunshine and the cold shade of trees along the sidewalk.

Their relaxed chatter jumped between work and their families, gossip about friends and coworkers. James had heard about Jean's pregnancy and upcoming marriage and asked her what she thought.

She shrugged. "I'm worried about her. She's so smart, and I can't imagine her stuck at home doing nothing."

"Doing nothing?" James' mouth hung open.

"Well, mothering. But—"

"That's not nothing, Elizabeth. Wife and mother is the most important calling in the world!"

A calling? A chuckle caught in her throat. James was serious, and she wouldn't laugh at such a belief.

"You feel very strongly about that, I see."

"I'm twenty-seven years old. Why wouldn't I feel strongly about having a family?"

She bit her bottom lip. "Well, true. I haven't given it much thought yet."

Elizabeth didn't know what else to say. She avoided looking at James. She could sense him staring at her.

"Should we go back?" she asked.

"Sure." James turned around slowly.

Lost in their own thoughts, they almost walked past the subway entrance.

In that moment, she experienced the day's first pang of guilt. His family lived in a cramped house in Brooklyn, a sibling, an uncle, and even a boarder. She couldn't imagine. Just being around James made her realize how spoiled she was. She took everything about her life for granted. And she wanted more, she hated to admit.

Elizabeth suggested they separate at the subway station and return home separately. James would hear none of it.

"What would your parents think?"

She didn't want to think about that at all.

On the sidewalk in front of her house, they talked about the work facing them in the morning. He had a staff meeting, and she was completing a research report.

He looked up at her house. "When you move out, it'll be quite a change. Can you manage it?"

She straightened her back and responded like a soldier to her commander. "I will make the adjustment!"

James bowed his head toward her and whispered near her ear, "Until tomorrow."

And he was gone. His back retreated the way they'd come and disappeared around the next corner.

Elizabeth walked inside, hoping her parents weren't around. Her father had delivered no ideas about her moving out, and she didn't want to have more discussion on the subject right now. She disappointed herself. Shouldn't an independent woman speak her mind boldly?

Chapter Fourteen

Elizabeth was astounded by James' embrace of dancing. They had settled into such a spirited routine, she should have known something would go wrong and ruin everything. Even if she had predicted a disaster, there was no way even she could have imagined the pending debacle and the pain it would cause.

One February Saturday night, they visited a dance hall they had never been inside before. The leaflet she'd found made it sound palatial and exquisite. Elizabeth was over the moon to see this place and experience splendid dancing with James, Anna, and all their friends.

The event featured a live ten-piece band. Jocelyn and Elizabeth had begged the doorman, John, at Jasper Hall, for information about how they might get in without waiting. He offered no help. Elizabeth crossed her fingers that things would go their way, and a long evening of leaning against a cold brick wall would not ruin the night.

The Brisbane was located just on the edge of the Tenderloin District. This area of New York was notable for its scandal, both exaggerated and real. The red-light district and what the newspapers referred to as the "vicious" element of the city lurked within its dingy streets.

And dance halls invited scandal, didn't they? The newspapers were filled with stories about lewd dancing, indecency, bare-skinned women, drinking, and associated sins. To Elizabeth, these stories emphasized the rarest happenings around the city.

She and her friends were fortunate they could attend dances in community halls, which attracted a more sedate crowd. The attendees at those dances weren't boring, but they certainly weren't having sex in the hallways, like the newspapers suggested.

Over the past year, Elizabeth had tried to ignore the women's groups that assembled to protest in the city, waving signs, screaming at scantily dressed young women in lines outside these supposed houses of ill repute. They were, in fact, just dance halls where young people listened to music and danced.

Still, a segment of the public maintained their opposition. Elizabeth and her friends agreed that the old fuddy-duddies were on a tear to dismantle both public dancing and the ills of this music called Jazz. An uphill battle for the dancers, for certain. They had heard all the arguments against public dancing from family members, yet they remained devoted to their weekend entertainment.

As they approached The Brisbane, their group was undeterred by the crowd outside. Knowing they had no special way into the building that evening, they lined up on the sidewalk with everyone else, hoping the wait would be brief. Winter promised to hang around longer, refusing to let the next season swagger in with much-needed warmth. The anxious dancers felt the promise of an early morning frost. Huddling and chatting closely together, the remains of their words rose in frothy clouds above them as the evening wore on.

They were nearly frozen to the bone by the time they

gained entry to the hall. The moment they walked into the lobby, the girls focused on the extravagantly painted ceiling and the dark walnut columns that supported it. The architectural detail in this old building overwhelmed the senses. Elizabeth thought she'd died and gone to heaven, and briefly, she forgot about dancing. But the live band had its own pull, and soon the soles of their shoes shuffled across the enormous dance floor. Large cream and red tiles formed a checkerboard on which more than a hundred dancers swayed and bumped. The room was a kaleidoscope of the vibrant silks and sequins the women wore. Only the smell of cigarette smoke marred the atmosphere, successfully competing with the scents of sweat and soap.

James and Elizabeth were doing a fast version of the two-step close to the group's table where Jocelyn and William were resting and talking, heads close together. Jocelyn was fanning herself. Elizabeth wasn't sure where Anna and Jocelyn's cousin Charles had gone. She was too intent on her footwork to care. James grabbed her hand, pulled her to him, and spun her around. The music was incredible and so was their dancing. Happiness had wormed its way into her heart.

The sound of the whistle didn't register over the trombone and saxophones and piano immediately. A din of feminine squeals and men's shouting erupted over at the entrance. Elizabeth heard someone say, "Police," and she froze, staring at James. He yanked her toward their table, where they grabbed their coats and bags. Elizabeth searched for her sister in the fray. People were stumbling in all directions. When the band's trumpeter stopped playing, it sounded like the comical punctuation of a clown skit.

With Anna nowhere in sight, James snatched the coat and bag she'd left on a chair. William found a likely path away from the police. Over James' shoulder, Elizabeth saw a scowling older matron pushing farther into the ballroom and watched a dancer wrestle a placard from the woman's wrinkled hands. Elizabeth, in her frightened state, couldn't recall the name of her mother's friend now studying her with sudden recognition.

Terror filled Elizabeth's throat. She thought she'd suffocate, as if someone had stuffed a rag in her mouth. James pushed her roughly through a door. A frigid column of air met them and stopped her in her tracks. A rush of anxiety doubled her over.

"Anna!" she gasped, her eyes darting like a trapped animal's.

"No, we're getting out of here. We can't be near this place if they circle the block," William said, helping Jocelyn into her coat as they trotted away. Jocelyn called over her shoulder, but William kept propelling her forward. Elizabeth glanced back at the door they'd come through. She couldn't leave Anna behind. James shifted Anna's coat and bag to his other hand. He cleared his throat.

"Elizabeth," he whispered, his tone steady, "William's right, we have to get out of here." The door crashed opened, and she peered through the darkness. Three couples stumbled through the opening, whooping and chatting as though they were leaving a grand party.

She grabbed a girl's bare arm.

"Are the police gone?"

"Don't think so."

Her dark curls swished as she shook her head. A young man put his tan wool coat over the girl's bare shoulders, and they moved away. Elizabeth brushed a tear from her cheek.

James grabbed her elbow.

"Let's go," he whispered close to her ear. She detected a fresh note of firmness in his voice. She looked him in the eye, their noses just inches apart. They turned and started down the alley together, their friends no longer in sight. Yelling voices in the distance told them that police activity continued at The Brisbane's main entrance.

A skinny policeman walked into the alley, slapping a billyclub against his thigh.

"James."

Elizabeth grabbed his arm, but he pushed her away. He left her side and approached the policeman.

"Sir. What's going on?"

"I'm just clearing the alley."

"Are we under arrest?"

Elizabeth's calm voice surprised her. She had to look upward, as he was at least a head taller than James. Beanpole came to mind, but she wisely kept it to herself. He adjusted his black hat and shook his head.

"Nah. You run along now. Stay outta the church ladies' way, would ya?" His voice faded away as he muttered something about old busybodies and wasting time.

"Thank you, sir," said James, who scowled back at Elizabeth. He grabbed her elbow and steered her down the alley, glancing over his shoulder every few seconds until they found the sidewalk.

The walk home seemed endless. Elizabeth's shoe rubbed her left heel, but that pain was nothing compared to the gnawing pain of dread and anxiety filling her gut.

James had grown silent as they neared her home, not that he'd muttered much over one-word responses to her nervous chatter. Though they weren't touching, Elizabeth could tell he was wound tight like a spring. She'd never seen him like this. In front of her house, she turned to face him. She faked a smile and looked hopeful at that moment. Would he talk to her now? Tell her what he was thinking?

"Good night, Elizabeth."

"Oh."

She brushed back a loose strand of hair from her forehead, not sure what to say. He nodded and turned, his lips tight and his eyes drawn down. He looked as tired as an old man.

She watched him walk away, his shape disappearing in between the streetlamps until his slim silhouette faded. Climbing the steps to the front door, worry for Anna and James overpowered her heel pain. Hot tears became icy on her lashes. She stayed on the porch waiting for her sister and hoping James would change his mind and come back to talk about what happened. She could withstand his anger. After a few frozen minutes, she slipped inside the quiet house and walked straight up the stairs to her room.

She examined her bleeding heel when she pulled off her shoes and stockings. They had walked at least twenty blocks in the frigid night air. Only one taxi had drifted by them along the way, and she'd wanted to flag it down. James pronounced they would walk. She convinced herself that he hadn't wanted to be in the close confines of the back seat, where he'd have to speak to her. He had started to push her away the moment they left The Brisbane. His taut body beside her, his lack of conversation, lent additional frostiness to their walk. She'd believed he was as worried about Anna as she was.

Into the wee hours, she replayed the night in her head until she heard the front door click. Jumping out of bed, she grabbed her robe and ran to top of the stairs. She hissed into the darkness.

"Oh my god, where were you? I've been going mad waiting for you!"

Not waiting for an answer, she dragged Anna into her room where they would not disturb their parents on the floor above. Once the door was closed, Elizabeth pulled her sister into a fierce hug. "Are you okay? Did the police see you?"

Anna was shaking her head and smiling wildly. She was bursting to say something, tell a secret, and Elizabeth stopped her questioning and frowned at Anna.

"Talk!"

"I'm okay, first. I wanted some fresh air and Charles wanted a cigarette. We were in front of the hall when the church ladies showed up. We drifted farther away up the sidewalk, so they didn't see us."

Anna took a deep, shaky breath.

"Then the police came zipping around the corner. They were going so fast. So fast we assumed they would keep driving past. Instead, they screeched to a stop and men in uniforms poured out the car doors."

Elizabeth hugged her robe more tightly around her and sat. She pulled Anna onto the end of the bed with her.

"What did you and Charles do? I mean, I didn't see you inside the ballroom for a while."

"We took off. But I didn't have my coat and bag. I nearly froze, I didn't realize we'd be outside that long.

We found a deli that was still open. Charles bought me coffee. We warmed up there. I…I'm sorry, Elizabeth, that I didn't come back to find you. Did you get in trouble?"

"No. William found a path in the melee and got us out to the back alley. While we waited there for you a bit, a policeman came into the alley. He let me and James go."

"You thought you'd be arrested? For dancing?"

"Clearly, you're not listening during family meals. Do you ever read the paper? It's actually worse in other cities. New York is lucky, I suppose."

Elizabeth wondered then if she should have mentioned her encounter with the police months earlier.

"The old biddies came inside?"

"'Fraid so. A dancer yanked a placard away from one of them." She hugged Anna. "And I was so worried about you. Oh my, your hands are still freezing."

She squeezed them between hers and looked in Anna's eyes.

"What else happened, Anna?"

"Charles kissed me!"

Elizabeth rolled her eyes.

"All right, let's get you to bed. I'm exhausted."

She pulled Anna from the bed and headed toward the door.

"Can't I stay with you tonight?"

"Fine. Get changed, and let's try to sleep."

Elizabeth sometimes took a parental tone with her sister, and this evening—or early morning, rather—called for it. She didn't need the distraction of her excited sister tonight, but she was too overwrought to argue.

Anna snuggled under Elizabeth's quilt and, to

Elizabeth's relief, her sister turned her back on her. Elizabeth stared at the ceiling, her imaginings accompanied by the soft sighs of her sleeping sister.

Chasing sleep was a turbulent business. Several times, Elizabeth untwisted her soft cotton nightgown from around her knees. Moonlight cast a knowing glow over the silver ballet shoes that hung from a pink satin ribbon on the wall.

Whatever would James do now, she wondered.

Chapter Fifteen

James tossed his lunch on the table in the courtyard. Surprised, Elizabeth glanced up from her bag to find him standing with his hands jammed in his coat pockets.

"I'm still furious."

"With me?"

He glared at her and pursed his lips.

"Fine. Blame me! I tipped off the police." She threw her hands dramatically into the air.

"Elizabeth. Don't you dare make light of Saturday night."

"So, you're daring me now?" She punched her forefinger on the tabletop. "That was not my fault. You've no right to be angry with me!"

"Let me start over."

"Please do."

She needed to watch what she said. She enjoyed their friendship, and she was immensely proud of how she'd turned him into a reliable dance partner. Pushing him while he was angry would be like poking a bear. Elizabeth had already experienced a police raid; he had not.

"I've never had a brush with any police. No one in my family has. Never. The longer I thought about it yesterday, the more mortified I became. What if we'd been arrested? That's just the memory I want to have with you. Huddled together in the cold dank slammer."

He snorted angrily.

"Oh, they wouldn't have done that."

"Really. How are you so certain? I think we just got lucky with that copper."

She waved her hand.

"Oh, well…how could they possibly arrest all those dancers? Too many for them to handle. Right?"

"They need only arrest a few to make an example. And there we stood alone in an alley. An arrest made in heaven."

"Mm. But he let us go. Shouldn't we just celebrate that?" A smile trembled on her lips.

James groaned. She gazed at the tree branches arching across the sky behind his head. He was being ridiculous about their near calamity. They could be more careful in the future.

"There's nothing to celebrate. Nothing to dance about. I'm finished."

"Finished? With?"

"With dancing."

"I thought you loved dancing with me."

"Elizabeth, be reasonable. We can just do other things. Explore more of the city. Take in a movie. Dinner. Whatever you want."

She bit into her sandwich. She didn't trust herself to say more.

James blew out a frosty breath and looked up at the faded blue sky. She pulled her coat tightly around her. She would've eaten in her office today, except for needing to see how James was doing.

"You're so smart. But in this one thing, you deny reality. The odds are, there'll be more police. I've read the papers. All of them! Those people won't stop. And we'll pay for it somehow."

He ran a shaking hand over his face. He was struggling to contain his temper. Elizabeth suspected most of his emotion was aimed at her.

"I won't be humiliated, Elizabeth."

"And I won't be cowed by some strange set of social misfits." Her voice sounded harsher than she'd intended.

"I'm asking again. Be reasonable."

"I don't know what that means, James. Enlighten me."

"I think I've explained myself quite well." He began packing up his lunch wrappings. "Why don't you think about it."

"Wait a minute. You've read the papers, you said?"

James sighed and shook his head.

Elizabeth persisted, even though he was clearly annoyed. "So, you already heard that dancing was a bit, um, controversial. Why are you so angry with me, then? You made your choice long before this weekend, didn't you? You took the risk for months, and now you won't."

He stalked to the courtyard door. She jumped when it banged shut.

"I've just lost my dance partner," she muttered to the empty courtyard. A cold breeze rattled the empty tree branches in reply. Elizabeth blinked back tears. But as she wrapped up her lunch things, an idea developed. She rushed back to her office and started furiously writing.

Balled up papers filled the wastebasket and spilled like snowballs onto the gray tile floor. Jean stopped at the doorway. When she saw the litter and Elizabeth's ferocious expression, Jean beat a path back to her desk.

****

Her first time late to work, Elizabeth attempted to

slip unseen into her office Tuesday morning, but Mr. Gerold appeared in her doorway as she removed her coat.

"A word, Miss Alter."

"Of course. I'm sorry I—"

"You attended Barnard, yes?"

"I did."

"I'd like you to pick up some materials from their library. Could you venture there today?"

"Of course! I'd love to see the grounds again." She smiled, meaning it. To be on her alma mater's grounds would bring back so many memories. She relished getting out of this building, too.

"You know who to see, then?"

"Is it still Mr. Thomas?"

Mr. Gerold nodded.

"I'll take care of it. I promise."

She stuck her head in Mr. Gerold's office at noon and said she was off to Barnard, and she'd also have to stop for lunch. After oversleeping and scurrying about her room like a rat on a sinking ship, Elizabeth had forgotten her lunch at home.

****

The library staff were ready with the requested materials, and she was disappointed that her visit on the campus was so brief. Strolling away from the library, the red brick of Milbank Hall caught her eye, and she made a detour.

The familiar black-and-white-tiled floors gleamed waxed and shiny as a bald man's head. She took the wide stairs swiftly, her hand trailing the smooth wood banister as she'd done only a year earlier. A mix of voices and laughter from down the hall elicited memories of debates between students, and sometimes with professors. The smell of paper and polish reminded her of how much she loved this place. She couldn't help but reminisce about her time here at Barnard—making friends with Jocelyn and having Dr. Claire Sporian for a professor and mentor.

Elizabeth's literature studies had given her opportunities to conduct research for her professors. She'd loved visiting Dr. Sporian's office and hearing her expound on Hume's skepticism or Locke's politics. Warm and funny, Clara Sporian had the rare faculty office. It was seldom empty, as students dropped in all the time. Books spilled out of their piles and onto the white notepads filled with Clara's tight scrawl. Her feet were often propped up on the desk, easy to do since she usually wore trousers. That had scandalized Elizabeth her first year at Barnard, until she envied her free-thinking professor.

In that office, Elizabeth had felt especially bright, a compliment Sporian had once offered, when she found her voice to take part in the lively give-and-take there. And if Dr. Sporian pointed at her and pronounced her comments "absolutely right," Elizabeth sat up a little straighter, but had learned painfully to avoid responding too openly to that praise.

"Oh my, Elizabeth! Are you preening?" Emma, a fellow English major, had exclaimed with raucous laughter.

At Elizabeth's mortified expression, Dr. Sporian had tossed her head back and laughed too.

"Just be yourself, Elizabeth. You're all right."

On this surprise visit months after her graduation, Elizabeth was happy to find Dr. Sporian's office door open wide; sunlight cast a long rhombus of light into the hallway. She could hear the faint shuffle of papers, but no voices. The hope of catching her former professor free to chat buoyed her.

Elizabeth found Dr. Sporian turned in profile, her feet up on another chair, crossed at the ankles. Her narrow feet sported a scuffed pair of brown lace-up ankle boots, her typical style. Elizabeth knocked on the wide wood doorjamb, and the professor startled slightly before turning toward the doorway. She exclaimed as she swept off her reading glasses and stood to her nearly six-foot height.

"Elizabeth, dear! How lovely, what a surprise. Come, come, sit down and tell me how you've been."

Elizabeth swept in bravely. After all, she was here with a purpose.

"I work in research at the public library. I had to pick up some materials from your library for my supervisor. And since I was here, I decided to stop by and say hello."

Dr. Sporian nodded in complete understanding. Professors were well aware of library partnerships in the city and beyond.

"So you're doing interesting work?"

Elizabeth beamed. "Oh yes, I love it! You know how much I like research."

"You've a keen eye and mind, indeed. What else is going on in your life?" Dr. Sporian didn't ask specifically if she'd gotten married, even though many of Elizabeth's classmates had done so by now. She'd been out of college nearly a year, plenty of time to get hitched.

She'd never hinted to Dr. Sporian about dating, being more focused on conducting research and learning more. Still, her professor likely wouldn't have been surprised if Elizabeth had drifted in with a dazzling ring on her left hand.

She shrugged. "Nothing really impressive. I want to move to my own place soon. Many things still to work out. Like finding a place, for starters."

Clara smiled. "I remember leaving home when I was twenty. It was funny, sad, exhilarating, and scary, all at once. But you've nothing to be scared of. It's a different time."

Elizabeth took a deep breath. "Since I'm here, I also wanted to ask you about the master's degree. You mentioned it before I graduated. Do you remember?"

"I do. I still think you're well-suited. Did we discuss the caveats then?

"Caveats? What does that mean?"

"Well, first, Barnard does not offer graduate studies. You'd have to go to Columbia, which is just across the street. No leap there, right?"

"That isn't a problem, I agree."

"You would have to apply there and be accepted, which for a woman of your caliber, well…" Clara held up a hand to brush off the idea that Columbia would deny her admission.

"The main issue lies in your options for study. Not everything is open to women. Engineering, for example." She squinted at Elizabeth and put her glasses on again.

"That's definitely not for me. Math!" She shuddered and laughed.

"Literature, journalism, and business, those may be your only choices."

Elizabeth pulled her bottom lip between her teeth.

"Elizabeth, you don't have to decide today.

109

But…admissions close May fifteenth, I think. It's only February, so there's time. That is, if you wanted to begin in the fall term."

"I have something to think on, then. Thank you, Dr. Sporian."

"Clara."

"Right. Clara. Can I visit you soon about this?"

"Please. I love seeing my favorite student. Any time." A knock sounded on the doorjamb and a flustered Elizabeth stood quickly. A young woman with a straight black bob stepped back to let her leave.

"I look forward to hearing from you, Elizabeth," Clara Sporian called after her.

As she walked down the massive stairway, she could hear the high-pitched voice of the student playing against the low, professorial tones of Clara. She was so relieved to have something substantial to consider rather than a college question wandering vaguely across her plans.

Plans. Such that they were. She knew nothing about tomorrow, let alone the rest of the decade or the rest of her life.

By the time she left the campus, it was nearly two in the afternoon, and she'd had nothing to eat since the cookie she had found in her desk drawer. She found a deli with a few late lunch patrons. Sitting on a stool at the counter, she cleaned a plate piled high with club sandwich corners.

Eating alone reminded her of lunches with James. She'd made a shamble of things with him. She hoped it wasn't a sign of how her trek toward independence would go.

****

Headed into the Research department, Elizabeth was

startled to see Lillie exiting Mr. Gerold's office. She watched the young girl sashay down the hallway, her pale green skirt swinging. Wait a minute, wasn't that the same green skirt she'd seen months ago in the stacks with James?

She shook the memory out of her head and peeked into Mr. Gerold's office. His head was down, his attention buried in a sheaf of papers.

"Hey!"

Matilda looked up and ran fingers through her dark curls.

"What's going on?"

"What was Lillie doing here?"

"I didn't know she was here."

"Well, she sauntered out of Mr. Gerold's office as I was coming in just now. It's curious. And odd, don't you think?"

Matilda frowned. She stood and pulled on the front of her cropped brown jacket. She stepped around Elizabeth and headed for their supervisor's office.

"Let's find out, shall we?"

"No, wait! You're just going to ask him?"

"Do you want to know or don't you? Honestly, girl."

Matilda shook her head and started walking again. Elizabeth sighed heavily and followed her friend.

"Mr. Gerold, we're curious about Lillie's visit today."

Matilda's boldness was just beyond belief, Elizabeth thought. She'd never have asked, or not like that, anyway. He didn't seem bothered by their interruption. Elizabeth peered at him from behind her friend, the top of Matilda's head just barely brushing Elizabeth's chin.

"Lillie is interested in Jean's position. She's finishing at Barnard this May."

"Ah, well, that's just grand." Matilda cut an eye over her shoulder at Elizabeth.

"Any other interest, Mr. Gerold?" Elizabeth asked.

"Um, not yet."

He dipped his head back to the papers strewn across his desk.

Matilda bumped into Elizabeth as she turned to leave, saying, "Thank you, sir."

"Oof, sorry. Gosh, not Lillie in here! Could you stand it?"

"I was afraid no one would take the position, and we'd be working after hours forever."

Matilda plopped down into her chair.

"She's insufferable!"

"Does this have anything to do with James?" Matilda raised her eyebrows.

"I need to get back to work."

Elizabeth's face flushed as she scooted away. She blushed more when she heard the chuckle coming from Matilda's office.

Chapter Sixteen

Early the next Saturday morning, Elizabeth and Maisie skipped down the front steps into the frosty air. She was on a mission. One quite different from that of her fox terrier, whose nose vigorously sniffed the environment for captivating scents. Uninterested in such carnal pursuits, Elizabeth turned purposefully to the left, away from their usual Central Park haunts.

"Come on, Maisie. I have a job today."

Headed home from work two nights ago, she thought she'd passed a "For Rent" sign in a window a few blocks over. It was time to investigate. Not that she wanted to live so terribly close to her mother, but with no lodging prospects on her list, she was getting increasingly desperate.

Accommodations for young women were few and far between. Or so she thought after scouring several newspapers and asking around the library staff. She'd unsuccessfully inquired in a few businesses near the library about possible upstairs apartments. Elizabeth patted herself on the back for being resourceful, even if her attempts yielded nothing. She was trying, for heaven's sake, and feeling empowered by each grownup step she took.

After doubling back around several blocks, Elizabeth finally found the sign in a window to the right of a dull gray door. Surveying the house and front garden, her nose twitched. The bushes on either side of the front stoop were overgrown and entwined with ivy, the glossy leaves hiding the true nature of its host shrub. Six brick steps led to the unadorned front porch; a lonely black umbrella leaned against the wall, fraying silk fluttered in the morning's soft breeze. She couldn't remember when it had last rained.

It looked rather bleak, she thought, shaking her head. She walked away and mused aloud, "Who would so neglect their home in Manhattan?"

That it could be less appealing than Jocelyn's new abode near The Tenderloin was certainly cause for dismay. She was doomed to live at home forever.

Maisie barked and scampered ahead, her tan ears bobbing.

"Good morning."

Curious, Elizabeth turned toward the sound of the tiny, feminine voice, but couldn't find its source. Movement at a nearby stone wall caught her attention, and she saw a spry, white-haired lady behind an iron gate.

"Hello."

From opposite directions, they both approached the sidewalk gate for a property that occupied the corner.

"I've seen you walk by before, young lady. Are you a new neighbor?"

"Oh, no, I live a few blocks over. I come by here to and from the subway most days. But I was looking at that house with the For Rent sign."

Elizabeth pointed to the house across the street.

The old lady peered over the gate.

"The Marsden place? Hmm, strange lot."

"Pardon me?"

Elizabeth stepped closer to the gate. Maisie poked her nose through the gateposts and sniffed the lady's leg.

"Stop it, Maisie." She grimaced meekly at the woman. "Sorry."

"The Marsden place. Only the old woman and her son live there now."

"There's a sign about a room for rent, but after seeing it in the daylight, I'm not certain I'm interested."

Elizabeth wrinkled her nose, causing the woman's aging face to crinkle more with a wide smile.

"You don't want to live there. I can't imagine." The old woman shuddered.

"I'll find something, eventually. Just started looking."

A light breeze lifted wisps of white hair that had escaped the old woman's bun. She reached up to smooth the top of her head.

"I should introduce myself. I'm Margaret Goldberg. I've lived here going on forty years."

"Pleased to meet you, Mrs. Goldberg. I'm Elizabeth Alter. My family's lived a few blocks over since before I was born."

"Alter? Don't tell me you're Henry's daughter!" Mrs. Goldberg's eyes narrowed as she studied her.

"Yes. You know my father?"

"He was friends with my son, John. Long ago. And I truly liked Henry's mother, Cora. How is she?"

"Oh my, Manhattan is such a small world!" Elizabeth exclaimed. "Gran lives in Philadelphia now. Did you know that?"

Mrs. Goldberg tilted her head in thought. She wagged a wrinkled finger.

"Hmm, I may have known that. Once. I've forgotten

so much."

Both women laughed and shook their heads in unison.

Elizabeth looked down at her dog sitting quietly, her rosy tongue hanging out. The silence stretched out while Mrs. Goldberg looked up at the waving branches of a Linden tree, apparently lost in thought. Elizabeth was about to bid her farewell when Mrs. Goldberg spoke again.

"Well, I should let you go. You young people are always so busy. Such a sweet dog, he is."

Maisie tilted her head to get a better head rub from the wrinkled hand poking through the gate.

"This dog is a good friend. It's been lovely to chat. I'll tell Father that I ran into you."

"Good luck with your search. Can't be easy for a young woman these days."

"No, it's hard to find a good place. It's like looking for a needle in a haystack." Elizabeth shrugged, a worried frown creasing her forehead.

She lifted her hand to wave, but the sweet old woman was already headed up her sidewalk.

****

Elizabeth nixed her usual Friday stroll through Central Park to catch a train to work. Her quick pace forced her breath into a thick fog in front of her face. Cars rumbled by in each direction.

"Elizabeth? Hello!" From across the street, Elizabeth saw Mrs. Goldberg coming down her front steps. She waved, looked both ways, and crossed swiftly to the front of the elderly lady's house.

"You're up early." Elizabeth smiled at her new friend, who was bundled tightly in a beige wool coat.

"I was hoping to see you. You're hurrying to work, so I won't take up much time."

Elizabeth approached the gate and slid her hands into her coat pockets.

"I slipped and fell in my kitchen on Monday morning, and—"

"Oh dear, are you all right?"

Elizabeth's eyes swept over the woman, seeking bodily damage.

"Yes, yes, just a bruised elbow." She waved away the discussion of her wounds. "It made me think. About living alone."

"Yes, I suppose it would. Do you have fam—?"

"I don't want to make you late for work. I was looking for you this morning, so I could ask if you'd like to discuss living here at my house?"

"Oh my! Yes, yes."

Elizabeth's eyes wandered to the tall house behind Mrs. Goldberg. What window might be the one she'd peer out of?

"Can you come by tomorrow or Sunday?"

Elizabeth nodded excitedly. "Tomorrow morning? Eleven o'clock?"

"Tomorrow at eleven. Now, run along. I fear I've caused you to be late."

Elizabeth walked away, but she spun around and raised her voice.

"Thank you, Mrs. Goldberg! Have a lovely day."

"You too, my dear."

Elizabeth's excitement bubbled through her body, and she was tempted to run all the way to the library. It was far too cold for that, so she boarded the train, granting a giant smile to everyone who looked her way.

117

She couldn't wait to tell Jocelyn and Matilda. In her eager brain, she'd already moved into her independent life.

She had trouble focusing on her work. So much so that, around noon, she heard Mr. Gerold clear his throat outside her office. He broke into her daydream, and she dropped her pen.

"Oh! Yes, Mr. Gerold?"

"I was asking if you had the Simpson file?"

She rummaged quickly through the piles on her table, pulling a brown folder out.

"And here it is!" She presented it to Mr. Gerold with a flourish. Her private exhilaration made her feel magnanimous toward the world.

"I expected no less. Thank you, Miss Alter." As he left, she put the pen between her teeth and returned to her reverie. She really was quite useless as a potentially independent woman.

She didn't have dancing plans that night and would be home. Should she talk to her father? She'd be wiser to approach him with more details, not less. He obviously wasn't as supportive as she'd first imagined he might be. Two months had passed since she had told him her dream of moving out, but he still hadn't returned with any suggestions.

Never mind him. Obviously, she could do things for herself. Finally.

****

Margaret Goldberg lived in an old three-story house on a corner. The side yard was a tangle of shrubs and wayward vines. The front of the house suffered from similar signs of neglect. White paint chipped off the windowsills where water had likely sat and caused damage. Iron railings bracketed the steps to the black front door on each side. Rust worked deliberately on a meal of black paint. Elizabeth wondered if the entire block was diseased with neglect. Still, it looked less grim than the Marsden house across the street.

Terracotta pots on each step were barren, and she wondered whether they'd held the same flowers her mother liked to plant in their gardens. The brass knocker was pitted with age. She lifted the ring and let it fall. The hammering sound echoed on the other side of the door. Soon, she heard footsteps, and the door opened.

"Good morning, Mrs. Goldberg."

"My dear, do come in." She swung the door wider. The aromas of sugar and vanilla broadcast a baking project in the works.

"Come with me to the kitchen. I've got sugar cookies in the oven. I love baking."

"Smells delicious." Her stomach rumbled; lunchtime was around the corner. She followed Margaret past a small overstuffed parlor and through the kitchen door. Elizabeth towered head and shoulders over this tiny woman, whose white hair was pulled back in a low bun from which no hair strayed. From the back, she was a column of black cut only by white apron ties.

She pulled a pan out of the oven; a dozen circles of crispy golden-edged sweetness teased her nostrils.

"Mm-mm." Elizabeth leaned over to sniff. Mrs. Goldberg laughed softly.

"We'll let these cool while I show you the room. Actually, rooms. They're in the basement."

Basement? *Dank and dark with cobwebs* entered her mind, a memory from her Aunt Amelia's vacation house in the Catskills. Elizabeth shivered involuntarily.

Mrs. Goldberg led the way to a door off the kitchen. She grabbed an oil lamp hung beside the door and lit it.

"Here we go." She walked down the stairs ahead of Elizabeth, the flame flickering into the darkness below. It didn't feel cold, a good sign. Elizabeth quietly sniffed for any sign of mustiness. Nothing.

Mrs. Goldberg put down the oil lamp and walked into a dark corner. Elizabeth heard the click of a lamp, and the space was suddenly illuminated. Elizabeth was astonished by how the room was furnished. Beside the tall floor lamp was a green damask sofa with cherrywood Queen Anne legs. At the opposite end of it stood a side table with dropped leaves on each side. It was large enough to be opened and used for dining, for two perhaps.

Mrs. Goldberg stood quietly while Elizabeth took it in. She hadn't moved from the bottom of the steps. The widow seemed to be waiting for her approval.

"This is beautiful."

"Alfred's mother lived down here for a short while. Before she…before she died a few years ago. We didn't move anything. Oh, there are personal things that I will have to move for you." She hesitated. "If you take it, that is."

"It's quite nice and has more space than I thought. There's a bedroom?"

"Through that door." She pointed a bony finger over the sofa.

Elizabeth stepped through the bedroom doorway into a heavily decorated Victorian boudoir. Dusty, thick lace hung limply around a small square window that looked out onto the front yard. Set partly below ground, this floor's windows were set with sills level to the ground.

The bed was a confection of texture: velvet, silk, lace, and cotton. It resembled an elaborate wedding gown designed in creams and whites. Four tall posts supported a fine mesh draping, designed to quiet a fear of mosquitoes, she supposed. In the far corner, a dark cherry wardrobe stood at attention. She didn't walk across to open it, as it likely contained the other Mrs. Goldberg's things.

"You don't like it?" Mrs. Goldberg stood in the doorway, surveying the room with a wistful look.

"It…it's very pretty. Maybe I'd want simpler bed coverings. Maybe?" She smiled over her shoulder at her prospective landlady.

"I have one more thing to show you."

They headed back through the parlor and past the staircase. She opened a narrow door built under the stairs. A moldy odor nearly knocked them both over. The little room contained a toilet and a sink with hot and cold water taps. It just needed a good clean, she thought to herself.

"A private bath! How nice!" Elizabeth put on a show of excitement. She had to admit that this apartment could be a magnificent spot to rent, with the added benefit of not having to share with roommates. She wanted to pinch herself for this good fortune.

"This basement has everything a girl could need." She was getting more excited by the minute, but she kept her tone even. If she appeared too enthusiastic, Mrs. Goldberg might think the rent should be higher.

"I thought you'd like it." Mrs. Goldberg picked up the oil lamp and made for the stairs. Elizabeth followed. With the widow's back to her, she decided to inquire about rent.

"Have you given thought to how much rent you'd charge?"

"Is thirty dollars a month too much? I'll be so relieved to have someone nearby." She peered questioningly at Elizabeth when they were back in the kitchen. Elizabeth was jumping inside, but her face remained impassive.

An apartment she'd looked at on Tuesday cost seventy dollars a month, far too much on her meager salary. It had been much more private, but Elizabeth needed to be careful about her expenses. Besides, the apartment building manager had peered down his nose at her, asking personal questions he'd probably never ask a man. This might be the perfect compromise.

"That seems fair to me."

"I forgot to mention, dear. There's a separate entrance, too. On the side of the house. Let's wander out there in a moment."

"I didn't notice a door downstairs."

"It's behind a thick curtain Alfred put up for his mother. Kept out the drafts."

"Ah."

"The doorknob just needs a little work. I'll ask Alfred's brother to inspect it."

"Mrs. Goldberg, I should be able to move in whenever you would be ready for me. You said, um, you said there were things you needed to remove."

Elizabeth wondered whether she should consult with her father before she made this decision. No, she told herself. Show him and Mother you are ready to be responsible for your own life.

Mrs. Goldberg nodded while she scooped the

cookies into a basket. She waved the spatula over them, indicating Elizabeth was to have one.

"What about next month? No, let's make it May. I need time to sort that space out for you. But it would be wise to move before it gets too hot, don't you think?"

"That's perfect, thank you. If you need help with sorting, I'm happy to help." Already, Elizabeth imagined her new life of freedom. Coming and going as she pleased, avoiding Minnie's inquisitions and verbal jabs. She crunched into a cookie, but quickly swallowed so she wouldn't talk with her mouth full.

"Oh, I do have a question. Two, actually. Taking a bath? Using the icebox in here?"

"You're welcome to use the bath at the top of the stairs whenever you like. You won't fill it to the top, will you?"

Elizabeth laughed and promised she wouldn't.

"The icebox is by the back door. I keep little in it— milk, butter. You may use it." She pointed around a wall behind her.

"Thank you. I like cereal and milk, and I take lunch to work most days. It's more economical."

"Smart girl." She pointed the spatula in Elizabeth's direction. "You're pretty, too."

"Oh! Thank you."

"Do you have a beau?" Worry briefly shadowed her face. "I'm not sure about gentlemen callers."

Elizabeth shook her head and waved a hand. "Oh no. I wouldn't. I…I don't have anyone. Not right now."

"Boy problems, I knew about those." Her faded blue eyes looked up at the kitchen light wistfully.

They grew quiet.

"Well! Let's go outside to your door." Mrs.

Goldberg hung her apron on a wall hook and moved nimbly to the front door. Elizabeth helped her into the beige wool coat she'd seen before.

The side yard's overgrowth blocked the way to the shallow stairs. Both women pulled at vines, but they broke off in their hands. Someone would need to pull them up from closer to the ground. Dirty work.

Thick wisteria vines created a canopy over the doorway. It would be lovely when it bloomed in a few months. The widow put her fists on her hips and surveyed the yard. She shook her head.

"This is going to cost something to clean up."

"I can do it." Elizabeth blurted out the offer. But...what did she know about pulling up vines and pruning shrubs? *How hard can it be?* She scanned the area, estimating how much time it might take.

Mrs. Goldberg nodded at her slowly, taking in her fine clothes and perfect posture. She couldn't disguise the doubt in her eyes.

"I'll come by tomorrow afternoon, poke around a bit, and see how much undergrowth there is. I should be able to manage it."

Mrs. Goldberg shrugged her thin shoulders and turned toward the front steps. "I'll see you tomorrow, then. Not too early. I sleep late on Sundays."

Elizabeth couldn't help but smile. She waved to the old woman as she opened the gate and stepped onto the sidewalk. The midday sun was bright overhead, and its gentle warmth portended good things for this new journey. She danced a solitary foxtrot when she got out of her future landlady's view.

Chapter Seventeen

Flames danced in the fireplace, a welcome heat on a frigid Friday night. The room's warmth was the main reason the sisters joined their parents in the parlor after dinner. Henry was reading and Minnie was replacing the button on a white blouse of Anna's. She held it up in Anna's direction and muttered something about her general carelessness with her clothes.

"Elizabeth, I'd like to discuss something with you. At your father's request, I waited until after dinner to bring this up."

Elizabeth closed the book on her lap. She knew it! More negative chatter about dancing. Her parents were about to ban them from going. They didn't know her big secret yet. This could be her night to spring her move on her mother and take the angry wind out of her sails.

The police raid had made all eleven newspapers in the city. The preachers were frothing over it, and some local politicians joined the complaints about public safety and public health. Elizabeth braced herself, certain her mother was going to make a point about "dance hall dangers."

Henry looked pointedly at Minnie. Was it a caution to go easy? She hoped so.

Minnie tied off the button thread and set the blouse aside.

Elizabeth decided to preempt her mother's diatribe.

"I listened to what you said at that Sunday dinner. I did. But I wish you understood. Public dances are just a fun way to pass time. There's no drinking. I'm—"

Elizabeth paused as Minnie stood suddenly and paced in front of the parlor's wide window. The gold damask floor-length drapes were still pulled back to take advantage of the last rays of the evening sun. It was an economy to prevent the use of lamplight before dusk, a lesson Minnie had learned as a young girl. But darkness had already settled around the windows, so Minnie pulled them closed. Rather forcefully, Elizabeth observed.

"Oh, it's not about that dinner debate. It's far worse. I've never prevented either of you from having your entertainment, no matter how I felt about it. We're trying to let you grow up. Find your own way to make the right decisions about your life."

Minnie paused and took a breath. The sisters looked at each other, unsure where this was going.

"But the way you've shamed us, Elizabeth. I thought you knew better than to embarrass our family."

A log on the fireplace chose that moment to spit orange sparks.

Elizabeth's mouth opened, then closed. What did they think she'd done? Her eyes flitted between her father and mother. Henry appeared to be engrossed in the paper. Minnie was seething quietly. Her lips pursed tightly, her eyes half-closed in anger. Both girls knew their mother's angriest expressions, and this one was possibly the worst.

"Mother…Father…"

"Enough! Haven't you said enough?" Minnie angrily turned to the chair where'd she sat and picked up a newspaper by its front leg. It was folded neatly into a small rectangle. Minnie held it up and said, "Let me read this. Perhaps then you can explain yourself."

And Minnie read from the newspaper. Elizabeth recognized the words she'd penned in a letter to one of the city's papers nearly two weeks ago. They printed her letter! Excitement was quickly overshadowed by a wave of nausea. Her mother's expression told her how much trouble she had caused.

"Dear Sir:

When I was four, my parents enrolled me in dance classes. I learned ballet, modern dance, and ballroom dancing. I also learned that practice and repetition lead to exquisite perfection. I came to understand heart and passion.

As a young woman today, I still practice dancing because I am passionate about it. Where do I practice? Why, of course, I dance at the dance halls around the city!

Elizabeth and Anna sat still as statues, staring at their mother. Anna hadn't dared look over at her sister. Minnie stopped reading to look at both of them, her gaze landing last on Elizabeth. It took the greatest restraint to keep Elizabeth from looking at Henry. She sensed his quiet stillness across the room on her right.

Minnie sputtered, "Indeed." She shook her head and returned to reading the letter.

I never imagined there would be people lined up against the idea of dancing. Yes, the music has changed dramatically, as have the wardrobes. But the young adults you know are no different than you were in your twenties. Who hasn't pushed against the constraints of old ideas? You cannot deny it. Every generation explores new things.

My generation wants to embrace all the remarkable changes arriving almost daily—the exciting music, the women's vote, new careers. And dancing!

Minnie paused again and sniffed. She shook her head as her eyes left Elizabeth's face and returned to the newspaper to read more.

You sent young men to a horrible war. Yet you think our dancing is an abomination and the end of the world.

I politely ask that you leave us alone,

Elizabeth Alter

New York"

Minnie threw the newspaper to the floor, spitting out the words "New York" as if they were curse words. Elizabeth stared at her hands folded in her lap. Silence was her wisest choice in the face of her mother's rage.

"These flappers are turning everyone's head! Such immorality they are sowing! Why must you carry on like that?"

"But Mother…" Elizabeth began.

"Mother, we are NOT flappers! How can you say such a thing?" Anna interrupted.

"Mother…" Elizabeth started again. "We merely want to dance with our friends." She couldn't win here, but having Anna in the room gave her the bravado to speak up, albeit in only mild protest. The strong opinions that danced in her head fled like cockroaches in the light of Minnie's flaming anger.

Anna sighed in exasperation.

"They hold the dances in community centers and renovated buildings around here. They're not in nightclubs, Mother. Nightclubs don't have the room."

Her face bright pink, Minnie whirled on Anna. She

was still blustering.

"And how would you know such a thing?" she shrieked.

A small sluice of spittle hung briefly on her lower lip and flew toward Anna, landing on the toe of her shoe. Part of Elizabeth wanted to laugh away her nervous tension, but this fight was getting out of hand.

To Elizabeth's surprise, Anna stammered. It was unlike her to be caught off-guard or at a loss for words. No flippant or funny retort tonight. Poor Anna. She'd inadvertently confessed nightclub knowledge to her parents.

"I—I—I've just heard…" Anna blubbered.

"I'm not having my daughters called good-time girls! You have no business in a nightclub. Rosemary Levara told me she saw you at that raid, Elizabeth! You have thoroughly embarrassed this family. I won't have you heap this shame on the Alter name!"

"Father…"

Elizabeth glanced at his quiet form, begging for relief and reason. The dark velvet chair enveloped him like a cocoon, lending him its protection from his wife's bullying and belligerence. He rarely got involved in Minnie's tirades, but Elizabeth couldn't believe Father was allowing his wife to insult his daughters. Elizabeth couldn't remember when she had last seen her mother's dander up so high.

Finally, having had enough of their mother's accusations and constant control, Elizabeth stood and spat out in anger, "Why must you be so distrustful?"

Minnie stepped swiftly toward her, right hand flying in a fast arc toward Elizabeth. The smack of skin to skin echoed through the room. Elizabeth's cheek stung, and she exclaimed in surprise. She looked at her mother in horror as her hand flew to her cheek. Gasps coming from both Elizabeth and Minnie filled the silence. They faced off, glaring at each other. Eye to eye in the center of the parlor, their willowy frames pulsed with indignation.

No shock or remorse showed on Minnie's face, her lip still curled upward in fury. Perspiration glistened around Minnie's hairline; her light brown hair matted in small dark curls on her forehead. The rest of Minnie's long hair remained tight in her chignon.

Elizabeth's glance shifted between Anna and Henry. Her father had lowered his paper as the tableau unfolded before him. Minnie's violence had suspended all of them in soundless shock, like a silent film rolling out in slow motion before her. The film screen in her mind flickered, and her reverie was broken by the sudden movement from the chair to her left.

"Minerva!" Henry barked as he leaped to his feet.

His wife's hand fell to her side. Trance-like, Minnie turned toward Henry. A wary expression briefly crossed Minnie's damp face, and then she sidestepped him and stalked out of the parlor. Maisie, the daughters' faithful furry friend, stood at quiet attention on her tufted green cushion in the corner. The proverbial cat had gotten the yappy dog's tongue.

Her father patiently folded his newspaper and neatly laid it in his chair. Clearly, he planned to come back to it. His head bounced once in a quick nod toward them, a tentative assurance that he might fix it all.

The girls said nothing as he marched out of the room. They listened to his footfalls on the staircase as he followed Minnie upstairs.

Anna ran across the room to Elizabeth.

"Oh my god, are you okay?"

She brushed her fingertips over the cherry-colored bloom on Elizabeth's cheek.

Elizabeth pulled Anna over to the divan and they sank facing each other into its creamy yellow damask. She wiped damp tendrils of hair from her face. The shock of the slap still vibrated through her and robbed her of her voice. Shaking her head, she began to cry. Tears stung her blazing skin. She fell into the back of the divan and buried her face into her mother's favorite embroidered pillow.

"There, there," Anna said as she awkwardly patted her distraught sister on the back. "You know, um, I'm thinking. I can't imagine Father is angry with you."

"I suppose," Elizabeth sniffled.

They lingered quietly in the parlor for a little while, listening to the usual evening noises. The grandfather clock ticked. A car horn blared outside. The occasional rumble of their parents' voices drifted down from the third floor. The sisters entertained their own thoughts while the tears slowly subsided.

"I'm hungry," said Elizabeth.

Anna laughed with relief. She pulled up her sister by both hands and they walked arm in arm to the kitchen.

"I'll fix you something," said Anna.

"You? Cook?" Elizabeth teased.

"Not cooking. A sandwich, a bowl of cereal? We already had dinner. Oh, Mary's chocolate cake!" she squealed and pointed at the glistening treat beneath an etched glass dome. Grabbing two white plates from the hutch, she prepared the sweet snack for her sister.

"Thank you," Elizabeth whispered as tears threatened again. This sweet, caring side of Anna appeared rarely and made her heart hurt.

"We don't have to talk about it if you don't want to," Anna offered as she forked a piece of the cake, afraid to look up. "But the paper published your letter. Aren't you a little excited about that?"

Elizabeth shook her head and put a hand to her mouth, struggling to hold back the tears.

"I can't believe it."

"Father will sort her out. She went too far." Anna placed a hand over Elizabeth's.

Elizabeth pushed the half-eaten cake away.

"I'm going to bed. See you in the morning."

"But it's too early!" Anna pleaded. Elizabeth knew her sister wouldn't want to be alone with her parents that evening. There was still no sign of them.

"Anna. Please. I need to be alone."

Elizabeth set her unfinished cake by the sink, assuming Anna would take care of the dishes. She patted Anna's hand and pushed through the door into the hallway.

Numb and not ready to see her parents, she ran quickly up the stairs. She locked her bedroom door so no one could disturb her. Right now, she had no interest in hearing her mother's voice, even if it was to offer an apology.

Chapter Eighteen

Bright moonbeams through the windowpanes etched a checkered outline on Elizabeth's blue carpet. Beyond the disk of the moon, the sky's inky blackness mirrored the dark place where her heart had gone. Elizabeth strained her eyes to detect something, anything, in the void. An empty pit of nothing was all she saw outside and felt in her heart.

She was primed to begin her new life. And then her mother humiliated her. Reduced her to a simpering child. Where had she gone wrong? Elizabeth worked through that puzzle in the darkness. Pressing her mother's words to the farthest recesses of her mind and shutting them behind a door hadn't helped. She couldn't help reaching through that imaginary doorway and pulling out the fight with her mother for yet another examination.

And there was James, too. He'd practically humiliated her as well, offering her a ridiculous ultimatum.

No. No. She would not lump James into her problems with gaining her independence. He'd been a roadblock she should have recognized from the start. She did know better, but she'd allowed her heart to rule her head, and waves of romance had crushed her against the jagged rocks of society's preferences.

She left the anger behind about three in the morning. Stewing on it had left her tired and nauseous. Yet sleep refused to come. She could feel a hot stream of exhaustion coursing through her veins. Her body thrummed with tired indecision.

As the morning sun cast a jaundiced shimmer across the sky, a kernel of resolve had formed in her heart. She sketched this determination into a plan. She needed a change of scenery, to get away from her mother's bossiness.

Her head was thick with the dregs of her night-long tears. From her bedside water pitcher, Elizabeth dampened a handkerchief and held the cool fabric over her puffy face. She dabbed at her burning eyes and peered into her mirror, using only the light from the window. She looked so dreadful even face powder wouldn't help cover the pink splotches above her lips and around her eyes.

From the bottom of her wardrobe, she pulled out a suitcase. Thankful she hadn't put it in the attic after the family's last trip to Connecticut, Elizabeth quietly flipped the latches. Its faint squeak made her cringe, and she listened for movement in the house. Dead silence. She thought she could hear faint snores coming from her parents' bedroom. Their bedroom was directly above hers, and she had occasionally heard her parents talking or snoring over the years. She'd have to be quiet while moving swiftly.

What should she take? She began pulling out dresses and tossing them on the bed. She folded two day dresses made of printed cotton and placed them in the suitcase. Her mother would insist upon folding them with soft tissue, but Elizabeth's mind was elsewhere, like how, when, and where she would wear these items. And she needed to pack light, something she wasn't certain she could do. The weather may be frigid for a few more weeks. She packed her favorite deep green wool dress with cream lace accents.

Back at the wardrobe doors, she rifled through the rest of her things. Dancing dresses were out of the question, impractical. She fingered the pale blue silk and smiled at the memory of the first time she and James danced. She pulled it out and considered packing it. Memories of James were the last thing she needed right now. She stuffed the dress into the back of the wardrobe and closed its doors.

Elizabeth tiptoed to the landing and leaned out, craning her ear toward her parents' room upstairs. No sounds. She listened at Anna's closed door. Six in the morning was too early for the party girl to be stirring.

Gathering her case, she surveyed her room, eyes touching upon the childish things that still littered the surfaces and hung on the walls. Ribbons for arts and crafts in school, a doll. Her ballet slippers dangled from a gilded hook. She turned to the door. It was time to go.

Terror struck her, and she looked back over her shoulder. God, what was she doing? Quickly, she rummaged through her jewelry and found her childhood prize. The gold brooch's garnets caught a tiny ray of sun, which was coloring the sky with its golden morning glow. Closing her fingers around the cool metal and stone, she quietly closed the bureau drawer.

She was ready now.

****

Elizabeth stood on the sidewalk in front of the house. She hadn't considered the availability of a taxi so early on a Saturday morning. Anger at herself made hot tears surface on her lids. She would have to walk, and that might mean taking a later train. She was still no good at planning.

Her body was leaden from lack of sleep, and the cold air wrapped around her thinly covered legs. Just as she shivered, she heard a clatter of rattling glass. Then, the grinding of engine gears reached her ears as the milk truck turned the corner. She waved.

Mr. Mackey pulled up beside her. "Morning, miss."

"I am headed to the train station. Can I ride with you?"

"Okay." He frowned.

"You don't have to take me to the station. Just, um… Can I get closer while you do your route? I can walk the rest."

"Glad to help, miss."

"Why are you here on Saturday? We aren't on your route today."

"Special delivery."

He grinned at her, revealing a row of bottom teeth that resembled ancient yellow piano keys.

"My lucky day." Elizabeth clambered into the front seat beside him. She pulled her case in front of her and held on. Though her legs were pinned uncomfortably against the seat, she nodded at Mr. Mackey, and he put the truck in gear. It grunted and lurched so hard, Elizabeth's head snapped forward.

"Ooh!"

"Sorry. It needs work, but I'd have to give up my route to fix it. One of these days."

Elizabeth's hand fluttered slightly to wave off his concern for her. She let her mind wander while the milkman chattered about the weather.

Soon, Grand Central Station loomed ahead. "Oh,

Mr. Mackey, you didn't have to! You're too kind."

"Can't have a pretty miss wandering the dark streets with her bags. No good can come of that."

Elizabeth's little adventure seemed even more ludicrous as she got closer to executing her escape plan. Staring out the truck window at the station's massive steps, self-doubt crept in again.

Hand on the door, she smiled wanly at Mr. Mackey, who was looking at her quizzically. "You all right, miss?"

"Yes. Yes, I will be when I catch my train." She offered him a nervous smile. "Thank you for bringing me all this way."

"Well, you have a nice day now."

Elizabeth stood at the base of the stone stairs and waved as the noisy truck pulled away.

****

Elizabeth stood inside Grand Central Station, taking it all in. She'd never been here alone. She always traveled with her family.

Mr. Mackey had looked at her with a question in his eyes. A young woman on the street so early on a Saturday morning was strange indeed. But she had made it this far. Grand Central Station! One step closer to… What? Freedom?

She breathed in the scent of warm bodies, grease, exhaust, and new stone. Under the lovely lighting, the pink marble floors shone like the inside of a seashell. This new building was the crème de la crème, the newspapers reported. It was awe-inspiring, and the latent energy in the walls gave her a new bravado. She marched toward the ticket desk with the shortest line. She did her best not to stare at others waiting in line. Noting the many families and couples who were traveling, she experienced a wave of loneliness.

She smiled at the attendant, certain he knew she didn't belong there. The attendant smiled back with a slight nod.

"Philadelphia, please," she spoke with a strange confidence.

"Have a pleasant trip," he said as he handed her the ticket.

She was really doing this. Going to Philadelphia. She had decided in the dark hours that it was time to seize control of her life.

"Silly girl, it's time to put your plan to work."

And then she thought, what plan? She shook her head.

Elizabeth squared her shoulders and headed through the station. She had an hour to kill before she could board her train. It was too early for the shops to be open, so she peered at the displays in the windows lining the station's main corridor.

A nagging growl began in her stomach. Elizabeth wanted to kick herself. Her mother always packed food and beverages for trips. In her haste to escape the house, food had been the last thing on her mind.

Elizabeth grappled with her suitcase and purse. She strutted into the oncoming crowd and allowed herself to be swept along by its momentum. Her case bumped into another. She smiled an apology at its owner and got a frown in return. Oh dear, she looked like a ridiculous first-time rider!

The train to Philadelphia was waiting for its passengers as they flowed out onto the broad platform. Some passengers ganged up on the doors to board, but

Elizabeth hesitated to join that fray.

She couldn't decide if it was best to stake an early claim on a seat or wait to take any old seat in any old car. So, she marched over to a conductor in a black cap who was inspecting a stairway.

The smell of grease and hot metal assaulted her nose. Reminded of fire and strength, a burst of resolve propelled her out of her nervous reserve.

"Excuse me, sir."

He looked up from his crouched position. He offered the perturbed expression of a man intent on getting his work done.

Undaunted, Elizabeth asked, "Which direction is the dining car?"

Barely moving, he thumbed back over his shoulder.

"Thank you!" she exclaimed and turned the opposite direction. One thing she knew from her family excursions—stay far away from the dining car. Her mother always huffed and puffed over all the people squeezing back and forth past their seats. "What is all the palaver about food cooked on a train?" Minnie didn't understand it, not at all.

Elizabeth hoofed it to a car where she saw few people sitting by windows. She hoped this might signal a less-packed car for the entire trip. What did she know, though? Father always selected their train car. He tried to select their seats as well, but Minnie usually won on that front.

No conductor or attendant stood at the foot of the car's stairs. She waited a moment in case he was helping a poor, lone woman like herself with her bags inside the car. The platform was less crowded now. Men, women, and children stood on the platform waiting for the train's departure. Arms were suspended in half-waves in anticipation of the big sendoff to Philadelphia, an inauspicious two-hour excursion.

Dragging her case up the steps, the wicked reality of her decision emerged. Muscles contracted in her calves and her arms now ached with the suitcase's weight that she'd carried for the last two hours.

Her responsibility.

What was she responsible for in reality?

Yes, she had a job. What else should she care about at twenty-three? She had friends who were married, pregnant even. Did she want that responsibility yet?

She pushed on down the aisle. Her eyes wandered from side to side, seeking an empty spot. She hoped for a window.

Luckily, she found one!

"May I sit here?" she asked a young girl in a brown wool coat already engrossed in a book. Brown eyes met Elizabeth's. An evaluation was taking place, so she stood taller and sported a jaunty smile. The little girl could see what was going on—a sales job.

Smiling slightly, she said, "I think you'll do."

"Well, thanks for that, young lady."

"My name's Maria. What's yours?" Elizabeth smiled at her and deposited her case overhead. Another struggle. So much for packing light.

Once seated, Elizabeth let out a deep breath.

"Why didn't you take the window seat, Maria? And I'm Elizabeth, pleased to meet you."

"I get sick if I look out the window too much."

"Ahh," said Elizabeth, "too bad. It's pretty between here and Philadelphia. I'm not sure whether it matters which side we're on, though."

"Hm." Maria smiled at Elizabeth and returned to reading her book, *My Antonia* by Willa Cather.

Glad to see I'm boring even to a kid, thought Elizabeth. Choosing not to be offended, she peered out the window to see the late passengers kiss and hug their goodbyes on the platform. A whistle blew and the startling whoosh of released steam urged stalling passengers to board quickly. Goodbyes ended, and the passengers were off like racers to find an empty seat. Vibrations of steps raising and doors slamming thundered through the floor. Another blast of the whistle, a jolt of movement, and they were on their way.

Elizabeth leaned her head against the cool glass and watched the passing scenery. The chill on her forehead tempered the searing weariness that remained around her eyes. She focused on the steady vibration of the tracks. The fight with her mother already seemed so far in the past. She wouldn't revisit that right now. She let her mind go blank, but thoughts of James wandered in. She hadn't had lunch with him for weeks since he told her he'd no longer be her dance partner. She'd resolved herself to not having him as a friend either. She missed his easy friendship and their brilliant conversations about his Army days, her college days, or things going on at the library. They'd seldom been at a loss for words.

So why hadn't she sought him out to apologize? Or to at least ask him back into the lunch routine they'd established months ago. Didn't she miss him? Did he miss her? Perhaps not, because he hadn't come looking for her either. He was the injured party. She'd been so angry with him, like he'd pulled the rug out from under her and left her lying on the hard ground. She thought he'd be her dance partner forever. Why had she believed that?

"Have you read this book?"

Maria's voice broke through the fog of sleep. Elizabeth struggled to pull herself out of it. As she straightened in the seat, the flattened skin of her forehead tingled from being stuck to the glass. Sleep had come so quickly, but then again, she hadn't slept a wink last night.

"Hmm?"

She looked at Maria, still trying to clear away the cobwebs.

"This book. Have you heard of it?"

"Oh, yes, I read it in college."

"College! But I'm only ten!"

"Well, they published it in 1918, my first year. I couldn't read it when I was ten, silly." She bumped her elbow into Maria to show she was teasing.

Maria pursed her lips. Elizabeth sensed a question coming.

"Is your mother still alive?"

"Yes, she is." Elizabeth hid her amusement. She turned sparkling brown eyes on the little girl and said, "I'm really not old enough to have dead parents."

"You could be an orphan."

Elizabeth tilted her head at the truth of this. "Why'd you ask?"

Maria whispered. "My mother is sick. It's supposed to be a secret."

"Can I ask where your mother is now?"

"Home. In New York."

"Are you going to Philadelphia like me?"

Maria closed her book. Sadness had turned off the light in her eyes.

Elizabeth reached around Maria and pulled her into

a hug against her left side.

"I'm going to my Gran's house. It's a surprise."

"She doesn't know you're coming? What if she's on a trip?" Maria's eyes brightened at the idea of a misadventure.

"I hope not!"

"I'm visiting my grandparents in Philadelphia, too."

"Perhaps we'll run into each other while we're visiting."

Maria shot her a quizzical look and shrugged.

"We should get our bags and be ready to get off."

Elizabeth pointed out the window to where the lush farmland vistas had shifted to cold metal fences and warehouses. Sunlight glinted off metal as they both squinted toward the window.

Elizabeth and her newfound friend Maria disembarked together. She helped Maria get her case onto the platform. Elizabeth told Maria she was a very brave young lady.

Quickly, the young girl was enveloped in the warm embraces of an elderly couple. Maria's voice rose in excitement as she described her trip to visit them all on her own.

Elizabeth, now feeling like a brave traveler herself, waited for the next available taxi. Who might be her next co-conspirator?

Chapter Nineteen

Elizabeth gazed up at the swirling cream scrollwork under the eaves. As a child, she had believed it was gingerbread icing, and it made her want something sweet to eat. Of course, she could count on many treats in this house when she was growing up.

Her suitcase was no longer a nuisance but a symbol of newly longed-for independence. The pursuit of that freedom was enough. She required a plan for her New York life, yet here she was in Philadelphia.

"Am I foolish?" She sighed and started up the steps.

The door flew open before she lifted the brass knocker.

"Lizzie-bit, my bay-bay!" Gran's housekeeper and cook, Pearl, enveloped Elizabeth in her smothering embrace. Though she had been in Philadelphia for thirty years, her strange southern accent still thickened everything she said. When she was excited, Pearl's pronunciation became very interesting as she mixed English and her family's African words into unintelligible phrases.

"You answered the door before I knocked. Were you going somewhere?"

"Oh, the phone!"

"The phone?"

"Anna called."

Anna had called here looking for her. Elizabeth

considered that for a moment. Her stomach clenched into a knot. Elizabeth should have left a note for Anna. Why had she been so impetuous?

"How long ago did she call?" she fidgeted with her coat buttons and wouldn't look at Pearl.

"Dear Jesus," Pearl raised her eyes to the ceiling in thought. "Two hours, I think. Not that long?"

"You told her I wasn't here. And you weren't expecting me? Right?"

"What is going on with you? You run away?"

"Now, Pearl, I'm not a child! It's a grownup trip." She straightened up as if for inspection for the second time that day.

Pearl crossed her arms over her ample bosom. Elizabeth spotted flour on her apron, and when she looked down, found a similar dusting on her dark coat.

"Oh!" Elizabeth began brushing herself off. "Pearl, where's Gran? She's not out, is she?"

Shaking her head, Flora repeated her question. "What is going on with you? Why you surprise us?"

A sudden chill made Elizabeth shiver. Weariness took over, so she sat in a chair in the entryway. Her hands slid over the deep gold velvet while she struggled to answer.

Sympathy radiated from Pearl's round brown eyes. A deep sadness she couldn't suppress overwhelmed her. Tears wet her cheeks and fell onto her coat.

"Dearie, it will be fine. Your Gran will fix you."

Pearl pulled out a handkerchief from her dress pocket and waved it in Elizabeth's face.

"Take care of your face before your Gran is home. She will be here soon enough. I'm makin' lunch." Her voice trailed off as she spun toward the kitchen.

145

Elizabeth blew her nose and pocketed the hankie for washing later. Pearl wouldn't ask for it, but she knew Elizabeth would return it.

"May I take my suitcase to my usual room, Pearl?"

"Uh, no. You must use Anna's room. Long story to tell you."

The carpet runner was threadbare. Over four decades of Alter footsteps had tripped up and down the stairs in the lovely old house. Elizabeth had wonderful memories from all her summers spent in this place. She lovingly slid her right hand along the banister as she climbed to the second floor. It was warm and slick from a recent polish. The overlook into the front hall revealed that all was not the expected perfection. Small cobwebs had formed between the ceiling and the chandelier.

Pearl would be mortified to learn she'd missed something in this home she had carefully tended for decades. Perhaps Gran had not noticed it either, or she had chosen to not call attention to it.

Elizabeth turned left to the room Anna always used. The dark wood door was pulled closed, so she set down her case to turn the knob. The polished brass knob was flecked with dark spots that revealed its age.

Loving care. The principal reason Elizabeth had fled to Gran's house. She smiled at the thought of Pearl purring over her in the coming days. Elizabeth relished that kind of attention right now.

The room had not changed much, though Anna's porcelain dolls that always nestled in a white wicker carriage basket were missing. The walls were still white. Heavy aubergine brocade curtains hung from ceiling to floor. The younger Anna's hiding place. She smiled at the memory. A dark mahogany four-poster commanded the room with its history and elegance. The soft bed covering was newer and featured delicate white floral crewelwork in the bed's center.

She threw open the drapery to let in some light. The sun shone brightly, straight overhead in a dazzling winter blue sky.

The lingering scent of mothballs greeted her, and she wrinkled her nose. Standing on the edge of the bed frame, she leaned up to unlatch the window. She pushed it open and regretted it the instant a burst of frigid air skimmed her arms. She'd wait to close it before going downstairs. Fresh air would do her some good.

Opening her case, Elizabeth heard Pearl moving around the kitchen, humming softly. It was a show tune Elizabeth had heard but couldn't place.

When they were children, Pearl would sit in the cream damask chair in the corner and sing songs with them. Elizabeth remembered fondly Pearl's tuneless voice belting out "The Itsy Bitsy Spider." The sisters played out the finger part, hands rising above their heads. They'd giggled and screamed, "Again!" Pearl nearly always obliged, but sometimes she would wave them off with a dusting cloth and say something they didn't understand about getting back to work.

Elizabeth laid out the few clothes she had brought on the bed. She set her suitcase in front of the wardrobe, unwilling to do anything else right then. The surrounding air sizzled slightly. The altercation with her mother plagued her. She touched her cheek, which still stung a little. Maybe her flight from New York contributed to these unsettled feelings. She hoped her Gran would make things better. If she could.

In the bathroom down the hall, she splashed her

cheeks with water. While drying her face with a thick lavender-scented towel, she noticed a razor on the windowsill. Strange, she thought. It couldn't belong to Gramps, could it? He'd been dead ten years. It wouldn't be like Gran to leave it out as a sentimental memory.

She twisted her fingers together nervously, fiddled with her hair, grabbed the banister, and headed downstairs. Her stomach tightened with dread. It was time to explain herself. She preferred to tell her story only once and hoped Pearl would let her wait. She'd been so hopeful Gran would understand her impulsive journey. Would she?

Reality now caught her in its ropes, that and the tangle of being away from home and her job. It made her as anxious as a mouse in a house of cats.

Elizabeth drifted into the warm, scented air of Pearl's kitchen. It was her kitchen, all right. The sparkling windows offered a view of a long, narrow garden. A few hardy herbs under the window swayed in the light midday breeze. Beyond, Gran's spectacular, prize-winning rosebushes hunkered down. Their deeply pruned branches promised a massive showing in a few months. Pearl and Gran would see to that.

The coffee's dark richness wafted up to her nose as Pearl poured some into a porcelain cup. She stared at Elizabeth quizzically. Stirring in cream, Elizabeth admired the green and gold pattern along the saucer's rim. Gran's china collection was beyond belief. Elizabeth promised herself a morning of exploration in the dining room. A little sentimental journey would be a comfort to her. Wasn't that why she was here?

Was that the one-hundredth question she'd asked herself in the last twelve hours? Where were the answers?

Gran arrived with much noisy fanfare just as Elizabeth took a sip. Pearl dropped the dishtowel on the counter and walked swiftly to the front hall. Elizabeth quickly dismissed the idea of following her. A lump formed in her throat as she heard their greetings and the indistinct murmur of conversation. They were not talking about Gran's shopping, she knew that.

The sound of footsteps headed her way. Elizabeth stood up beside the table and pasted a smile on her face. Tears threatened, and she squeezed her eyes tightly to push them back. She couldn't cry now. It wouldn't be fair to Gran. She was not the type who brushed away tears and kissed boo-boos. Had Elizabeth ever seen Gran cry?

"What have we here?" Gran queried, her gaze studying Elizabeth's tear-stained face.

She bit her bottom lip, then took a deep breath to press down the threatening tears. "Hi, Gran. I—I'm sorry for this…surprise."

"A pleasant one! You're a sight for sore eyes. I missed you at Christmas. Come here, let me look at you."

Elizabeth walked toward her grandmother, Cora Eugenie Alter, who stood straight in a black silk dress with long full sleeves. Black and cream lace adorned the cuffs and bodice. Beautiful jet buttons carved with a floral design embellished the front, from the waistline almost to her neck. A small vee revealed the aging decolletage of a sixty-seven-year-old woman. Her skin was lightly tanned from years spent in her garden. Another woman might look severe in this dress, but Gran's nearly smooth face offered a loving smile for this young woman she adored.

Elizabeth stepped into Gran's open arms and relaxed into her embrace. Nothing could stop the tears. Compared to her white lace pillow back in New York, Gran's firm shoulder was the better place to absorb Elizabeth's grief. Grief over a loss of innocence, the shock of her mother's unapologetic violence.

Elizabeth had come to Philadelphia because she needed Gran to sort through her confusion about her place in the world. Gran would help her make things right again.

Chapter Twenty

"Elizabeth, since your sister has called here looking for you, you must call home."

"Oh, Gran! No!" Elizabeth huffed.

"My dear, it's for the best. Think of it this way. You tell them where you are, and they settle on the idea. You and I can work from there."

Elizabeth didn't like this, but Gran was right. She had to call home.

"All right."

She brushed her shaking hands down the sides of her navy dress as she walked into the foyer. Picking up the phone, she glanced expectantly at her grandmother, who nodded in encouragement.

Elizabeth looked in the mirror and brushed her bangs with her fingers. A delaying tactic.

"Okay," she muttered to herself. She took another deep breath. It didn't shake that time, so she supposed she was ready. Now or never.

Minnie picked up on the second ring.

"Hello, Mother?"

"Elizabeth! Oh my god. Where the devil are you? I cannot believe—"

"Mother, I'm at Gran's."

"Your father and I were worried to death about you. What possessed you to leave in the middle of the night? I am—"

"Perhaps you've forgotten that you hit me!"

"Well…"

"Mother, I'm very sorry—" Elizabeth stopped talking when Gran shook her head.

"Elizabeth, you need to come home now! Cora is ill-equipped to handle your problems."

"My problems?"

Minnie laughed. "You—"

"Mother, is Father there? I want to speak to him."

"No. He is out."

Elizabeth thought for a moment. Why would her father be out on a Saturday afternoon? That was out of character.

"Anna, come talk to your sister." Minnie's voice was muffled while she pleaded with Anna.

"Go, Mother," Anna hissed. Elizabeth pictured her sister waving their mother out of the foyer.

"Oh, Elizabeth!" Anna exclaimed softly, in relief.

"Anna! Thank goodness, a voice of sanity."

"What do you mean? Why in heaven's name did you sneak out of here and leave me this mess?"

Elizabeth rolled her eyes at Gran and mouthed, "Anna."

"I just… I needed time to think." Surely her sister understood that.

"Did you think about your job? The one you have to go to two days from now? Mother is concerned about that, of all things. Another part of your life she's disapproved of all along and suddenly she's concerned you'll lose it. And she's aiming all her sermons at me!"

Elizabeth heard Anna sigh heavily over the phone.

"Where's Father? Is he really out?"

"Today has been strange. I miss you!"

"I miss you, too, Anna."

Elizabeth didn't get her question about her father answered before they rang off, promising to stay in touch. She had no answers for her sister about her plans to return home. Her heart ached as she returned to the parlor.

Elizabeth quietly examined the framed photos around the room. Elizabeth could tell Cora enjoyed sharing titillating tales of the cousins and uncles in the photos. She laughed along. She'd made the right choice coming to Philadelphia, no matter how spontaneous it was. Gran would be the fresh ear she needed to help her comb through the tangle of thoughts, the ones making both her heart and her head ache.

She didn't know how she would resolve her problems, though. Leaving New York was obviously not a permanent solution. Anna was right. She had a job, and she had just abandoned the city and the library.

"Gran, I need to get back home. I escaped with no word to my supervisor. How stupid was I? I can't just—"

Cora raised a hand to halt the tumble of words.

"I hate seeing you so anxious, my dear. We can work through these things."

"But I…"

"No buts. Let's make a plan. You're a bright girl."

Elizabeth bit her lip and looked away. There was that compliment again, "bright." She appreciated her brain but failed to see how her intelligence had advanced her in the world so far. Her personal life lay in tatters on Gran's Persian carpet, and the mess she'd made with James belied the keen intelligence ever present in her clear brown eyes.

They spent the afternoon discussing what was going on in Elizabeth's life. Gran beamed proudly while Elizabeth talked about the research she was handling at the library. Elizabeth's excitement was contagious. Gran asked many questions, eager to learn new things, too.

Pearl brought in tea and asked Cora about dinner. Elizabeth didn't listen closely while they discussed whether chicken or fish should be on the menu. Her mind wandered back to Jocelyn and Mrs. Goldberg and so engrossed was she in her memories that the older women's voices became a distant murmur.

"That's a good girl. You're smiling." Gran stood. "Let's take advantage of what little sunlight is left. That glare is in my eyes." The setting sun made shadows and light perform a staggering dance with the patterns on the rug. She pulled the gold moiré drapes half-closed. She looked over her shoulder at the velvet settee that had been her perch to ensure the sun's rays weren't shining over her space. "There, that's better."

"I could have done that for you, Gran."

"Well, now you know, tomorrow it can be your job." She winked at her lovely granddaughter. Elizabeth sensed Gran's great delight in this surprising turn of events.

"I'll pour the tea, then. What did you and Pearl decide about dinner?"

"Since it's just the two of us this evening, we'll have the fish."

Elizabeth handed a teacup to her Gran.

Later that evening, the two of them dined at one end of the dark walnut dining table. An electric chandelier cast shimmers of light across the table's highly polished sheen. The scalloped gold edges of the china gleamed like jewels adorning an alabaster neckline. Baked halibut swam in a delicate and tasty sauce of herbs and butter. Roasted potatoes with crisp edges melted in their mouths.

Pearl's welcome dinner was a hit with them both and Gran praised her. "You've outdone yourself again, Pearl. We're so fortunate."

"I had seconds of everything, Pearl. I can't possibly have dessert. Tomorrow, I'll save room." Elizabeth stood to help Pearl clear the table.

After Cora settled herself with a book in the parlor, Elizabeth retreated to her room to hang all her things, but Pearl had already taken care of it. She searched the wardrobe and under the bed, but the suitcase was nowhere in sight. The two old women had apparently decided she was staying.

Soft snores emanated from the parlor, drifting halfway up the stairs. Elizabeth grinned. Book in hand, she tiptoed over to the chair, slid over an ottoman for her feet, and turned on the lamp. Light cut through the glass prisms on the shade, casting a jewel-like sparkle over the pages of her book.

Her grandmother dozed on. She had a good relationship with Gran, but she couldn't get over feeling foolish about showing up unannounced that morning. Perhaps she had taken advantage of Gran's lifetime of love for her. Gran had taken it all in stride, offering a surprising shoulder to cry on and some helpful advice about tomorrow and the day after.

The weariness of an emotional day washed over her. It was too early to retire to bed, so she opened her book. Soon, the granddaughter joined her grandmother in the land of Nod, both of them slumped in the parlor like vagrants in a railway station.

****

She'd been asleep in bed for a few hours when she heard a noise. Elizabeth turned over on her back and stared at the ceiling. Disoriented, she blinked. She was looking at the ceiling of her Gran's house! Relief oozed out of her. So tired from the last twenty-four hours of emotional turmoil, she barely remembered waking Gran and then getting into the bed.

Squinting through the blackness of her room, she tossed back the covers and touched her bare feet to the floor. The thick wool rug greeted her toes. Her white cotton nightdress skimmed lightly around her ankles. In the room's coolness, she was grateful for long sleeves. Elizabeth felt her way in the dark. Wood against wood squeaked as she pulled open the heavy door. The hallway was lit by a single lamp at the far end near Gran's bedroom and beyond her usual bedroom door.

What noise had wakened her? The house was silent.

Curiosity got the best of her, so she slipped up the hall. The room where she'd spent many a childhood summer was off-limits now, and she didn't know why. Pearl had never had the chance to tell her why she'd been relegated to Anna's old room.

The floorboard squeaked outside her old room, like it always had. Elizabeth was reaching her hand forward to the doorknob when the bathroom door flew open behind her. She nearly jumped out of her skin.

"Oh!" she shrieked and crossed her arms over her chest.

A man stood in the bathroom's doorway. Long strands of wet black hair hung over his forehead and water dripped onto his unbuttoned white shirt.

"I…who…who are you?" She was tempted to wake Gran with her raised voice, until she remembered the shaving razor on the windowsill. Mystery solved.

He pulled a white towel from around his shoulders and rubbed it over his hair. He studied her from head to toe. Puzzlement and a few other emotions flickered over his face before Elizabeth stepped back. She bumped into the door frame behind her.

"George?" He offered in confusion.

"George? You're asking me?"

George sniffed and tipped his chin up.

"Who are you?"

"Elizabeth, Gran's… I'm Cora's granddaughter. Who are you again?"

George was tall, even taller than James. It was hard not to focus on the fine detail of his abdomen and chest where the wet shirt clung. His arms were muscular, his shirtsleeves tight around them. Elizabeth finally looked up at his face. He watched her, an amused smile playing on his full lips.

Heat crept up her neck. She hoped the dim light in the hallway hid her reaction.

"Nice to meet you, George," Elizabeth huffed as she skirted past him and strutted back to her room.

"Sure, Stick. Nice ta meet ya too."

She didn't dare glance back as she swept into her bedroom and firmly shut the door, as if she were shutting him out of her thoughts, too. She leaned back against the door and closed her eyes. Hair prickled on the back of her neck. Go to bed, she scolded herself. Elizabeth hiked up her long white nightgown, climbed onto the high mattress, and slid under the covers again.

She didn't understand what had just happened.

Whyever did Gran have a man, a young man, staying here? Was he living here? She wished fervently that she had asked Pearl about the razor that morning.

Ready to drift off, she remembered he had called her "Stick."

"Ooof!" She hit her pillow with her hand and squeaked in embarrassment. How insulting.

****

Elizabeth woke to the warm, sweet scent of cinnamon and apples. Like a siren's song, Pearl's cooking beckoned her downstairs.

Gran, her fork poised midair, greeted Elizabeth. Gran's eyes cut quickly to George, who was filling his plate at the sideboard.

"Elizabeth, this is George. And…"

"We've met, Gran. Late last night in the hall." She cast him a sideways glance while perusing Pearl's breakfast offerings. She sure knew how to put on a Sunday breakfast, Elizabeth thought. Her stomach growled loudly.

"Good morning, Stick." He grinned.

Elizabeth glared at him. A sarcastic comeback was not forthcoming, and she wanted to kick the cat that had her tongue in its claws. Ignoring him would have to be her best offense for now.

"Did you sleep well, Gran?"

"Yes, I slept just fine."

For a few moments, silence settled in the dining room, with only the sounds of forks clinking on the gold-rimmed plates.

"George, why don't you tell Elizabeth about your music?" Gran beamed at him like a doting grandmother. Elizabeth looked at them in disbelief. His music?

"Sure. I play piano. We just got here from Chicago. A couple months ago, was it?" He looked over at Gran for confirmation.

"Oh. How interesting." While she looked pointedly at her grandmother, she asked him in a firm voice, "And exactly how did you meet my Gran?"

A guffaw filled the room, and it didn't come from George. Gran was holding her cup of coffee with both hands, her fingertips poised on both sides. She was shaking with laughter. Elizabeth could hardly stand it. The camaraderie between her grandmother and George was mystifying. But should it be? Her mother too often clucked when hearing news about Gran from Henry, who called her about once a month.

Gran was too much of a free spirit, in Minnie's opinion. Gran didn't "act her age" as Minnie wished every person would do. Except children, they were to act like adults, and if they couldn't manage that, they should be invisible. Minnie's two daughters had experienced that attitude all too often.

Because Elizabeth was staring at Cora, George shared no more about his music. She changed tactics.

"So, what brought you here? You're in a band?"

"Yeah, Stick, I play piano in a band." He repeated it slowly, humor playing on his lips. Why was she focused on his mouth? She crossed her arms.

"Elizabeth."

"Huh?"

"That's my name. Elizabeth." Mimicking him, she sounded out her name slowly, lifted her coffee cup primly, and peered at him over its rim. Challenge issued.

"I'll try to remember that." He winked at her, coaxing a pink flush up her cheeks.

Elizabeth stood with her plate and walked through the dining room into the kitchen, muttering "pardon me" on her way.

Her plate clattered on the countertop as Elizabeth groaned, "Ugh."

Pearl swung around with a coffeepot in her hand. Seeing no cup, she leaned on the counter across from Elizabeth. Her bosom straining against her gray-blue cotton bodice.

"You met George, eh?"

Rolling her eyes at Pearl, Elizabeth also leaned on the counter and rested her chin in her hand. She played with the food on her plate, hoping her appetite would return.

"Gran seems to think he's a hoot. I'm not amused."

"Well, my dear, he has been very good for your grandmother. He came along right when her best friend, Olivia, died."

"Oh, no, I knew nothing about that." Her bottom lip came out. Elizabeth cut a glance at Pearl. "You like this George person?"

Pearl chuckled. "Oh my, he is so good to have in the house. Like having you. Young people make this old house buzz. Is that how you young'uns say it?"

Chapter Twenty-One

Elizabeth felt bloated from the eggs and toast she'd eaten, so much more filling than her usual morning cereal and milk. She liked the relaxed feeling of a Sunday morning with no responsibilities around the house. No family dinner, no fussing.

George had decided to walk over to another band member's place. But Gran wasn't finished discussing Elizabeth's future.

"Elizabeth. What do you want in life? You must answer that for yourself. No one else can tell you. If you let someone else plan your life, you will be miserable."

"You surely experienced worse pressures from society way back then."

"Oh, yes, way back then."

Elizabeth gasped and shook her head vehemently.

"No, I didn't mean you're old! But things were even more confining before 1900, weren't they? For women, I mean."

"Indeed, they were. Still today, your mother's generation and mine don't want to let these bold changes take root without fighting them."

Elizabeth snorted and touched her cheek. "I learned that harsh lesson."

"Even at my age, there's been pressure. When your grandfather died ten years ago, I was only fifty-seven years old. Still marriageable, by most people's standards, and apparently unable to carry on without a man." She brushed a hand down the burgundy silk of her skirt.

"Oh, dear. Did people say that to you?"

"There were little comments, sideways remarks. I ignored them all. I'm quite happy, as you can tell."

Gran put a vein-marked hand over Elizabeth's. "Now, answer the question. What do you want out of life?"

So many expectations had weighed upon her as she finished college and started her job at the library. Elizabeth had only begun grappling with the conflict between the world's expectations and her own desires. She was desperate to find her own way, but society's boundaries vexed her and made her confused about how she could have it all. Did she want it all? She wasn't even sure of that, either. How could she put all that into words her Gran would understand?

She started her answer by telling her grandmother about the dance hall debacle, James' terrible anger directed at her, and how much she liked him.

"I'm certain I won't be seeing him anymore. He wants a different life than I do right now. And I had always planned on us being just friends."

Gran nodded and said, "Of course, you've now learned that such a friendship could be fraught with problems."

Elizabeth grimaced and shook her head. "I can't think of a single friendship like that, unless Ginger Rogers and Fred Astaire are just friends. James has already squashed any future for me as Ginger to his Fred. And I hate to say this too, Gran. It's really all my fault. What happened with James. I am so obstinate. I wonder at times if I'm even likable." Elizabeth slumped back into her chair.

"You have friends?"

"Oh, I suppose. I've been wondering if they're just around out of courtesy. Like my coworkers asking me to dinner or to see a film." She shrugged. "They're being polite."

"I think you're being ridiculous, dear." Gran slid her cup and saucer back with a rattle. "You are a delightful young woman. You're smart and funny."

"I appreciate that, though you're meant to be biased toward me. But there's another sign," Elizabeth continued. "My old friends from high school and college. I never see them anymore."

"Why is that? Have you tried to talk to them?"

"They're all married! With babies!" Elizabeth complained.

Gran refused to commiserate. "My dear, you're wallowing. I'm sorry to say that. Appreciate what you have. Your friend from college. Jocelyn, is it? Don't you still see her, a year past college? Surely she's not forced to hang about."

"Oh, Gran. I am being juvenile, aren't I? My supervisor has always seemed to like me, too. Well, until… That remains to be seen."

She was dreading calling Mr. Gerold tomorrow with her news. Keeping her eyes cast to the floor, she ran her hands down her legs to smooth her thick black tights. Brooding felt good at the moment.

The two women chatted until the coffee ran out. Gran asked a lot of questions to coax Elizabeth into considering many options for her future. Gran wasn't focused on marriage and children, to Elizabeth's relief. But hearing Gran list Elizabeth's many choices sent her head spinning.

She had so much to consider. Navigating an independent life meant repairing relationships, convincing her parents she could work, live alone, and return to school. Perhaps she should first convince herself that all of that was possible.

After they helped Pearl get the breakfast dishes to the kitchen, Gran and Elizabeth settled in the parlor with the newspaper. A few pages in, Gran dropped the paper in her lap and cleared her throat.

"Dear, let's discuss why you came here. You didn't think I had all the answers, did you?"

Trust Gran to drive home the uncomfortable question. Elizabeth wondered if her tears may have kept Gran from prying open that nasty can of worms yesterday.

Elizabeth floundered around, not sure where to start again. She explained about Dr. Sporian's master's degree suggestion.

Gran had leaned forward. "You would like to study more, my dear?"

Elizabeth had shrugged. "I don't know. I was ambitious to get a job too. It seemed like what I should do."

"What does your father say?"

"Very little, Gran." Elizabeth hesitated to criticize her father to his mother. Besides, she adored Father. She had some lovely memories of playing games and chase in the back garden with him, in Philadelphia especially. When he got away from work, he became more relaxed and funnier.

Gran remained quiet, so Elizabeth rushed to his defense.

"You know what he's like with Mother. He lets her rule the roost. Till she goes too far, that is. She has strong opinions about what Anna and I are supposed to do. He has not been one to counter them."

"Talk to him about college."

Elizabeth studied her grandmother as if she were speaking in code. She sat down and rested her forehead in her hands. She did too much thinking, but now it appeared she needed to engage in even more pondering.

"There's more to tell. Do you remember Margaret Goldberg?"

"Maggie Goldberg," Gran said wistfully. "What a dear woman. Her son and your father were great friends when they were young."

"Yes, she told me. I'm going to live in her basement."

"What? Live where?" Gran's brows furrowed, and she fingered the pendant at her throat.

"Oh. It's not horrible. It's lovely!" Elizabeth described how she met the sweet old woman and her offer to live in the basement of her house.

"Well, that sounds quite nice for you. Living on your own but having someone around. Maggie will be good to you."

"I haven't told Mother or Father yet." The words tumbled guiltily into the room.

"Oh, my dear. The plot thickens." Gran chuckled. "You must do that very soon."

"You're right. Father knows. Well, actually, I only told him I wanted to find a place of my own. That was before I found Mrs. Goldberg. Or she found me, truth be told. But I've yet to tell him about moving in May." She smiled at Gran, still feeling a bit like a naughty child.

Gran was right, her parents needed to hear this news. And they needed to know about her college dreams.

How was she going to convince them she was capable of managing her own life? Had she convinced herself yet?

****

Elizabeth got ready to call Mr. Gerold at the library. Standing in Gran's foyer, she stared into the mirror, took a deep breath, and picked up the phone's earpiece. She dialed and got put through to his office.

When he answered, she took a deep breath. Then the words came out in a tumble.

"Hello, Mr. Gerold? This is Elizabeth Alter. I'm calling to tell you that I left in a hurry this weekend and I'm in Philadelphia with my grandmother. Um. That's why I'm not in my office right now."

Elizabeth cringed as she waited for his querying into the why's and wherefore's, but it did not come. He was always pleasant to her, so his directness surprised her.

"Well, this does put our office in a bind, Miss Alter. When will you be home? Soon, I hope?"

"Um, I haven't thought about the day I'll return. Perhaps on Saturday."

"Saturday? You'll be gone the entire week? I see. Most unfortunate, Miss Alter."

Elizabeth grimaced.

"Mr. Gerold, I am so very sorry to inconvenience you and everyone else in research. I do feel badly."

"Yes, well. It's done now, isn't it? Shall we say I'll see you on the Monday? Hopefully, before."

"Yes, yes. I will hurry home, I promise. I'll work extra hours to get my projects caught up. You'll see."

She hung up the phone and looked into the parlor.

Gran had disappeared while she took the minor verbal beating from her supervisor. Mr. Gerold was too mild-mannered, she supposed, to give her the tongue-lashing her impetuous self actually deserved.

The house was quiet, other than the distant sound of Pearl singing while she cleaned. Regardless of the signs that Pearl might be slowing down—a stained tablecloth, the cobwebs—Pearl's energy was astounding, particularly in the kitchen. She wished she could stay longer and have a cooking lesson or two.

In her room, Elizabeth sprawled across her bed and pondered what Mr. Gerold had said to her. He was displeased with her, an unusual state of affairs. But what had she expected? Leave with no warning and expect him to throw her a bon voyage party?

Gran had left the house, and there was no predicting when she might return. She pondered how she could get to the library and work on some research. Maybe if Elizabeth found a rare resource in Philadelphia, Mr. Gerold would smile at her again one day. He wouldn't question her commitment ever again. She could hope, anyway.

She'd been working on a research project about westward migration in the 1880s. And it was one she loved sinking her inquisitive teeth into. Jean and Matilda had happily passed on this request to Elizabeth. They both had strong preferences about the assignments they wanted. Elizabeth often saw Jean in Mr. Gerold's office, posing seductively and asking for the list of incoming requests so she could get her project preferences fulfilled.

Elizabeth didn't mind her coworkers' selectivity because she enjoyed the challenges of unique research questions and the chance to escape into the stacks and archives. No passage between boxes or any aisle between shelves had remained a mystery once Elizabeth had started working at the library. She developed her own code names for some dark, musty paths in the basement: Teapot Harbor for the Revolutionary War section and Sanctum Jefferson for the boxes on the Declaration and Constitution that rose to ceiling height.

The rooms smelled of old dust layered on inky paper, and she loved that. While her workmates were quick to leave the archives, claiming to be overcome by the staleness, she relished each chance to visit. Housed there were the stories upon which much of American literature rested—the archives of human workmanship, service, and valor.

Chin in her hand, she flipped over a leaflet she'd found in the newspapers yesterday and started reading. It was an advertisement for an upcoming dance. The dance hall featured live music every Friday and Saturday night. She loved live music and dancing. Her thoughts switched to George. Did he bring this leaflet to the house? Was this place nearby, perhaps? She knew little of the street names outside of Gran's neighborhood.

She wouldn't be around long enough to learn the local geography. She loved New York and the predictable grid structure that made it difficult to get lost there. Time to learn a little about Gran's placement in the city, she decided.

Mind racing about dancing and research, Elizabeth raced down the stairs and into the kitchen to question Pearl.

Elizabeth heard the low mumble of voices as she approached the closed kitchen door off the front hall.

One was male. Was it the milkman chatting up Pearl? Or was George up? She grimaced at the thought of having to be friendly to him. Only one way to find out. She wouldn't let George keep her out of any room in Gran's house. Still, she snuck a quick glance in the gilt-framed mirror and fingered her dark bangs. Even though her hair needed a trim, it looked pretty, its soft shiny strands draped against her neck. Catching herself possibly caring about what that ridiculous man might think, she stuck out her tongue at her reflection.

Elizabeth pushed open the door into the kitchen to find Pearl and George holding an enormous silver pan. Tool in hand, George was finishing up the job of tightening a handle.

"Good morning, Stick." George set down the pan and dramatically wiped his forearm across his brow. "Starting my day off with hard labor."

"Starting... Yes, indeed." She placed the leaflet on the sideboard and crossed her arms over her chest.

Georgie shook his head and chuckled. "You're a hard one."

Pearl frowned and held up a hand. "Now, now, children."

Elizabeth straightened and got down to business. "I need some help. Where's the public library? I have some work to do."

"You can't walk there from here. It's a long way," Pearl said.

"How many blocks, do you think? I could use the fresh air. I'm accustomed to walking a lot at home."

Pearl turned to the stove and stirred a pot. "First, eat lunch."

"Hey, hey, no way. You can't walk across town to

the library." George ran a hand through his shiny black hair. His eyebrows knitted together while he thought of a way to talk her out of this mad plan. "You don't know your way around here good enough."

"I'll have you know I spent summers here for years. My sister and I wandered quite far afield sometimes. And…my sense of direction is impeccable!"

"No, George's right. Bad part of town you have to cross."

"Look, my pal is coming to pick me up for practice this afternoon. We'll take you."

Elizabeth lifted her chin. Trapped into accepting a kind gesture from this…person. Pearl's gaze bounced between them, her hand still holding the long spoon in the pot. The hearty aroma of chicken soup caused Elizabeth's stomach to rumble so loudly her hand flew to her abdomen and she blushed.

"Comin' up." Pearl waved the two wary adults over to the kitchen table with her apron.

In minutes, steaming bowls of chicken soup sat in front of George and Elizabeth, each working diligently to avoid the other's gaze.

Halfway through the lunch, Elizabeth remembered the leaflet. She jumped up to fetch it.

"What do you know about this?"

George gave the leaflet a cursory glance. "Dance place a few blocks over. We've played there."

"I'd like to go."

"Bad idea."

"Why?"

"Not your kind of place."

"You don't know my kind of place. I go dancing in New York."

George's eyebrows shot up. He shook his head.

Elizabeth frowned. Did he consider her a sheltered princess who didn't get out much?

"I can take care of myself. You don't know me."

"Ha, true enough. Know your type, though."

Elizabeth lifted the bowl to her lips and slurped the last drops of broth. She set the bowl noisily on the table and ran the back of her arm across her mouth. "Mm."

His eyes, so dark brown they were nearly black, danced.

Chapter Twenty-Two

Elizabeth stood at her bedroom window, peering through the gossamer sheers, her body shielded by the velvet curtain that brushed the back of her hand.

After lunch, she'd retreated to her room to think about her research assignment. She made little progress remembering what questions she might get answered at a different library.

Daydreams assailed her. She thought about James, his kindness in stark contrast to the stinging candor she had received from the exasperating George. James had treated her with kid gloves, and she had enjoyed being with him. He was comfortable to be around.

George made her terribly uncomfortable. His commentary was a challenge. He had her pegged as a delicate poodle, trying to tease her into snapping. She fought off the image of his grin. She hated the way his eyes lit up in that strangely entrancing way.

She heard a loud sputtering sound long before she saw the offending vehicle. It reminded her of the milk truck she'd ridden in only days before. The most marked difference was its color. It appeared to be hand-painted in a revolting golden hue. Musical instruments painted black and white appeared to dance across the side panel she could see. Painted swirls created the impression of movement for a saxophone, drums, two other instruments. The painted piano keyboard had keys depressed by invisible fingers. The entire visual effect was a jaunty quintet playing jazz music.

This was her transportation this afternoon? Of all the insults. Had she given the offer any thought, which she hadn't, she would have concluded that her ride would not be a brand-new Model T. This was George's "pal" after all, and he continued to deliver on her low expectations of him.

A second ride in a truck in as many days did not fit her definition of adventure, but she would rise to the occasion for the sake of her job. She was enthusiastic about visiting the library and making good use of her impetuous trip. Reminded of that, she shut the wardrobe door with her snobbery buried inside.

After checking her reflection in the bureau's mirror, she headed downstairs. George stood by the front door, brown tweed hat in hand. He wore a threadbare tan coat that ended mid-thigh, accentuating his height and his unhealthy narrow frame. Its sleeves barely touched his wrist bones. Were he a five-year-old on the street, she'd mark him as a pitiful urchin.

She poked her head into the parlor, but Gran wasn't there. Elizabeth remembered hearing Gran huffing up the stairs earlier that afternoon.

From the coat rack, she lifted her navy wool coat and put it on. George was immediately at her side, attempting to help her with it. An awkward dance ensued because she resisted his help. George stepped back and bowed slightly with that smile playing on his lips. Rosy warmth flooded her face, and she feared George would detect her mood and make hay with it.

"I've forgotten my hat. One moment." She ran up the stairs. In her room, she took a deep, shaky breath. She grabbed her hat off the chair and returned to the landing at the top of the staircase. George stood at the front door, looking expectantly at the place where she now stood.

"Got it." She held up the navy wool hat while she walked down.

He opened the front door and touched her elbow briefly as they navigated the front steps.

Elizabeth approached the truck slowly and glanced over her shoulder at George. How were they going to do this? She quickly deduced that all three of them were riding in the front seat. She would have to grin and bear it, it seemed.

George opened the door, which creaked as metal squeezed metal. The sound reverberated down the street and she cringed. George waved a hand toward the truck. "After you."

She frowned at him, then glanced into the cab at the driver. Had George mentioned his friend's name?

To its credit, the truck sported running boards, which allowed her to enter the truck cab gracefully. She hated to give George a view of her backside and legs. She quickly heaved herself into the truck and slid over a bit toward the center. But not too far.

"I'm Marty."

"I'm Elizabeth."

"Great, you've met. You need to scootch over so I can shut the door, Stick." George slid onto the seat.

Elizabeth blushed and glanced at Marty like he'd bite. Marty chuckled and slid himself over a little, too.

"Marty, the little lady needs to go to the library. It's a couple blocks past our club. Just keep straight."

Elizabeth considered politely quizzing Marty about their band, but the truck's close quarters kept her mum.

Every bump and turn meant her thigh touched George's. She suspected he got a subtle pleasure from her discomfort, and she wouldn't let him think he had pushed her personal sensitivities.

Soon, a dozen or more blocks from Gran's house—honestly, she'd lost count—the library loomed ahead on the left.

Marty pulled to the curb. George leaped out and held out a hand to Elizabeth. She dropped to the ground and released his hand like a hot potato.

"Now, Stick. When you're finished, walk down Twelfth Street. See it there? Go two blocks and you'll see the sign for the Tangle Club?"

"What—"

"We'll give you a ride home after practice."

Elizabeth's mouth worked and her mind whirled as she grappled with the solution George offered. It was too far to walk back to Gran's; she had to admit it. She nodded.

"Twelfth Street, two blocks, Tango Club."

"Tan-gle Club." Georgie sounded it out slowly, like she was simple.

"Okay. I'm off." She waved and looked both ways before crossing the street. Out of the corner of her eye, she caught him shaking his head at her caution. Well, it was who she was.

On the opposite sidewalk, she turned and waved. From this vantage point, she saw the other side of the truck. They had painted the words, "The Legacy Quintet," in fancy white letters, with the same flourishes that gave movement to the instruments on the other side of the truck.

Knowing she was being watched, she skipped

lightly up the cement stairs to the main doors.

****

She found the research manager when she arrived at the circulation desk. Overcoming her surprise that the manager was a woman, Elizabeth explained her situation.

The manager introduced herself as Florence Welden. She listened as they strode through tall wooden shelves that reminded Elizabeth of her own workplace. She sneaked a deep breath to confirm that the Philadelphia library had the same gracious scent of paper, leather, dust, and sunlight. While there were some who'd debate whether sunlight had a smell, Elizabeth would win that debate. The sizzle of light stealing through the long windows in her library's Reading Room imbued the air with the warm scent of sunbeams. Weightless and heavy all at once. She couldn't describe it perfectly, but she knew it when it draped around her.

"You can settle here." Miss Welden broke into Elizabeth's distraction. "I've shown you the shelves you'll want to peruse, and I'll go down into our archives. I have some ideas."

Elizabeth thanked her. She put her handbag down and returned to the relevant shelves. With a foot-high stack of books, she tottered back to the table and chair Miss Welden had assigned to her.

She opened her notepad and got to work.

Miss Welden interrupted her a half an hour later with a sheaf of papers, some of them quite delicate.

Hours passed, and when employees made motions of ending their day, Elizabeth continued her note-taking. She heard a soft throat-clearing and found the manager standing over her. "We're closing."

"Oh, no. May I come back tomorrow to finish? Your materials need more than three hours of my attention; this may take a few days. I'm not certain."

"Not to worry. I'll lock the archival documents in my office. The books can stay there for now."

Elizabeth expressed her gratitude for being allowed to continue the research project again in the morning.

The woman's back was ramrod straight as she walked to her office, her gray dress a simple column from the back. Following her, Elizabeth stuck her head into the office, her eyes widening at finding a place enrobed with femininity and warmth. Photographs of Florence with another young woman with the same shade of blonde hair and one of an older couple, her parents most likely, occupied several spaces on the cluttered desk.

She smiled at Florence while checking to see if she was wearing a wedding band. She wasn't. That a professional young woman could have what appeared to be a happy, unmarried life warmed her heart.

They walked out together, both in navy wool coats, while Elizabeth peppered Florence with questions about the building's history. They turned in opposite directions at the bottom of the steps.

"Good night," Elizabeth tossed over her shoulder. Florence's hand came up in response, but she didn't turn around.

****

Walking a block from the library, she looked around. Elizabeth could not remember how to find George's band. Frustrated by her absentmindedness, she spun on her heels and walked back to where she'd started.

Crossing the street was challenging now that many had finished work for the evening. The swishing noise of tires on pavement and the oily smell of exhaust reminded her of New York City. If she closed her eyes—which she'd never do in this part of town—she could imagine herself headed home after work.

Leaping onto the sidewalk from the street, Elizabeth nearly collided with an elderly man.

"Excuse me, do you know where the Tangle Club is?"

He leaned toward her, babbling, and she realized he was drunk. Her smile wavered. She backed away and headed down a narrow side street. Shaken, she looked over her shoulder, feeling desperately alone in a city she didn't know. The evening shadows emerged, and she no longer felt the faultless protection of the library.

She saw a sign for 12th Street and exhaled a shaky breath. A hand over her heart, she darted up another block.

The sign for the Tangle Club was missing lights, but the syncopated beat of piano keys and the low moan of a saxophone assured her she was in the right place. Across the street, a man flew out a black door preceded by his hand holding a cigarette. A woman's riotous laughter followed him, and the owner of this gleeful noise stepped through the doorway. She lost her balance on the tiny step down and her laughter faded. The music inside stopped, and the sudden silence provided a backdrop to the couple's mumbling conversation.

Elizabeth stood still about ten feet from the Tangle Club's doorway. The couple, as they engaged in an inept dance, found their sea legs and moved down the sidewalk away from her. The woman seemed tipsy, and her fellow practiced a clumsy chivalry to get her walking in rhythm with him. With his arm wrapped around her waist, the thin white fabric of her narrow sheath rose above the lining. Her gold and white feather headband, a childish tiara, slid sideways in her platinum hair. The young woman was probably Elizabeth's age and in need of intervention, but Elizabeth suppressed the urge to assist the poor girl away from this man. They retreated with the music of mumblings and laughter and the light drumming of shoes on stone.

She heard the music start up again, muffled behind the club's heavy wooden door. Its green paint had worn away around the edges, an abandoned building feel to it all. No light emanated from the dark-paned windows. Maybe painted black on the inside, she thought.

Taking a deep breath of desperate bravado, she pulled open the green door and found herself in a four-foot vestibule and faced another thick wooden barrier to the full impact of the instruments and a female vocalist's playful staccato.

The door stuck tight, and Elizabeth wondered if she should knock. But she pulled it with both hands, and it jerked open. She stepped into half-darkness and heavy stale air. Silvery-gray light fingered its way from the bright stage and barely touched her. Remaining in near darkness, Elizabeth watched the musicians sway, playing their parts.

The woman singing wore a plain navy dress with a dropped waist, its hem ending below her knees, much like one Elizabeth owned. Still, her throaty voice oozed with sexual undertones and her hands caressed the microphone in its stand. She twirled her hand in the air to signal a repeat, and the band slid easily back to the refrain. It was sloppy; the notes fell over each other, inviting and alive. Elizabeth's foot was tapping to the beat, and if a man had offered a hand in invitation, her shoes would have spiraled across the dance floor.

The song ended abruptly, and she heard George call to her. Her eyes flew open as he yelled, "Stick!"

Elizabeth didn't want to leave her hiding place yet. Didn't want to exit the space inside the music's energizing beat. But George stepped off the low stage and came toward her, a hand running through his slick-backed hair to reset its glossy black strands. Elizabeth had not noticed him playing the piano on the stage because she was so entranced by the singer's sensual vocal performance. She bit her lower lip as he approached.

"Glad you found us. Easy, was it?"

Muted by the strangeness of the moment, she barely nodded.

"Come on, let me introduce you. Then I can get you home."

George's bandmates came forward to shake her hand, head-nodding with polite utterances of "pleased to meet ya" in soft Southern accents. He saved Serene, the singer, for last. Serene held out her hand palm down and Elizabeth nearly curtsied, awed by this woman's talent.

"I love that song you were just singing. Your voice, it's… I'm speechless." Elizabeth giggled and blushed.

Serene bowed her blonde head slightly in apparent natural modesty, and her cheeks flushed under her makeup when she looked over at George.

"Bring her to the show, Georgie." Serene turned and glided to the back of the stage, disappearing behind a faded red taffeta curtain edged in dull gold cording. The queen had left her supplicants, and they remained silent as though commanded to do so. Elizabeth shivered in the unheated space and her motion snapped George out of his trance.

"Marty, let's go. See you guys back here tomorrow." The scrape of chairs on the hollow stage floor followed them out the door.

The ride home gave Elizabeth no chance to ask about what Serene had called him or the drunk couple she'd encountered. "Georgie" sounded brotherly, affectionate, intimate. Marty and George bantered, argued, and discussed the band's set list. Crushed between them, she just listened. Tuning them out in the small truck cab was impossible. The banter was fascinating for a dancer like her, the music they discussed like one of her favorite books. Before she knew it, they were back at Gran's. A gaslight on the porch illuminated the front door.

George followed her up the steps, and she stopped on the porch as if they were ending a date. Elizabeth looked up at George and opened her mouth to speak when she remembered they were both going inside. The awkwardness was hers alone because he reached around her and pushed open the door for her to enter.

****

"I hope you called your supervisor!" Anna sounded like a parent, not a younger sister.

"Anna, of course I did." Elizabeth rolled her eyes.

"Are you in trouble?" Anna whispered into the phone, privacy in their front hall impossible.

"Well, he wasn't thrilled with me. And—"

Anna interrupted in a stressed whisper, "Of course he wasn't!"

"Well, I'll have you know that today I went to the Philadelphia library and kept working on one of my projects. I'll have something to show for this time. It might get me back in his good graces."

"I wish you were here, Elizabeth," Anna whined.

"What is going on there? How are Mother and Father?"

"Father's the same. Quiet. Mother is stalking through the house like a Sioux warrior. Lots of slamming doors. I'm staying out of her way."

"Since I am here, I plan to stay until Saturday. Or Sunday."

"Sunday!" Anna squealed into the phone so loudly, Elizabeth had to pull the earpiece away from her head.

"You're screaming into the phone. What is Mother doing?"

"She's upstairs. I need to go anyway. Should I tell them when you're returning? No, wait, I will tell Father we spoke. He can tell her."

"Thank you, dear Anna. I am sorry you feel like a target with me away. I'll see you soon."

"Not soon enough," Anna complained.

"Goodbye now."

"Toodles, big sister."

Elizabeth sighed and picked up the phone again. She called Jocelyn, who was surprised to get a Monday night call from her best friend.

"I didn't know you were away. Why didn't you tell me your plans?" Elizabeth could sense Jocelyn pouting on the other end of the phone.

Elizabeth told Jocelyn what her mother had done three nights before.

Jocelyn gasped. "No, she didn't! That's awful. Now

what're you going to do?"

"I'll be home this weekend. Can we meet for lunch early next week? We should plan another dance outing. Would you look around for a band playing?"

"Consider it done," Jocelyn answered with an amusing forcefulness. It usually fell to Elizabeth to find the locations and set up meeting times. She enjoyed being in charge of details. It was a relief to let something fall upon her friend for a change.

"Um, Jocelyn? There's something else. I might as well tell you now."

"Are you in even more trouble? I can't believe it!"

"Not really. Everything has been happening so fast, my head's been spinning and we've not had lunch or anything—"

"What's the matter? You're scaring me."

"No, it's not scary or anything. But…it's about James. The Brisbane thing, well, it…" Elizabeth sighed. "It's just that…I suppose he broke up with me."

"What? That's impossible! He adores you—"

"It's over, I'm sure. He told me to think about it all, on the Monday after, and he walked off. Haven't talked to him since."

"Well, I'll be. Ain't that something? Hm." Elizabeth smiled at the vision of her friend tapping her leg and contemplating this news. Jocelyn interrupted Elizabeth's thoughts, "Are you all right?"

"Oh yes, my Gran's been wonderful. And I…I think it's going to be fine. Maybe James was an unnecessary distraction."

"Perhaps you're right. I'm not sure he understood you can take care of yourself."

Elizabeth grunted. This telephone call was costing

her Gran, so she pulled herself together.

"How's your father?" Elizabeth asked.

"Oh, he is grand. He's been cooking my favorite meals at least twice a week, so I will come home to visit."

"You're so lucky, Jocelyn," Elizabeth said wistfully. Would she receive invitations for Mary's fabulous cooking? Even occasionally?

"Hey? Where'd you go? Thinking again, right?" Jocelyn laughed.

"Um, yes. Thinking about home-cooked meals after I move."

"Ahh. Well, I'll try to wrangle you an invitation to Chez Weber. How's that sound?"

"I'd beat you there after work!" Elizabeth laughed out loud. She loved talking about life with Jocelyn.

"Just get home soon."

"I'll let you know when I'm back. Good night, Jocelyn."

"Good night, my friend." Jocelyn started humming, and then she hung up her phone.

Elizabeth smiled as she returned the earpiece to the phone stand. Ending the long day with Jocelyn calling her "friend" was what she had needed.

Did she know what she was getting into? Was an apartment and college more than she could chew at once? She wanted desperately to believe she had the strength to manage it all.

Chapter Twenty-Three

At the library, Miss Welden insisted they work on a first-name basis. And so Elizabeth and Florence peppered their research conversations with personal information.

On Wednesday morning, Florence walked excitedly to Elizabeth's makeshift desk and plunked down a small stack of documents.

"You're going to love this lady!" Florence exclaimed, patting a long-fingered hand on the papers.

"Who?" Elizabeth asked as she read from the first paper on the pile. "Mary Elizabeth Lease. Well, I like her name!" She grinned at her newfound friend.

Florence flashed her a bright smile. "She seems a bit like you. Rebellious."

"Me? Rebellious?" Elizabeth's dark brown eyebrows arched in disbelief. She shook her head and said, "No, I'm just a silly runaway."

"Mrs. Lease was married. With four children. She studied the law, passed the Kansas State Bar, worked as a journalist." Florence ticked off these details on her fingers.

Elizabeth's face grew serious, and she began pawing through the papers anxiously.

"Oh, I'm sorry. Thank you so much for finding this for me. I have nothing like this in my westward expansion project back home."

"Of course you're welcome! She was born in Pennsylvania. I suppose that's why we have this." Florence's hand gestured to the papers now spread in front of Elizabeth.

"Let me find out more about this real rebel lady." Elizabeth laughed and picked up a pen.

"Hope it's fun for you. Let me know if you need anything. I'll be in my office."

Elizabeth dug into this new branch of ideas for her project for the rest of the day. She hoped the patron who requested this would enjoy learning about Mary Lease, a sturdy, brash pioneer woman. She certainly did.

****

Elizabeth was impatient to go dancing while in Philadelphia, so she got up the courage to ask Florence her opinion of dancing. When she was a little girl, Florence's parents had also invested in a few years of dance lessons, but she'd found other interests—horses, for one.

"That turned out to be quite an expensive endeavor!" Florence shook her head. She pointed to the black velvet riding hat in the case behind her. "All I have left, and the memories."

"What happened?"

"I fell from a horse and my parents made me stop riding." She shrugged, but her mouth turned down at the corners. Elizabeth could only imagine how her new friend felt about losing a beloved hobby.

"You weren't hurt badly, were you?"

"Oh no, just shook up, I suppose. Shaken enough that I made no fuss when my mother announced I could no longer ride. It wasn't until some weeks had passed that I longed to be back on top of the world, on a horse.

186

But I was never going to ride again, in my parents' minds."

"Would you like to have some Friday night fun after work tomorrow?"

"Horseback riding?"

"Dancing?" Elizabeth was wide-eyed and hopeful. How could Florence say no?

"Oh, I don't know." Florence frowned. "There's been some trouble in the city with the dancing."

"Same in New York. It's ridiculous. I refuse to stop dancing because of closed-minded people."

"Where?" Florence smiled nervously.

Elizabeth leaned forward and described the nearby club where George's band was playing.

She resisted dancing a pirouette back to her makeshift research desk. She hummed a quick beat, her feet tapped, and her ankles swiveled in the shadows beneath the table.

Though George had not followed Serene's suggestion to invite her to their show, that was indeed where she planned to take Florence in two days. They'd go straight after work and bring their own little meal to indulge in while they waited in line. She knew enough about dance halls to know that waiting in line could be an endless slog. With live music at the Tangle Club, they might have a long wait. They would need a little sustenance to dance the night away.

Elizabeth had talked herself out of exploring the dance hall near Gran's. Having the company of Florence would make any dance adventure more palatable to Gran and George, but they wouldn't know until after the fact. Since the Tangle Club was so close to the library, it made sense to get a taste of Philadelphia's nightlife there.

George would look out for her in the club, she was certain of that. Whether he liked it or not.

She was finishing her stay here in Philadelphia. It was time to get out on the town, like a young woman should. George was about to get a little surprise.

****

The band's practice went longer on Thursday afternoon because their show would be live for the next three nights. Daytime rest was on their docket for show days. Elizabeth had become an enthusiastic fan of the quintet. They worked like a team, or so it appeared to her. There was the occasional fuss over a note, a beat, or which song they'd use for their open and close. Marty told her that many patrons returned night after night, and like true entertainers, the band strove to offer variety and surprise. They were proud their band had a local following already.

This evening, she had more time to survey the club's interior. Round tables and chairs bordered the main room, which contained the bandstand and the dance floor. Without tablecloths yet, she could see the mismatch of the furnishings, which lent some charm to the place. Her chair was velvet covered on the seat cushion and up its narrow back. Its twin was opposite her and two other solid wood chairs completed the setting. Plain wooden utilitarian chairs flanked many tables. In the dim light, Elizabeth counted about twenty-five table settings. A wide opening framed by what appeared to be two street lights led to another smaller room. Tables and chairs filled it, leaving no room for dancing. She tried calculating how many dancers might take to the small dance floor. It could get crowded, she was sure.

While the band debated an arrangement, Elizabeth's

curiosity got the better of her and she drifted over to a closed door to the left of the stage. Pushing it open, a pungent smell greeted her. She assumed it could be spilled alcohol. Sweet tobacco also mingled in the swish of air that rushed past her. She heard nothing, no tinkle of glass, no voices. Too dark to see well, she leaned into the door harder and found her right foot dangling over a staircase. She tottered for a few seconds. Only the heavy door swinging back her way kept her from falling forward.

She crossed back into the room, this time walking straight across the wood dance floor to her seat. A narrow band of glossy shellac edged the floor, but dancing feet had scuffed the rest of the pale gold wood. Dark splotches dotting the dance floor strengthened the unkempt atmosphere. In the brighter pools of light falling off the stage, stains on the carpet created extra patterns inside the diamond shapes formed by blue and black yarns. George yelped for her as she passed by. She squinted into the light. Serene's eyes were closed as her powerful vibrato ended the story of lost love. His hands crashed onto the keys and he showed off a jaunty run up the keyboard, a crescendo of tinkling ivories with his right hand.

Applause clamored from the entrance. A large man clothed in all black pushed himself off the wall where he hid in near darkness. Elizabeth's hand rose toward her lips and she glanced guiltily at the doorway to the downstairs bar. How long had he been in the room? Had he seen her open the door and release the aromatic evidence of lawbreaking?

George leaped off the stage and yelled, "Hey!"

The men shook hands and the hulking man pulled

George into a chest bump, clapping him on the back like burping a baby. George pointed back to the stage, arms waving to emphasize his excited conversation. Eventually, he caught Elizabeth's eye. He held his arm out to coax her over, and she learned that "Tiny" Brocadero worked for the club owner. He eyed her curiously but didn't say more than a quiet "hello." The band wrapped up while they chatted, and Serene had disappeared by the time Marty led them out onto the sidewalk.

Arriving home later than usual, they found Gran nodding off in the parlor. A newspaper drifted sideways off her lap. Elizabeth grinned slyly at George and held a finger to her lips, and said, "Watch this."

She pulled him back from the open doorway into the foyer. "Hell-oh-oh," Elizabeth cooed, mimicking her mother. Gran startled, and the newsprint fluttered around her.

"Oh, you horrible child! I thought Minnie had arrived." She shuddered in mock horror.

George clapped softly and asked her about her day.

Gran waved him off with a chuckle, saying they needed to have supper. They escaped to the kitchen. Pearl had left a pot of soup and a pan of bread on the stovetop. Elizabeth got everything to the table for them, while George found some wine.

"Wine? Where'd you get this?"

"Cora keeps a decent stash hidden in the pantry." He poured the shimmering red liquid into stemmed glasses.

"She won't mind?"

"Nah, she's poured for me many times. She showed me where she hid it!" He leaned in, whispering conspiratorially, "I think we're safe."

Elizabeth touched the stem of the glass but didn't drink. She focused on the soup.

"This is marvelous." She circled her spoon over her bowl. "I wish I could cook like Pearl."

George raised his eyebrows.

"We have a cook, Mary. The Alter women don't get into the kitchen much. Mother even has her prepare food for Sundays."

"Sundays?"

"Oh, once a month, Mary comes over and cooks a family dinner. About a dozen of us. My mother's sisters, my cousins." Elizabeth paused, tilting her head. "At the last one, dancing was the dinner topic. I tried unsuccessfully to keep out of it."

"And?"

"It was heated." She scooped up another potato and chewed. The threat of tears tightened in her throat.

"Ahh, family. Gotta love 'em."

"Do we?" She twisted her lips on the question.

"Must be more to the story."

She nodded and continued to eat. She became as interested in her food as her father got when he was avoiding involvement in his wife's drama.

"Gran didn't tell you why I'm here, then." She sipped some courage from the wineglass. The wine warmed her tongue and throat with dark richness, a peppery flavor playing briefly on the back of her tongue. "My, that's delicious."

"Cora does not talk about people, I've learned. She lets them tell their own stories."

He lifted his wineglass to her. She raised hers, and their crystal clinked musically in the silent kitchen.

"I ran away from home."

He threw his head back and laughed. "Grown women don't run away from home." His gaze pierced right through her, and she stumbled forward with her confession.

"I wasn't feeling very grown up, I suppose. My mother slapped me during a heated argument. She'd never done that before."

"In front of your entire family? That's terrible."

"Just in front of Father and Anna. It happened a few weeks after the last family dinner."

"Anna?"

"My younger sister. Gran really hasn't told you much."

George waved his hand.

"Doesn't matter. Because of my band schedule and sleeping more during the day, we don't see much of each other. Having dinner with her…and you…the other night isn't the usual. It was just because you're here, I guess." He dabbed a napkin at the corner of his mouth and continued, "She's been good to me."

"How did you end up sleeping here?"

"Cora is friends with John, the owner of Tangle."

"Really?" Elizabeth pursed her lips in thought. The plot of Gran's life thickened. "Is that where she gets her wine?"

He shrugged. "Probably not all of it."

She held her glass in both hands. The light played hypnotically on the moving liquid. She pondered her own house, dry as dinosaur bones. In more ways than one.

His banking career kept her father on the rule-following side of the ledger. Minnie was overtly conscious of what others thought. Breaking a law like the

Volstead Act would be a betrayal of the upright image she'd concocted all her life. Their daughters, especially Anna, knew how to access alcohol in or out of speakeasies. Elizabeth, however, had never been in a speakeasy, a classification she supposed the authorities would give to the Tangle Club. Her first official visit was around the corner, but she kept quiet about her Friday night plans.

"Penny for your thoughts. Or another glass of wine?" George held up the bottle.

"No more for me. I don't drink much, hardly ever, really. That's what I was thinking about. I live in a boring, bone-dry house." She snickered at her description.

"Takes all kinds," he offered gently. "I've got no kin left 'cept a brother I lost track of. Wish I had them to go home to sometimes, like at Christmas. I used to love that time of year. We were dirt poor. So poor, even the dirt didn't want us around. My brother, Nathan, and I would get a small thing, a wooden toy or new dungarees. My parents smiled sometimes at Christmas."

She nodded quietly. This conversation had gotten too somber. Sadness descended like a cloud over the table.

Pushing out of the gray fog, Elizabeth stood and reached for his empty bowl. He grabbed it too, his fingers brushing hers. Clumsily, they worked together to assemble the dishes in the sink. "I'll wash." Georgie rolled up the sleeves of his white shirt.

She noted the fraying edge on the cuffs. The taut muscles of his forearms stretched and moved under his skin, making her blush.

"Then I will dry." She whipped out a drying towel

from the sideboard drawer and twirled toward him. His hands drummed on the side of the sink. Unsteady from the wine, she leaned against the counter so he wouldn't notice.

Dishes dried and put away, George bid Elizabeth a good night. With late nights ahead, he said he needed to rest up.

****

Elizabeth went into the parlor to check on Gran, but she was gone. The newspaper lay in neat folds on the floor by her chair. Elizabeth turned out the light.

George was still in the hallway bathroom, so she sat at the vanity and brushed her hair, contemplating the home-going she needed to plan. She missed home, she truly did. Philadelphia had its own city rhythm, which she was learning to appreciate, but the air did not thrum like the atmosphere on New York's busy streets. There was no comparison.

Thinking about the familiar New York streets reminded her of James. They had taken a few city walks, showing each other their favorite spots, sometimes sharing an ice cream. She had a thing for architecture, and their city was rich with textures of stone, brick, and wood. One couldn't walk ten feet without seeing something interesting.

On one of their last walks, she'd dashed up steps to a private stoop so she could point out a specific detail of woodcut she admired. She'd put her hands on her hips and laughed when he wagged his finger at her like a naughty girl. Back on the sidewalk, he had moved so close to her she thought he might kiss her. She stood still, bracing for it. Surely, it would happen this time. But a barking dog broke the spell. She must have imagined he was about to kiss her, because he resumed their walk without comment. What she remembered now about that moment was the bitter scent of smoke from the chimneys overhead and the chill of the February wind. And confusion about the wished-for kiss.

Once she heard George's bedroom door close, she slipped down the hall to finish getting ready for bed. Cold water on her face washed away the last of the wine's tipsiness, even though its shimmering warmth still coursed through her veins.

She danced a waltz to the bed. Childish exuberance about dancing tomorrow night nudged aside the anxiety of facing a different kind of music in New York. Staring up at the ceiling, she thought again of James.

She remembered his promise to her at Jasper Hall, "Is it too soon to tell you I'd do anything for you?"

Obviously, he hadn't meant it. In only weeks, he'd broken that promise.

Could she rekindle their friendship, even if he wouldn't dance with her anymore? No matter how angry she was, she couldn't stop liking James. She flipped on her side, pulling the coverlet under her chin. For a woman bent on having her way, she surely was a fool for wanting a man in her life.

While knowing him for only a few days, she couldn't resist George. His quirky humor and his impertinent teasing had grown on her. She felt sad for him, too. He'd had a hard life, even more limited than James' upbringing. But George admitted he'd chosen his exciting life of music and travel, leaving little room for a life of permanence. He seemed to accept the temporary nature of his days so matter-of-factly. Why weren't women permitted to make that choice too?

During dinner, George had talked about the drain of the hot lights and the tension of performing for a crowd in small confines. He described how the crowd filled the club and pushed from the dance floor up close to the stage. Sometimes they had to push away men who wanted to dance with or touch the lovely and sexy Serene.

She was desperate to see all of that before she left Philadelphia.

Chapter Twenty-Four

Without a ride to the library on Friday, Elizabeth called a taxi to take her to work after eating lunch with Gran. She dressed in a deep green dress that reminded her of a snowy forest—its long sleeves were trimmed at the wrist with off-white lace, and a sheer lace panel covered the bodice from its round neck to the dropped waist, making her appear even more slender, and taller. Creamy lace stockings and her comfortable black Mary Jane's completed the outfit. A little dressy for work, but she was certain her ensemble wouldn't telegraph her evening plans to Gran.

She lacked the courage to admit her plans to Gran, and she was deeply disappointed in herself. Trying to avoid warnings and negative murmurs was a child's maneuver. Had she not grown any over these past few days?

Gran's pearls of wisdom rolled around her head day and night. Her grandmother's encouragement and probing questions had given Elizabeth an inner strength and a new vision about finding her place in the world.

She'd finally developed the resolve to go after all she sought.

To ensure they could dance to their heart's content, Florence and Elizabeth nibbled on their sandwiches in line so they would not have to spend time in a deli before their dance date. Being in line early should almost guarantee they would get a table for the show. It also meant they were subjected to the late February cold, plus the moaning and groaning of the rest of the dancers in line. Elizabeth would be happiest, though, to escape the pungent odor of garbage from the nearby alley.

As luck would have it, Tiny Brocadero manned the club's door. Though a man of few words to club patrons, Tiny wandered up the line checking for regulars he liked to give entry privileges to. He did a double take when his gaze fell on Elizabeth. "You're George's girl."

"Um." Elizabeth nodded.

"Come with me."

"I have a friend, too."

"She's good. Come on."

Elizabeth grabbed Florence's elbow, who glanced nervously at the people they were passing. Night had fallen fast and cold. Couples huddled together to keep warm and whisper secrets into frigid ears, just as they did outside New York City's dance halls. No one paid the two women any mind as they followed their newfound protector. He unhooked the faded purple rope and ushered them inside like royalty.

Elizabeth guided Florence on a quick walk around the dance floor to a table for two by the private room's archway. The out-of-place streetlight caught Florence's curiosity, and she ran her hand down the ridges of its wrought-iron post.

Elizabeth eyed the dance floor, which was not yet bursting at the seams, as George had described. The evening, though, was still young. A handful of dancers were foxtrotting their way across the scuffed wood. Feet slid sideways, the men guided their partners gently backward, and vice versa.

She cocked her head toward the dancers. Florence nodded and tossed her coat on her chair and followed Elizabeth to the dance floor. Florence wore a wine-colored sleeveless sheath that showed off thin arms and a long creamy neck. Together, they resembled a Christmas decoration.

A single light created a halo's glow in Serene's platinum hair, who sang a quiet Al Jolson ballad accompanied by George on the piano. Florence couldn't take her eyes off the singer, her head swiveling awkwardly when the dance steps put her back to the stage.

The band slid into a quirky rag, so Elizabeth and Florence broke apart and began a jaunty version of the two-step. Florence proved to be a fun dance partner, as she knew all the required steps and moves. About the same height, they could easily watch each other's expressions and know the other's next move, no bumping or toe-stepping between them. The floor got more crowded with the quicker beat, forcing the friends to the edge of the dance floor to avoid getting bumped around or separated from each other.

They sat out the next few songs to settle in their spot and get a cold drink from a serving table in the corner. The beverage was a sweet punch with no alcohol in it. They were busy talking when a loud "whoop" from the crowd caught their attention. The music still played, but the dance crowd parted and there was George approaching their table. He stuck his arm straight out, hand in front of Elizabeth. She bit her bottom lip and looked at Florence, whose eyes sparkled with excitement. Elizabeth stood and gracefully placed her hand in his. He pulled her in a spin onto the dance floor and dipped her back. She smacked him on his shoulder and mouthed, "Show-off."

They danced that number and then the next one. George had rhythm and holding back was not part of his nature. He swayed with Elizabeth across the floor, his legs and hers blurred together. He spun her around like a top and pulled her back like a string connected them. To Elizabeth, this was genuine dancing with their timing and movement in perfect synchronicity. George's touch made her feel beautiful and wanted.

When the band finished that number, Serene sulkily asked the crowd, "Hey, you dancers, anybody seen my pie-anny player?"

"Gotta go." George hugged her so fiercely that, when he let her go, she flopped like a rag doll. He skirted the edge of the dance floor and leaped back onto the stage. The crowd whooped again.

"Well, that was fun!" Florence clapped for her friend.

Elizabeth dropped breathlessly into her seat. She sipped at her punch to give herself time to marshal her thoughts. Her damp hair clung to her neck.

"And that's George." She shrugged. Telling Florence that she knew a band member had been the most convincing way to get her agreement to come to the Tangle Club. Florence didn't know the place, and when she expressed her fear of the dance hall police that had terrorized Philadelphia's dance halls, Elizabeth had reassured her by explaining she knew the band.

"He's quite the musician and dancer." Florence bounced her fingers on the table like it was a keyboard.

They didn't see George on the dance floor anymore. During a band break, George came over to see if they wanted a "better" drink, but they shook their heads in unison. Marty called to him, and they didn't see him again. At nearly midnight, they tumbled through the green door and said, "Night," to Tiny, who bowed slightly. They headed up the narrow street the same way they'd come.

Back in front of the library, they hailed a cab to share.

Florence regarded her. "It surprised me to see you talking earlier today to a little girl in the library."

"She was looking for her mother—her lost mother, according to the child." Elizabeth giggled.

"She was so beautiful," Florence said.

Elizabeth frowned in puzzlement.

"I dream all the time that one day I'll have a little girl like that. Don't you?"

"I haven't given it much thought. But, no, I can't imagine having a child right now." Elizabeth pulled her coat tighter and looked out the taxi window.

"I can imagine it. But, without any prospects—"

"Florence, did you see the men looking at you in there?"

Florence shook her head. "Really? They must have been looking at you. You're so lovely."

"No, they were ogling you and only you. Your hair is the loveliest color, like the color of sunshine. And your smile is infectious."

"I have dated little in my life. How will I find the one? I'm nearly thirty!"

Elizabeth shook her head. "We're young. We have plenty of time."

"If you say so." Florence smiled tentatively.

The cab got Elizabeth home first. They chatted

about staying in touch after Elizabeth got back to New York. Elizabeth had thanked her new friend profusely for the research help and the chance to dance in another city. She'd miss Florence and hoped they could remain friends.

The cab driver, impatient to get on with it, pulled away from the curb with a screech. Florence's head snapped back as red taillights lit up the pavement where Elizabeth stood watching her friend leave. Her mood shifted to maudlin, thinking about facing her family and Mr. Gerold.

What would her New York homecoming be like?

****

Her feet ached, so she spent time in the bathroom to wash them tenderly with warm water and soap. She inhaled the soap deeply, its masculine scent reminding her of George. He didn't wear cologne, but this soapy scent brought his face right in front of her. She imagined his arms around her again as when they'd danced hours before. He'd had full control of her movements and he hadn't been afraid to pull her up against his solid frame, and they'd swayed as one. His eyes lit up when she spun away and moved her hips tantalizingly. She'd been one with the music too.

Elizabeth folded the cloth neatly on the edge of the footed tub and started back to her room to change into her gown and fall into bed. With a glance at the foyer down below, she debated turning on the light for George. She'd already moved around a lot upstairs since she'd returned home and didn't want anything to disturb Gran's sleep. She crept down the dark stairs, the wool carpet runner scratching the soles of her bare feet.

She started across the front hall to the switch. The

kitchen door swung open, and she nearly jumped out of her skin. Before she could make a sound, George whispered, "Hey, hey…sorry to scare you." He didn't sound sorry at all, a wreath of amusement circling his words.

She leaned against the wall with a hand to her chest, puffing. Her heart thudded against her ribs.

"Wow, I did scare you."

He came closer to check on her. Standing in front of her, he blocked her way to the stairs.

"I thought you and Cora would both be asleep, so I slipped in real quiet-like."

She nodded, her breath settling down, the thudding of her heart slowing. His warm breath brushed past her. It smelled of hops and something salty. He held a sandwich in his hand.

"You came home hungry! Taxing night?"

He studied her. Perhaps he'd found her remark sarcastic. But it was an innocent question. Performing in a band looked exhausting to her. Dancing was tiring, but she did it only for herself. But was that true? What about the way she'd swayed against George at the club? Had that been just for her?

Being in George's arms had filled her with a heady excitement she hadn't experienced since…since she'd watched James' face while they practiced dancing in the basement hallway. James. She shouldn't be having stirring thoughts about James, either. She shook her head to clear them.

"Elizabeth."

She straightened, her body barely an inch from George. She glanced to her left and slid in that direction. The walls were closing in and the chandelier suddenly glowed brighter. She squeezed her eyes shut.

"Elizabeth."

She opened her eyes and scrutinized him, finally hearing him say her actual name. No "Stick" coming from his mouth. His mouth—she studied his lips with that tantalizing divot on the top lip, the shape of a Cupid's bow. She shivered as a chill prickled her scalp. A fiery circle spun around her navel.

"I..." She pointed halfheartedly to the stairs. She was frozen to the spot, feet in ice blocks so heavy she couldn't move.

He touched her wrist and said, "Come here."

Like iron shavings pulled to a magnet, she moved behind him as he walked toward the kitchen. His broad shoulders a wall in front of her, her brain simmered with questions about what they were doing. A buzzing around her ears made her feel stupid, thick and slow. The sizzling blood flowing through her core was working against her logical mind. Her body sent confused signals to her brain. She shivered again. Even her long-sleeved dress provided little warmth.

George reached into a cabinet.

"I could use another drink. I think you need one too."

She sank heavily into a chair at the table. Her fingers worked the hem of the tablecloth while he poured red wine into goblets. He handed her a glass and clinked his into hers. As if they had something to toast. The ring of crystal barely penetrated the thickness of desire filling her. The dancing, standing close in the dark foyer, him finally saying her name, had capped off all the resistance she'd used to cut him down.

Elizabeth sipped her wine and kept her gaze on the

tablecloth. Her forefinger and thumb rubbed the base of the glass. The spiciness of the alcohol hovered on the back of her tongue, emphasizing her heady confusion. She didn't trust herself to speak. She wasn't certain her voice box was in working order, anyway.

"Hey."

His finger tipped her chin up. His eyes were hooded. It was dark, but through the kitchen window the moon offered a silvery glimmer slanted across half his face. She swallowed. His eyes mirrored desire back at her. Her stomach clenched in fear.

She tossed back the last of the wine and stood. "I should go to bed. G'night."

She fled.

Back in her room, she heaved a deep breath. She pressed her back against the door, assailed by a jumble of emotions. The soft rap on the door didn't startle her. She'd expected that vibration against her skin, and wanted it.

With her hand on the doorknob, she contemplated the consequences of opening the door. Rationality abandoned her. Elizabeth opened the door slowly, struggling to draw from within a modicum of resolve. She held her chin high. She'd be polite. She would take the high road.

George's arm flew out and pulled her against him, his long fingers splayed across her back. His other hand went straight into her hair. The resistance in her brain failed to communicate with her muscles. She gave in completely. She tilted her head up and his lips crushed hers.

Her fingers were plowing through his slick hair before she knew what she was doing. Their lips sucked and pulled; his tongue swept hot across her bottom lip. Her knees became jelly. His whiskers scraped her chin. Reason seeped into the edges of her swirling thoughts. Her body challenged that reason, not ready for the intimate moment to end.

Elizabeth placed her hands flat on his chest and pushed, reluctantly pulling herself out of the steamy embrace. She thought of her Gran, worried about waking her. But she would not pull him into the quiet of her room. Oh, she was tempted to do it, to give in to this foreign impulse. The air around them felt tropical, and she was an exotic flower. George made her feel that way.

Remembering her future was always in the balance, she let reason win. She stepped back, the sound of breathing filling, the hallway.

"I can't." She looked down, shuddering. His hands still rested on her shoulders lightly. He ducked his head to make eye contact.

"Hey?"

"No! We can't…do this." Tears choked the words. She pulled away from him, unable to meet his gaze, and retreated backward into her bedroom. She gripped the edge of the door and closed it slowly but firmly. She willed him to stop its movement yet hoped he too would be sensible. Elizabeth sank to her knees, her fingers curled into the nap of the carpet. Tears burned raw and hot in the back of her throat, the pain at odds with the storm of passion still rumbling through her.

She crawled away from the door and rose unsteadily in the middle of the room. She turned to the door, knowing George stood on the other side or waited in his room a few steps down the hallway.

"No," she spoke to the empty room. She flung her

body across the bed and pulled the covers around her.

The heavy coverlet pinned her to the mattress, a captor that held her back from her heart's desire. She closed her eyes against the foolish heartache she had created. Again.

She'd made another mistake. So absurd! Getting involved with George, or James, or anyone else would forever halt her dreams.

Chapter Twenty-Five

Blinding sunlight streamed into the room because Elizabeth hadn't closed the curtains the night before. She groaned as her limbs woke. She stretched her arms overhead. Her eyes were puffed and sticky from tears shed into the early morning hours. What had gotten into her of late? Crying herself to sleep, confused by the messes she found herself in…

Speaking of messes. Her lips burned. Her chin stung. She remembered the kiss, the hot press of George's lips on hers.

She pushed the covers back and climbed out of bed before she succumbed to the decadent memory of the night before.

Listening for sounds of the house, she poked her head into the hallway. Saturday. Pearl wasn't here today. Please, Gran, don't go out and leave me. Alone. With him.

Elizabeth scooted down the hall to the bathroom and ran a washcloth over her face. She chided herself for leaning over and inhaling the scent of George's soap. Leaving the bathroom, she frowned at his closed door. What would be the repercussions of that kiss? Her stomach tightened at the thought of seeing him today, so she scooted back to her room to dress.

While she brushed her hair, she took stock of her appearance. Her dark hair shone, gleaming like the Mona

Lisa's. She turned right to left, taking in her profile. But when she looked at her lips, George's kiss came flooding back. She swiveled away from the mirror, unable to meet her own gaze. A traitor to her own dreams.

She stepped into the plain navy dress she'd worn exactly a week ago on her trip here. Buttoning it up to her neck, she contemplated her next steps. She had no plans for the day, except for talking to Gran about returning to New York the next morning.

Elizabeth was first downstairs and started the coffee percolating, one of the few domestication lessons she'd gleaned from Mary. She sliced Pearl's scrumptious bread and toasted it in the oven, watching it so it didn't burn. A new gadget called the toaster hadn't made its way into either of the Alter homes. She'd heard of it, but just toasting bread in the oven struck intense fear of a house fire. The new toaster provoked only more unease.

After she stacked the toast on a plate, she pulled Gran's lovely china jam jar from the icebox. Narrow green and gold bands circled the jar. She removed the top and sniffed. The tang of orange marmalade, Gran's favorite, warmed her nose and made her smile. She loved marmalade too.

Floorboards creaked above her. She froze. Panic grabbed her by the shoulders and propelled her out into the back garden. She felt like a coward and incredibly stupid at the same time. Her heart hung in her throat so heavily she couldn't swallow.

The back door opened. George's head poked out, and he grinned. Already frozen, her arms were crossed over her chest. "Good morning. Um, aren't you freezing out there?" The sun glistened on his dark hair and his clean-shaven face. He wore a dingy white shirt, the cuffs unbuttoned.

Her worst nightmare. Mr. Chipper. She groaned and dragged herself through the back door and into the warm kitchen. Heaven help her.

George handed her a cup as she came through the door. The domestic scene was too cozy for words. She dipped her nose to the coffee and took in the rich aroma. Anything to avoid his eyes. She strode past him and pushed open the door into the dining room. When he walked in, she was spreading marmalade on toast.

"Ah, no." He turned back the way he'd just come.

"Come in here," he yelled from the kitchen.

She stayed in her chair. When he opened the door again, she was wiping marmalade from the corner of her mouth. Her eyes flashed with challenge.

"You don't know how to cook a single thing, do ya?"

She licked her finger and ignored him.

He stalked into the room and stood above her. "You want to live on your own, huh? You'll starve." He gestured dismissively at her plate of toast.

When she stood, he was dangerously close. George ran a hand through his hair in frustration. He took one step backward, swiveled, and left her standing there. Incredulous, she followed him in defiance.

"Let's fry an egg. How 'bout it?"

"Okay." Her eyes darted around the kitchen for the right implements.

He held up a pan and an egg. He's such a hoot, she thought derisively. She didn't trust herself to speak, even to say something sarcastic. It would come out wrong. Why didn't she ever say the right things to the men in her life?

Ignoring her insolent posture, George waved a wooden spoon to get her over to the stove. Kindly, patiently, he taught her how to fry an egg. And how to scramble one. The earthy aroma of butter filled the kitchen.

Eggs, she learned, were quite versatile and easy to cook. At least George made it look easy. She mostly watched. He handed her a spatula to turn over a frying egg, nodded his head encouragingly. When she was too tentative in flipping it over, he put his hand over hers and pushed under the egg and helped her turn it. She'd smiled with the simple joy of this success. And he'd pecked her on the cheek. His lips could have been tongues of fire, for what they did to her concentration.

They continued the pretense of domesticity, stuttering though it was, by polishing off their eggs and Elizabeth's toast in the dining room. He told her about the kitchen lessons he received from his frail, loving grandmother: flapjacks and eggs. The basics for a life worth living, according to his grandmother. Elizabeth had little to add, other than her knowledge of coffee and toast, of course. She could live on breakfast now that George had taught her something new.

He'd suggested showing her his poached egg trick the next day, but she hated to encourage him. So she did what young women of her social status knew how to do well, made excuses about their schedules, Pearl, and basically gave him the stiff arm.

Of course, she'd been trying to keep George at arm's length the entire week. And he'd continued his flirtation, undaunted by her haughty attitude. Look where that had gotten her. A steamy, unforgettable kissing session outside her bedroom. She was her own worst enemy.

211

She didn't mention leaving the next day, and she wasn't sure why she left out that important detail. Was she afraid of their goodbye? Afraid she'd have to experience an awkward moment of reckoning about their mutual attraction?

Things needed saying, but which of them would be brave enough to say them? He intrigued her like a forbidden fruit. She was leaving tomorrow, and before she fell asleep the night before, she'd convinced herself how easy it was going to be to put this temptation behind her.

George played the role of a good soldier. He took her hand in his, thumb running across the tips of her fingers. He focused his gaze on their hands. "Stick, look, I travel too much. My life is crazy. You know, all the women throwing themselves at us." He grinned impishly at her. He shook his head. "I'm not your man. Am I?"

Her eyes shuffled back and forth between his eyes and his mouth while he spoke. It was his decision to brush her off gently, but then he asked her that.

Am I?

It was both statement and question, hers to choose. She had enough tough choices to make.

Silence was her answer. George had said it best.

****

"Well, good afternoon." Sarcasm dripped from her lips.

Elizabeth had been reading a book in the parlor when she heard his loud footfalls on the stairs. Soft singing accompanied the wood squeaks and shoe taps echoing in the foyer. It was George joining the living after what she assumed was a very long morning nap. There'd been nothing but silence from his room directly above her head. Cooking eggs had worn him out, she mused.

"Stick, I bid you *adieu*."

She rolled her eyes. "That's 'goodbye,' George. Do you mean *bonjour*?"

He smacked a hand to his forehead. "I still need your help, Stick. Don't leave yet."

Elizabeth eyed him suspiciously and looked down, brushing an invisible piece of lint from her dress.

He waved dismissively in the air and kept walking into the kitchen. She could hear him asking Pearl something, but it didn't concern her.

His allusion to playing the field in every city had stung at first, but he said what she needed to hear this morning. He might have forgotten their kiss. She didn't think so, though. Over breakfast, she had caught him studying her, and she wasn't sure if she imagined a cloud of soft pain in his dark eyes. He looked away too quickly, his mood subdued.

She groaned and ran up the stairs to her room to get her coat. She would walk around the block and get some air. Elizabeth had things to figure out.

****

When Gran came home from her Saturday shopping, George and Elizabeth were eating lunch together in the kitchen. He had just asked Elizabeth about the brooch on her dress. Its red gemstones caught the winter sunlight coming through the window, and a prism of reds and pinks fanned across the white tablecloth. While her fingers traced the wiggling streaks of color, she told him how her Gramps had bought it for her at an antique shop. Until he died, he enjoyed browsing books and what-nots with her when he felt up to it.

"We'd just walked past this shop, and it had mannequins in the window. They were covered in masses of different laces, some faded and discolored, others creamy and white. Practically bridal. The garnet brooch was holding pieces of lace together across the bodice, and it caught my eye."

Gran joined them at the table, listening intently.

"Gramps came back to stand by me. He asked me what I saw."

"The red diamond pin."

"Gramps laughed and nodded and said, 'Let's go inside, then.'"

"I never thought he would buy me diamonds. But my heart soared in that moment to think he might buy something I thought was terribly expensive."

Gran pulled out a creamy lace handkerchief and dabbed the corners of her eyes. "Nothing was too good for his little Lizzy."

"Yes. He bargained with the shopkeeper and got 'a good deal' on the brooch. So he said."

George cleared his throat. "Well, I best be going."

"I didn't think you practiced on Saturdays," Gran said.

"Marty and I are working on the truck this afternoon. Oil leak, we think."

"Do be careful," Gran said, sounding like his grandmother.

"Yes, ma'am." He bowed his head at them. "You two have a delightful afternoon."

Elizabeth dished up something for Gran to eat while they talked about her morning.

"So Gran, I explored the delights of your china cabinet this morning and I found something." She went into the dining room to collect a photograph.

She handed it to Gran. "Did Father have a brother I don't know about?"

Gran stared at the photograph and said, "No. This is your father."

"It is?" She stood behind to look at the photo again. "But this woman…that's Mother? It doesn't look a thing like her."

"That's Imogen. Imogen Parker Alter." Gran licked her dry lips. "Your father's first wife."

"What?"

"She died in childbirth right after their first anniversary. So sad. She was a lovely person." Gran sniffed and dabbed the lace around her eyes.

"What year was that?"

Gran thought for a moment. "I think she died in 1895. He met your mother in 1897."

"Hm. How do you think my mother feels about his having a previous wife?"

"She would like to be his first love, I think."

"Perhaps this explains a few things about Mother. You know? Maybe she's a little insecure. She tries so hard around Father at times. Seeking compliments, things like that." Elizabeth smiled at her grandmother.

"I suppose this is a new insight into your mother."

"Do you think my mother is really unsure of herself?"

"Insecurity is common for women."

"Well, we are told a lot of things that aren't true." Elizabeth laughed.

"I hope you remember that when you decide your life's path. It is *your* life's path, remember?"

"Yes, Gran, you've no idea how much you've

helped me this week. I won't forget that when I get home."

"Going home? You're thinking about that already?"

"Gran, I must go tomorrow. I mentioned it to you on Monday after Anna called."

"Oh, my. I'd foolishly hoped that you'd stay another week. So silly of me." Gran fiddled with her handkerchief.

"Gran, I have a job to get back to on Monday. And I need to sort things out with Mother. Besides, I need to talk to them both about Mrs. Goldberg's place. Who knows how that will go?"

Elizabeth smiled ruefully as she gathered dishes from the table. "You've been grand to me. This has been a special time. I'm going to miss you so much."

"Don't worry about me. I'm just an old woman enjoying the attention of her beautiful, brilliant granddaughter."

"I love you, Gran." Tears stung her eyes.

****

"Who could that be calling so late?"

"Shall I answer it for you, Gran?"

"Please, dear."

Elizabeth scooted into the front hall and picked up the receiver.

"Hello?"

"Oh god, thank goodness you answered." Anna's harsh whisper crossed over the miles of phone lines, yet it wasn't difficult to hear the emotion in her voice.

"What's going on?" Elizabeth turned her back to Gran and fiddled with her bangs in the mirror.

"Oh, you don't want to know. But then again, you must. When you didn't turn up today, I knew I had to warn you."

"Warn me?" Elizabeth's voice dropped. She looked in the mirror for Gran's reflection. Gran appeared to be reading.

"It's Mother."

"Of course, it is. What's she done now?"

"She has thrown most of your clothes onto the floor of your room."

"What? Why?"

"A fit, I suppose. She's been raging off and on all week since you left. I've been staying at the library and having dinner out with friends when I can."

Elizabeth couldn't help but smile at the image of her sister spending extra time in a college library.

"What's she and Father saying, though?"

"Father, as best I can tell, has tried to reason with her. Honestly, I think he slept in his study last night."

"Oh, dear. I've caused all this."

"Look. What you did…it wasn't wrong. I thought you very brave. It's just…um…"

"I'm coming home on the train tomorrow, arriving late afternoon. Can I even walk through the front door? Do you think?"

"I don't know. Honestly. I have no advice. It's horrible around here."

The gears in Elizabeth's mind started to whir. Where else could she stay? Jocelyn? No. Matilda? No. She blew out a breath.

"Hey? I know you're thinking. What are you going to do? Can I help you?"

"So, you don't think I should come home?"

"Um, I didn't say that, but…what about your apartment around the corner?"

"Anna, it's not ready! I can't move in a month early. Well, I can't show up on her doorstep tomorrow night, at least."

She glanced into the parlor. Gran looked up and raised an eyebrow. Elizabeth mouthed "Anna" just as she'd done a week earlier. Gran nodded and returned to her book.

"Elizabeth? I can't talk much longer. Tell me what to do. I can help, I promise. I just don't see how, right now."

"No, no. It's all right. I caused all this. I need to think. Don't know what I'll do when I get back to New York tomorrow."

"But how will I know you're safe?"

"Safe? Um, if I don't come home, can you stop by the library on Monday? We'll talk then."

"Oh. Okay. I don't like this, you wandering the streets tomorrow night."

"Anna! What an imagination you have. Of course I can take care of myself."

Anna snorted. Elizabeth frowned at herself in the mirror. Not a soul believed she could take care of herself.

"I must go. Bye, Elizabeth. Take care!"

"Good—" Elizabeth stopped speaking into thin air, as her sister had rung off.

She blew out a breath and tucked hair behind her right ear. Plastering a smile on her taut face, she spun around to face Gran's inevitable questions.

"What did Anna want?" Straight to the point.

"Oh, nothing really. Just anxious about my return home tomorrow. I'm just not sure of the time. Told her I'd flag a taxi home."

Elizabeth's stomach did a flip. She didn't see the lie

coming until it rolled off her tongue. Her forked tongue.

"You sounded a bit anxious on the phone."

"Not at all, Gran. I was calming Anna down. Mother's gotten on her nerves more than ever. My absence, I guess."

Elizabeth managed a taut smile. She patted her knees and looked around the room. This parlor had felt so warm and welcoming this past week. Hardly anything like home, where Minnie perched on the damask sofa. Like a queen bee.

"Mm."

Gran's gaze caused Elizabeth to squirm.

"I need to get my book. I'll be right back."

Elizabeth swept out of the room, leaving her Gran with a furrowed brow.

She closed the bedroom door and leaned her forehead against the dark wood. Tears spilled over her lower lashes. What was she going to do? She couldn't stay here at Gran's any longer, but going straight home seemed unfeasible for now.

Elizabeth brushed her hair, carefully arranging her features into the face of a girl with no worries. She dabbed her eyes.

Elizabeth felt panic bubble into her throat. Once she arrived in New York, she had no place to go. Perhaps she could talk to Jocelyn. What would Jocelyn be able to do? She was grasping at straws.

What a disaster. And it was all her doing.

She smoothed her shaking hands down her skirt. Her breath came out jumpy, tears still simmering. As she opened the door, she remembered her book. She snatched it off her pillow and started back downstairs to face Gran's questioning blue eyes.

219

Chapter Twenty-Six

Elizabeth woke on Sunday morning, listening to the movements of Pearl and Gran. Her eyes burned and the hairs on her head ached at the roots. She didn't know when she'd finally fallen asleep. How many times had she flipped her pillow and crushed her head into it willing herself to fall asleep? Her worries had kept her brain stewing. Fear was eating away at the resolve her Gran had helped her build this past week.

While here in Philadelphia, not only had the calendar changed from February to March, but she had also changed. The silly girl who ran away a week ago had run headlong into herself, a person she hadn't truly understood. Yesterday, she'd entertained life on her own, potentially fearless.

But this last morning at her Gran's brought fear about that life on her own. It wasn't arriving on her own terms, was it? Oh, how right George had been. She was terribly spoiled, having everything in life poured over her in perfect time. Like a coating of silver gloss. But her actions, while hardly criminal, had delivered her to this fear-tinged, tearstained moment.

Her brain had processed a lot these past few days, and she'd made a few cautious decisions. First, when she got back to work, she would speak privately with Mr. Gerold to ensure she had not damaged her chances for preferred projects. She would be smart, apologetic, and reasonable. Her extra research in Philadelphia should strengthen her case. With childlike faith, she saw her supervisor beaming about her initiative. That idea had made her laugh yesterday. Yesterday, those innocent hours before news of her mother's lingering anger chased away the calm.

She'd planned to talk to her parents together, not just Mother alone. Oh, what plans she'd made to smooth the waters! She'd hoped for time to speak alone with her father upon her return. Gran had suggested she do this. Father would listen to her ideas and ask probing questions. He'd be encouraging and helpful, she and Gran agreed on that. But now? What was Father thinking or doing about Mother's behavior?

Perhaps she should have written him as soon as she'd arrived here. Too late for that now.

Elizabeth sighed loudly as she threw back the bedcovers. It was time to start this horrible day.

There was another decision she had made this week. University. She needed to visit Dr. Sporian soon, before the spring term ended. She was definitely returning to school.

Gran had been not only a sounding board but a wise adviser. Not one to tell another how to live their life, she was adamant that Elizabeth should live on her own before she made other major life decisions. Gran understood her so well, and Elizabeth had learned more in this short time in Philadelphia than she had in her first months of working toward a career.

While she was in the bathroom washing her face and brushing her hair, she heard the ooh-gah of a truck horn. It sounded like the band's truck, so she hurriedly packed the brush back in her suitcase.

Yesterday morning, George had been visibly disappointed by her news about leaving. Elizabeth put a brave face on it all. Since their kiss, he'd returned to a brotherly posture and his annoying nickname for her.

"Stick, your grandmother is going to be lost without you here. And now you'll get no more cooking lessons. I was looking forward to expanding your repert—um, what's the word? Dang it." His southern twang lengthened the exclamation. She'd laughed.

"Repertoire. I think that's what you mean."

"See, I guess I will be lost without you, too." George grinned, but his gaze slid away quickly.

"You must find me if you ever come to New York City. Okay?" She doubted the quintet would get an invitation to her illustrious city. An easy overture for her to make, never to be fulfilled.

Now he was outside waiting, having insisted on providing transportation to the station. She'd tried vehemently to get out of it, anxious about being pressed together one last time. Gran stepped into their childish arguments and told Elizabeth to accept George's offer.

She bit her lip, looked in the mirror a final time, and dragged her suitcase down the stairs. Her throat tightened with dread.

Going home shouldn't feel like entering a courtroom, but she'd brought all this on herself. When she'd left New York a week ago, she anticipated meeting each of her "co-conspirators" on her little adventure. Now, her stomach clenched at the thought of facing a house of accusers. People who considered her selfish and unyielding. But before she faced them, she may have to face a night lost in her city. Whatever was she going to do?

Stepping out on the front stoop, Elizabeth waved at George and Marty as the truck slid to the curb in front of Gran's house. She left her case and turned back inside.

Gran and Pearl were standing in the foyer, sadness filling the lines of age on their faces. Pearl's age-spotted hand was stroking Elizabeth's navy wool coat folded over her arm. Elizabeth hadn't noticed the wrinkles and brown spots on the ladies who'd cared for her this week. She'd been so absorbed in her problems and selfishly happy to soak in their love and care. And their heartache over her departure only emphasized the toll time had taken on Gran and Pearl.

Elizabeth practically ran into Gran's arms, squeezing her tightly. Gran's lingering scent would be a reminder of the sage advice offered every day this past week. Pearl choked back a sob as she patted and rubbed on Elizabeth's back.

"There you go, Lizzie. Be a good girl."

Elizabeth stepped back, blinking tears away. She smiled wanly at them both.

"Oof! I packed you a sandwich." Pearl bustled through the swinging kitchen door and returned with the bag held high.

"Thank you. Thank you both! I promise to write to you when I get home."

"I want to hear all about your apartment, dear. And don't fret. Minnie'll come around. You'll see." Gran pulled Elizabeth in for another hug. Elizabeth squeezed her eyes shut, a silent prayer that Gran was right about Minnie, even though she didn't know the half of it.

Pearl helped her into her coat.

"Okay, then. I'm off." Elizabeth headed for the front door. She turned once to smile at them and pulled it open.

"Here she comes!" George announced to no one in particular as he stood on the sidewalk looking up at her.

He waved her into the truck, just like he'd done on Monday.

"Goodbye!" A chorus of voices reached her as she slid across the seat toward a smiling Marty. Looking past George, she saw Gran and Pearl waving. Their eyes sparkled with tears.

"Let's do this," George said as he slammed the door shut.

Marty ground the truck into gear, and they pulled off. Too quickly. Elizabeth could no longer see the house where she'd confronted her personal failings and found then lost her resolve.

****

"Can you stop there, Marty? It's a quick walk inside." Elizabeth pointed to the curb in front of the wide steps leading to the station entrance.

She hopped out, after telling Marty how much she appreciated his driving. George pulled her case from the back of the truck.

"Thank you for handling my case. It had slipped my silly mind." *Keep it light, Elizabeth, keep it light.* She forced a smile to press down the urgent tears threatening to choke her.

"Well, Stick." His head dipped to hide a smile at his repeated impertinence. She'd forgive him this time.

"Yes, well, it was…" Elizabeth didn't know how to finish it. *It was nice meeting you* wasn't the thing to say to someone who'd passionately kissed her two nights before. She looked down at her feet.

"Hey, can I really see you if the band comes to New York? I mean, we've gotta make it there eventually, right?" George blinked. A gust of wind blew a long lock over his forehead.

She wanted to push it back into place, but they were already standing too close for comfort.

Elizabeth nodded. "I'd like that. Your band is good, as good as any I dance to at home."

George chucked a finger under her chin.

"Save me a dance, Elizabeth."

Tears pricked the corners of her dark brown eyes. "Bye, Georgie." Something flickered in his eyes at her use of his nickname. A lump rose in her throat, tightening at the intimacy she'd unexpectedly created by uttering it.

She reached for her case and started lugging it up the steps. George appeared beside her and grabbed the suitcase from her hands. She smiled up at him, unable to chide him for overriding her wish to go inside alone.

With quick movements, he held the door open for her and followed behind her into the main hall of the train station. People sounds swirled around them: families chattering and their cases hitting the marble floor filled the air.

"Another goodbye," Elizabeth's voice hitched with unwelcome tears.

"*Adieu*," George said softly into her ear. She closed her eyes, almost leaning in but holding back. His lips grazed her cheek as he pulled away. She watched the door swing shut between her and his retreating figure.

Elizabeth stood there, lost in the moment, until a woman and a little girl came through the door George had just exited.

What would she do without Gran's warm smile and the heat of George's gaze?

She exhaled and carried her suitcase to the ticket

window. She should have been relieved there were still seats on the noon train, but all she wanted was to avoid New York entirely. What was going to happen when she arrived in the city?

****

When Elizabeth was younger, she'd watch Mary cooking the family's evening dinner. She'd sit at the table in the kitchen and talk to Mary about her school day. She asked questions about Mary's two children, who were much older than the Alter girls.

Like any child, Elizabeth was amused by the occasional funny disasters that Mary experienced while wrangling various pots and serving dishes. Perhaps her favorite "funny" was the behavior of the lid on a stewpot. That lid was light enough that when the contents of the stewpot got to boiling, it would rattle and shake from the ribbons of steam trying to escape.

Warned never to touch the stove's knobs, Elizabeth had occasionally watched in fear and amusement as the lid danced to its own clattering music while Mary was out of the kitchen. Nothing terrible had ever happened, even though Mary usually flew in, flapping her apron and squealing.

As she stared out the train window, Elizabeth herself was stewing. Everything that had happened in the past month bubbled through her brain. She wished she could turn down the heat of her thoughts and worries to keep the lid from bouncing off. By the time her train arrived in Grand Central Station, the clattering lid covering her thoughts and emotions threatened to fall in an enormous clatter.

She had much to do and much to say before she could move beyond her anxiety about her future. She wanted things settled, but that wouldn't happen overnight. Two days ago, she was fully ready to tackle the problems with her mother, but the script she'd practiced in her head might not work anymore.

Since she had no ideas about where to go, Elizabeth lingered in the main lobby of the station. On a hard bench, she closed her eyes and willed herself to relax.

Chapter Twenty-Seven

"Miss? Miss?"

Elizabeth jolted out of her stupor. A white-haired man gently shook Elizabeth's shoulder. She took in his black coat and his gold-and-black stationmaster's hat. Where she was slowly dawned on her.

She straightened, her back aching from her sleeping posture across her case. She'd slept in a strange position. She didn't remember putting her case beside her on the bench. Her right hand flew to her hair—she was sure it was flattened or crimped on that side.

"What time is it?" She scanned the grand hall. The man glanced at the clock behind him.

"It's nearly five o'clock, miss. Are you waiting for a train? May I help you with your bag?"

All these questions. Easy to answer, but they were hardly the ones she needed to figure out.

"Oh, no. I'm all right." Though she didn't directly answer his questions, he nodded and began to walk away.

"Um, sir. I do have a question. Is there a hotel nearby?"

"Of course, yes. Are you travelling with someone?" The gentleman looked around the hall.

"No, I'm alone."

He tilted his head. Elizabeth thought he was debating what to say.

"There's a women's hotel," he said, pausing to scratch his cheek.

Elizabeth nodded in encouragement.

"It's on Lexington." He pointed to the main door. "That's Forty-Second. Go left, then turn right on Lexington. You'll see the blue sign a few blocks down."

"All right. Thank you, sir."

Elizabeth pulled her suitcase off the bench and started toward the main door.

"And miss?"

She turned halfway around.

"It's dark now. Be careful."

"Thank you again. You've been so kind." She smiled wanly. Being pleasant and polite was the last thing she wanted to be. Her body was stiff and tired. She couldn't remember ever feeling so desperate for a soft pillow and warm covers.

Out on the sidewalk, she shivered. Her stomach growled, reminding her that she'd gobbled down Pearl's sandwich the moment she found a seat on the train. That was at least five hours ago.

****

Elizabeth stumbled against her suitcase as she emerged through the hotel's glass door onto the sidewalk. Humiliated, she rubbed her forearm across her runny nose. She'd held back her tears until she turned away from the hotel front desk.

She slid her coin purse into her handbag and looked around. Where could she find some dinner, she wondered. She had only two dollars, an embarrassing circumstance revealed to the desk clerk and a nearby hotel guest when she was informed a night's stay cost an exorbitant three dollars. She'd bitten her bottom lip to keep from crying and from questioning the true value of a night's stay.

Elizabeth shook her head and scanned the businesses across the street. A blinking diner sign a block away caught her attention. She turned back the way she'd come. The cost of dinner wouldn't be more than fifty cents, so she pushed through the door.

A waitress with a wavy blonde bob greeted Elizabeth with a menu as she slid into a booth.

"Passing through?" The waitress nodded toward the suitcase perched beside Elizabeth on the banquette.

Elizabeth yawned.

"Oh, I'm sorry. Um, no, I live in the city. Just coming home." She smiled at the waitress.

"Coffee?"

"Perfect." Elizabeth smiled and picked up the menu. "I already know what I'd like. A club sandwich, please."

"Got it. Coffee on the way!"

Elizabeth ran her hands across the tabletop. Anything to keep herself awake. Her eyelids were so heavy, even the clattering of dishes and silverware in the kitchen couldn't invigorate her.

Penny, her sweet waitress, kept her warmed and lubricated with hot coffee for over an hour. Elizabeth ate slowly, watching customers come and go.

She had nowhere to go. Miserable, she swung her case ahead of her as she walked out of the diner. Her breath coiled out like silver smoke in the frigid night.

Seeing the lights of Grand Central Station up on the left, Elizabeth started walking. What if she went home tonight?

****

Sleeping in the family's car had left its mark all over

her. Her shoulder twinged while she finger-combed her hair. Running her fingers through her hair again, she encountered a tangle that pulled. "Ow!"

Having arrived at work early on a Monday morning, she had the room to herself. Mondays started slowly in her office, but Mr. Gerold never offered recriminations to the tardy.

"Miss Alter. Welcome back." Did his voice carry a trace of sarcasm?

His eyes wandered over her wrinkled dress, then back up to her face. She'd pinched her cheeks in the ladies room moments before. Did her tired eyes betray her night spent in a car?

The man nodded when she reported her daily trips to the Philadelphia library to continue her Westward Expansion research. She'd hoped he would share her excitement about the unique materials she'd found there. Had she expected any praise for her initiative? Not really. Perhaps she'd expected he might raise his bushy eyebrows, showing the slightest pleasure in her commitment.

The best Elizabeth could do was plunge back into work and complete the assignments that had piled up on her desk. Hadn't she made that promise to her supervisor exactly a week ago?

Jean and Matilda tried to extract details about her sudden flight out of the city. Elizabeth said only that she had gone to see her grandmother.

That answer would not be satisfactory at home, so Elizabeth chose the coward's way and worked late into the evening.

By the time she walked through the front door, her parents had already gone to bed. She found Anna reading in her room.

"Hi," Elizabeth whispered softly from the doorway. Anna flew off her bed and pulled her bedraggled sister into a tight hug.

"Oh, Elizabeth. It's so…" Anna was speechless with worry apparently. Elizabeth hugged her again.

"I'm home. I just have to get through the inquisition or flogging or what other horror Mother's dreamed up."

"At dinner tonight, they questioned where you might be. Thank goodness I could honestly say I had no idea." Anna pulled back and asked, "Where have you been today? When did you get home?"

Anna looked poised to continue the questioning. Elizabeth shushed her.

"Let's sit. I'm frayed around the edges and want to have a bath and sleep in my own bed."

"And…?"

"Anna, I arrived yesterday. I slept in Father's car last night." She paused when Anna gasped. "Went to work this morning. All is well there. And I worked late to avoid…you know."

Anna touched her sister's hair. "I'm so happy you're home!"

"I still have to face Mother and Father. I'll get up early in the morning and see if I can have a quick quarrel and go to work."

"A quick quarrel?"

Elizabeth raised her eyebrows at her sister.

"Am I receiving a hero's welcome?"

"No. Mother is beside herself."

"And that's why I'm hoping to give her a short time to dig in and off I go to the library. Silly strategy, I know."

"You may be right. I'll sleep in so you can have them all to yourself!" Anna grinned.

Elizabeth smacked her arm lightly and stood up from the white-covered bed.

"Good night, Anna."

Elizabeth sighed deeply when she remembered the suitcase in the garage. She started a bath and went to her bedroom. Clothes lay strewn all over the floor. *Mother!* She pushed them aside into piles to create a path to her bed and left the room.

Sliding into the white porcelain tub, she allowed the hot water to cover her shoulders. Steam rose to circle her head, and she closed her eyes. Tension seeped out into the water.

"I will not cry. I will not cry." She repeated the refrain from the night before.

****

"Elizabeth." Minnie stood by the stove, coffee cup in hand.

"Good morning, Mother, Father." Elizabeth nodded in Henry's direction. He set his cup on its saucer and looked at his wife.

"Minnie…" Henry spoke firmly, as though in warning. Elizabeth looked between them both, fear etched on her face.

"May I say something first?" Elizabeth asked as she sat at the kitchen table beside her father.

"You always have plenty to say," Minnie quipped. Elizabeth nodded, knowing it was best to be agreeable and contrite.

"I am very, very sorry that I left the city without a word. I caused you to worry. That was wrong." Her voice grew softer at the end as she looked into her father's eyes. He looked so sad.

Minnie sniffed. "Is that all you have to say?"

"I think the less I say the better."

"What?"

"Go ahead, Mother, let me have it. I'm sure you're angry and have things to say."

"Elizabeth." She looked up from her hands to see her father with tears in his eyes as he continued, "I, for one, am happy to see you back home. It's been a difficult week. But we must go back to being a family under this roof. Your mother and I—"

"Are furious!" Minnie interrupted, her face pink with rage.

Elizabeth shrank into the chair. She bit her bottom lip.

Minnie began to cry. She pulled a white linen hanky from the pocket of her black skirt. Dabbing her eyes, she looked at both Henry and Elizabeth.

"I *am* furious with you, Elizabeth..." Minnie's breath shuddered. "But I am willing to meet you halfway."

"Halfway?"

Elizabeth frowned. Halfway to what? She didn't like the sound of that.

"Clearly, you insist on this dancing nonsense. And if we're going to go along with you..."

Dancing is not nonsense, Elizabeth thought. Minnie was still talking.

"... a young man at the bank."

Elizabeth snapped to attention.

"Pardon me?" Bile rose in her throat.

"Your father's hired a nice young man and he's coming here on Friday night. We want you here for dinner."

Elizabeth spun in her chair to face her father, who had returned to reading the newspaper. Part of it tore when Elizabeth pushed it down to make him look her in the eye.

"No! Father?" Would he really allow her to be displayed like that? A wife for sale?

Henry patted her hand gently.

"Remember what Shakespeare said, dear. 'It's not in the stars to hold our destiny but ourselves.'" Henry looked into her eyes. Understanding passed between them.

Resigned, Elizabeth pushed the chair back with a scraping sound. "Better get to work. I have lots of work to catch up on."

"You've only yourself to blame for that." Minnie pursed her lips, her hazel eyes daring her daughter to respond.

Elizabeth nodded and walked stiffly from the room. It was only eight o'clock and she was already exhausted.

****

Elizabeth had dreaded this evening ever since her mother demanded her attendance four days earlier.

Minnie had pulled out all the stops. White candlesticks stood at attention in Minnie's favorite silver-and-crystal candlesticks. Blue-and-white china and the best silverware sparkled on top of the crisply ironed linen tablecloth.

The fragrance of rosemary and thyme warmed the air. The kitchen had become a hive of activity after everyone left that morning. Mary's special talents were being employed to their fullest.

Elizabeth had caught a glimpse of angel food cake

when she scooted through the kitchen after work. She'd hugged Mary, and asked after her two children. Mary had taken the time to fix her a cup of tea and ask about Cora.

When the doorbell rang, Henry left the comfort of his wingchair to welcome Robert, his new employee. Elizabeth watched all this transpire through a crack in her bedroom door. She would delay her mother's humiliating parade of female flesh as long as possible.

She looked down at the simple black crepe dress she'd chosen for this evening. The neckline draped softly across her collarbones, the fabric forming soft caps at the top of her arms. It flared slightly from the hips to below the knees.

It was funereal, just the look Elizabeth was going for. Strange that Minnie hadn't ordered a costume for the evening. Would Minnie get the message of the dress or would her eyes just sparkle with matrimonial glee? Elizabeth shook her head and then closed her bedroom door behind her.

She began the death march, her slender fingers skimming the banister on the way down. Robert sat on the settee across from the doorway and watched her descend the staircase. She smiled. His mouth dropped open, then closed.

Elizabeth knew what he was thinking. She looked beautiful. She'd brushed her dark hair until it was as smooth and shiny as a placid lake. Peach blush shimmered on her cheekbones. Helena Rubenstein lipstick in a demure pink glossed her lips.

A command performance is what her mother had requested. Elizabeth was stage ready.

Gliding into the parlor, she held out her hand to

Robert. He stood and looked confused. Elizabeth nearly giggled as she tried to read that little mind. Was he wondering, *Do I kiss it or shake it?*

"Robert, lovely to meet you. You're in for a treat."

Henry cleared his throat, as though he could intuit a hidden meaning in her words.

"Mary is cooking tonight. And she's a prize. We're so lucky." Elizabeth smiled brightly at Henry. "Father, shall we go in?"

They crossed the hall to the dining room just as Minnie entered it from the kitchen.

"Oh!" Minnie squealed in surprise.

She looked Elizabeth up and down, but if she found fault she kept the critique to herself.

"Robert, do sit here. Elizabeth is right across from you."

Could she be more obvious? Elizabeth blushed as she pulled back her chair.

And then Minnie's inquisition began. Elizabeth and Henry played witnesses to the entire spectacle, and filled up on the succulent roast beef while they watched. Poor Robert could barely finish a mouthful.

Henry rescued him occasionally, interrupting the questioning to explain something or direct a comment to Elizabeth. Still, the entire dinner conversation was rather lopsided.

After dinner, Minnie sent Henry for something upstairs and she disappeared into the kitchen. This left Elizabeth and Robert alone in the parlor.

She relaxed into a corner of the settee and smiled up at Robert. He studied the seating, wondering where to sit.

"Well, you know that's Father's chair, and Mother likes that one. You're either stuck by me or over in that corner by the dog bed. Don't worry, Maisie won't bite."

Robert snorted and ran a hand across his black hair while he decided.

"But will you?" he asked as he sat at the other end of the settee.

"Ha-ha. You should probably be more afraid of Mother."

Elizabeth winked at him. He blushed deep red.

Henry entered the parlor and held up a book. "Here's that book I was telling you about, young man. You may borrow it, if you'd like."

"Thank you, sir."

"Well, you'll have to come back to dinner, won't you?"

Minnie beamed from the doorway.

"This has been a very nice evening, Mrs. Alter. Thank you for welcoming me to this great city. I should be going, I suppose."

Elizabeth stood when he did. Robert turned to shake her hand.

"Pleasure to meet you, Elizabeth."

"Delighted as well."

She meant it. He was the perfect combination for a dinner guest: handsome and funny.

But definitely not for her.

Chapter Twenty-Eight

Besides catching up on library research, Elizabeth's other pressing project was clearing out the side garden at Mrs. Goldberg's. She desperately wanted to get the area cleaned up and gain access to the private entrance. Doing the cleanup would make it feel all her own.

Her escape to Philadelphia had seriously delayed progress on that front. And she still hadn't told her parents about it even though she'd been home for weeks. She felt less grown up and capable each day she spent wrapped in fear of discussing her moving plans.

Elizabeth waited until late morning on Sunday to drop by to see her future landlady. The door knocker echoed inside like it had the first time she came to view the apartment.

"Coming!" She heard Mrs. Goldberg on the other side of the door.

Elizabeth straightened and put on a smile as the heavy black door opened.

"Oh, my dear. How nice to see you! It's been a long while, hasn't it?"

"Yes, it has been. I'm very sorry. I went to see my Gran in Philadelphia weeks ago, and it's been terribly busy since I got home."

Elizabeth entered, taking in the high ceiling in the foyer, which she hadn't noticed the first time.

"Not to worry. Let's go in here and talk."

The old woman gestured to the parlor. The room felt much like the living area down in the basement, with its dark wood and deep green fabric.

As she sat down, Elizabeth said, "Well, I know I said I'd work on clearing the side garden, so I came dressed to work on that today."

Mrs. Goldberg nodded distractedly.

"Dear, are you a flapper girl?" The widow cut right to the chase and asked the surprising question. Elizabeth stirred around for the right response that said 'no' but didn't insult her future landlady.

"No, I'm not, Mrs. Goldberg. May I ask where you got that idea?"

"I heard you go to dance halls. I don't want any trouble here."

"Oh, I see. That is true, I must be honest. I started dancing as a very little girl and I love it. But I don't dress like a flapper. I don't go to speakeasies. I just like to dance."

Mrs. Goldberg took all this in and looked at Elizabeth, who waited for a shoe to fall. She was rummaging around her brain for how this gossip had reached her landlady. She was part angry but mostly terrified of losing grip on the dream of independence.

"I don't want any trouble," Mrs. Goldberg repeated. Her fingers played with the edge of her thick black cardigan. Elizabeth wondered if she was just looking for more reassurance about becoming a landlady.

"I promise you, I won't bring any trouble to your doorstep. You have my word. You know my father. He was a good boy, don't you think? He raised two very well-behaved daughters, I assure you."

Mrs. Goldberg stared out through the window. The

late morning sun cast a golden hue into the room. It ran its fingers through the old woman's silver hair. Elizabeth had the feeling she was with an angel each time she visited. The old woman was so goodhearted, one could only hope to be a teeny bit as good.

"Lillie seems to think you're trouble."

"Lillie?" The tumblers fell into place. Elizabeth would have pounced on that silly girl if she were near.

"She lives down the road. Says she knows you."

"Hmm. Right. We work together at the library." Elizabeth held her tongue. No point maligning poor Lillie and appearing like a shrew for criticizing her.

"I should think some more about taking in a tenant." Mrs. Goldberg looked straight into Elizabeth's eyes.

Elizabeth bit her bottom lip to keep from blurting out something she'd regret. She had already gone to some expense for her new home by purchasing a new rug last week. Jocelyn had shopped with her for curtain fabric, too.

She could throttle that little…jealous brat! That's what Lillie was. Wait till they were in the same room at work. Not prone to violence, she'd have to come up with a plan to set her straight, tell her off, something.

Heat rose into her neck, her desperation in this moment palpable. How could things be falling apart already? She had to convince Mrs. Goldberg of the wisdom of renting to her.

"Mrs. Goldberg, I understand your caution. You've never done this before. But I will be the best tenant you can imagine, I promise!"

The old woman blinked at her, so Elizabeth continued, "And…remember, you liked the idea of having someone around. I'll be a great help, like the garden work I came to do this morning."

"My dear. You'll let me think about it, won't you?"

"Yes, Mrs. Goldberg. But even if you decide not to rent to me, I'm going to go out in your garden right now to start clearing it out. I'm happy to do it for you."

Elizabeth stood and buttoned her coat. Just a bit of guilt might bring Mrs. G around.

****

So it was, on that cool but sunny March day, Elizabeth found herself up to her chest in vines. With no suitable gardening attire, she'd created a casual ensemble of an old black cotton wrap dress she hadn't worn in ages and some flat ankle boots. Her thick tights were speckled with dirt and leaves, along with pulls in the weave all over. One of her father's old straw hats contributed the only hint at the gardener look she'd tried to achieve. Play the part, you're halfway there, or so she'd heard.

In her parents' garage, she'd dug out a pair of stiff work gloves. After an hour, she ventured back into the tiny shed to find a shovel. Several of the wisteria vines were tree-like, several inches thick near the ground, and hacking them with a heavier implement proved magic. Feeling quite proud of herself, she surveyed the pile of rejected greenery in the back yard. A path from the front walk to the side door had emerged.

Neighbors on Sunday strolls or nosy expeditions had wandered by, some of them offering greetings. No one asked who she was or what her goal might be.

Resting on the shovel and swiping her forearm across her damp forehead, she thought about her parents. Today might have been the day Elizabeth mentioned this apartment to them, but now her life was once again in limbo.

Pulling at the gloves, she dropped down onto the stoop at what should be her first apartment. Whatever was she going to do if Mrs. Goldberg did change her mind about renting?

She sniffled and dragged a dirty sleeve across her nose.

****

Elizabeth pushed her food around the plate while Minnie peppered Henry with questions about another man he'd hired in his office. She wanted to know where he'd come from, whether he was married, if he had a family. Anna barely stifled a yawn, earning a quick squint from Minnie.

Later, as Elizabeth brought in the dessert, Minnie asked, "What were you up to today, Elizabeth? You looked a bit bedraggled when you came home this afternoon."

"Oh. Um," she stammered.

Minnie raised her eyebrows and maintained her stare. Elizabeth told her stomach to stop its tumbling.

"I was at Margaret Goldberg's. She's John's mother... Um, Father's old friend?"

"Whatever were you doing there?"

"Working in her garden, clearing the brush outside what was supposed to be my new apartment." There, she said it.

"Your what!" Minnie's fork clattered onto her dessert plate. Her lips trembled and her eyes radiated disbelief.

"I bumped into Mrs. Goldberg months ago on my way to work. She showed me her basement apartment, but now..." Elizabeth took a deep breath to press tears back.

She sighed and continued, "But now Mrs. Goldberg is uncertain about having a tenant. Or me in particular."

"What do you mean?" Minnie pushed away the cake.

"She asked about my dancing, and…"

Elizabeth wanted to kick herself for giving away too much detail. She was so tired from today's gardening and working extra hours at the library she could barely think straight.

"Like most people, she's concerned about the morals of society. And now, you are paying the price of—"

"Mother, please."

"You've certainly been a busy girl. I never imagined you were the sneaky one."

Fidgeting with the napkin on her lap, she glanced between her parents, sitting at opposite ends of the white-covered table. "I didn't sneak around. Um, I… It's just that things have been so busy, and I wanted to…um…make progress before sharing any details."

Anna's attention bounced between their parents and Elizabeth like she was watching a tennis game. She smiled at her sister from across the table.

"Did you know about this apartment, Henry?" Minnie's voice dripped with accusation.

"This is entirely Elizabeth's doing." Henry patted his mouth with his napkin. Elizabeth thought he sounded proud of her.

Minnie blinked back tears.

"I don't know what you're doing. But we had an agreement."

"You mean agreeing that you may pawn me off to the next new fellow at Father's work? I don't imagine things will work out with Robert. Did he seem interested to you?"

Minnie stood and said to Henry, "I'm going upstairs."

And Minnie was gone. Elizabeth let out an audible breath.

In bed that night, Elizabeth replayed the conversation about the apartment over and over. Had her mother surrendered to the news of Elizabeth pursuing an independent life? Or was this just the calm before another frightening storm?

But Elizabeth hadn't yet reached the goal. Not until Mrs. G decided in Elizabeth's favor.

She sighed. Pulling the covers around her, Elizabeth turned over and tried to fall asleep.

And then, Gran's words about Imogene and Henry returned. Father had lost a child, too, as well as a wife. Did that memory still break his heart sometimes?

Her family lived in a lovely home and their lives seemed quite uncomplicated. She'd never really considered Minnie and Henry as people with pain and sadness.

Her youthful self-centeredness had blinded her to her parents' feelings about the future. Perhaps she could be more considerate and gentle.

Chapter Twenty-Nine

"Good afternoon, Mrs. Goldberg, sorry to drop by unannounced. I haven't seen you in two weeks and wanted to see how you're doing." *And find out if I have an apartment.*

The past two weeks had passed in a fog. The uncertainty about Mrs. Goldberg's decision and her mother's angry silence had driven Elizabeth nearly mad. She had nothing but bad luck these days, taking one step forward and two back, it seemed.

The only positive outcome recently was that Minnie's plan to match her to the bank fellow had fizzled. Apparently, he had a fiancée in Boston. Elizabeth was elated for him.

"Let's have tea, shall we?" And just like that, Mrs. G turned away from the front door, back straight, ready to make tea.

Following her into the warm kitchen, Elizabeth silently pleaded with the sun, moon, and stars that Mrs. G had come around. Elizabeth helped with teacups and plated some freshly baked cookies.

They chatted in front of the window overlooking the garden that was showing some life. Elizabeth went along with this strange situation and waited for a sign.

Out of the blue, as though there'd never been a question about Elizabeth becoming her tenant, Mrs. Goldberg said, "My dear, will you be ready to start moving in around early May?"

Elizabeth's teacup clattered onto its saucer.

"Oh goodness, yes."

Mrs. G admitted the bedroom wasn't quite ready for her since the bedding and dingy lace curtain were still there. She'd only removed the dearly departed mother-in-law's clothing so far. Her brother-in-law had fixed the side door.

"Perhaps in late April, you'd allow me to bring over a few clothes and start organizing things? Oh, and I want to tackle that bathroom before I sleep here. May I start that soon?"

Mrs. G nodded over her silver-rimmed teacup, her smile lighting her blue eyes from within.

****

Elizabeth called her grandmother on the second Saturday in April. Gran had left her a message, and she was keen to find out why. They caught up on the basics quickly, and Elizabeth told her about the hard labor she'd been putting in at the apartment. Gran filled her in on Pearl's recent cold.

"George isn't here right now." Elizabeth hadn't asked, but Gran shifted the topic.

"Really? Where is he, then?"

"The band is traveling, which is wonderful for them, of course. I miss the young lad."

Elizabeth giggled. At age thirty, George could hardly be called a young lad.

"Do you expect him back?" She couldn't imagine George installing himself permanently in Gran's house. Father would have an opinion about that situation. She didn't think George would take advantage, but what did she know?

247

Gran was answering, and she'd missed the first part.

"Did you say he's playing in New York? He's here, in the city?" Elizabeth's heart lurched into her throat.

"I don't know. His itinerary was quite busy, lots of places. He left it here somewhere. Let me look." Elizabeth heard the clatter of the earpiece on the table. Then Gran was asking, "Is there a Brisbane there? Club something or other?"

Elizabeth groaned inside. That fateful place would be forever etched in her memory.

"I've been there. It's a nice place. Very large. His band is lucky to get to play it."

"Talent. It gets you places," she said it like a proud grandmother.

"His band's very good, I agree. When is he here?" She prayed it wasn't soon. How could she manage more stomach somersaults and confusion?

"I can't see that here. No, in May, I think. You must find out for yourself. I can't promise I'm reading his handwriting properly."

"Well, Gran, you're full of interesting news today. What are your morning plans? Shopping? Lunching out?"

"You caught me on a rare day in. Pearl and I are tackling the garden this afternoon after the sun comes over."

Elizabeth smiled, remembering the roses pruned back to nubs.

"How are your roses?"

"They are going to be magnificent in a month! The bushes are getting so lush. I wish the post would allow me to send you some. You'd love them. I'm smelling a few early blooms here on the table." As Gran breathed in deeply, she did the same, willing the sweet scent across the miles.

"I wish you could too, Gran. I must come back to see them. Next year?"

"You know I'd love that. You needn't wait till next summer. Come anytime."

"Thank you again, Gran, for taking in this sad runaway. You took good care of me."

"My dear, what is a grandmother to do but love her granddaughter? And you are that—grand."

Elizabeth sniffled, and before she could speak, Gran was talking again.

"Pearl's waving at me, so I must go. You take care, Elizabeth. Send me a note about how your visit with George goes, if you do see him."

"I will, I promise."

They rang off. Elizabeth ran up to her room to finish getting ready.

She was crossing the front hall when Minnie called her name. She did an about-face and walked into the front parlor, where her mother was holding a book in her hand. For all her overbearing parenting faults, Minnie had read to her girls for years and instilled a great love of books in Elizabeth. Anna, not so much.

"You look nice," Minnie offered, taking in the pleated gray skirt that fell just below her knees and the soft gray sweater with white cuffs and collar.

She smiled at Minnie. She started backing out of the room to avoid more questions.

"Did you get your grandmother's message?"

"Yes, thank you. Just talked to her."

"What was she calling about?" Minnie stared her down. Her intolerance of Cora was no secret.

"Oh, nothing really. Just checking on me." She shrugged and turned.

Elizabeth waved and nearly ran out the front door and down the steps. She lifted her face toward the sun and took a deep breath. It was a gorgeous day. She slipped her hands in her skirt pockets and crossed the street on her way to her future apartment. She was helping Mrs. G pack the last items left over from her mother-in-law.

****

She slipped downstairs to make a cup of tea. Mary didn't arrive until later in the day, and cooking breakfast would be futile this morning. Thank heavens for cereal and milk. She ate quickly and quietly, not wanting to stir up unwanted company.

She'd had more sleepless nights in the past year than in the entire span of her life. A headache threatened to ruin her morning, if not her entire day.

Maisie was nowhere in sight, which meant the dog was sleeping in Anna's room and stuck there until Anna woke for classes. Elizabeth smiled at the silly thought that she'd miss that dog more than her parents when she spent her first night in the apartment. Her first step to independence was only days away. She suspected she'd feel a smidgeon of Maisie's enthusiasm when Elizabeth untied her leash in Central Park. Would Elizabeth bound around Mrs. Goldberg's garden like a clumsy puppy?

Elizabeth sneaked out of the house before seven-thirty without speaking to a soul. The day might turn out right. A girl could hope. Her plan for the morning involved a stroll through half of Central Park, then a hop on the subway to the library.

She needed fresh spring air to advise her. The glossy

green shrubs sparkled with evaporating dew. The early sun's rays cajoled a steamy mist off the benches like a snake charmer.

She thought of Maisie again. She'd miss her walks with that silly dog when she moved out. A seed of worry stopped her in her tracks. Moving out in three days. She couldn't believe she'd be on her own. Would she enjoy having her evenings to herself?

She had given little thought to carting dishes up and down the basement steps if she wanted to eat alone downstairs. Did Mrs. G expect them to dine together each night? She sat on a park bench and pondered how to approach the topic with her landlady. If she wanted, she could always eat out with Jocelyn. If she could afford it.

Jocelyn. She'd been a fabulous friend this past month. Helping Elizabeth figure out some details of living on her own. She'd joined Elizabeth and Matilda on the quest for curtain fabric for the bedroom. The three of them enjoyed shopping and lunch, sharing secrets to save money on food, the subway, and clothes. Elizabeth was humbled by how much she needed to learn.

Jocelyn liked her rooming house well enough. Not all the tenants were perfect roommates. Someone kept leaving things about, dripped water on the bathroom floor. Irritating, said Jocelyn. Still, having absent parents was the ultimate goal of these young women's independent lives.

Her parents were still good for something, though. They'd allowed her to store her winter clothes in the attic, so she only had to pack her summer wardrobe. Her mother had stayed quiet about the new apartment. Minnie hadn't offered any help, and she'd yet to see

Elizabeth's basement home.

****

Elizabeth scrubbed the little bathroom on her hands and knees. Using her crack investigative skills, she'd determined that the smell was mold.

On her first visit to a hardware store, she left armed with cleaners, brushes, and sponges. The bathroom wouldn't know what hit it. She didn't know what she was in for, though. She coughed from breathing in the chemicals, and her hands, even though encased in rubber gloves, were red and sore for days. Still, she was so proud of her handiwork that she returned to the hardware store and purchased paint, brushes, and a dropcloth to protect her now beautiful floor. She chose a marine blue, the color of the sea, a place she had loved as a child. She rarely made time for it anymore.

Minnie had adjusted her mothering style not long after Elizabeth announced her apartment move. Questions had replaced her prior curt, meddling advice. Sometimes the questions were pointed, yet couched in concern. She would ask things like "Are you certain you'll have enough money?" or "Will you be safe?"

Elizabeth glanced around the apartment, trying to see it as her mother would. The side table held two framed photos: one of her with her sister and parents, and another of her paternal grandparents. Mrs. G's brother-in-law had carted off a large oriental rug. A new rug was the largest item Elizabeth had purchased out of her own savings. She loved the simplicity of the unusual navy carpet with gray filigree designs she'd found in a SoHo warehouse, her personal art deco touch in the old-fashioned room. On either side of the door to the garden she'd placed two ladderback chairs with rush seats, which she could use for dining at the dropleaf side table.

The bedroom was free of the mother-in-law's velvet-and-lace explosion. Though it had been a beautiful, creamy confection, Elizabeth wanted something simpler and less dramatic. Her bedcovers were green and blue. With Jocelyn's help, she'd hung blue moiré curtains, plain with no fussy trim. Underneath, however, they'd added thickly embroidered cream lace curtains that gave privacy from the garden and let just enough light into the basement room. Henry had allowed her to bring an old bureau from the house. Her extensive clothing collection required more storage, so things were going to be a little crammed.

Elizabeth had decided that morning to invite Minnie over for a look at the apartment. An olive branch. It was the least she could do, given all the tension between them.

Minnie seemed to like it, fingering the fabrics and running a hand over the polished wood bureau. "You may need more light in here. Let me know if I can find you another lamp."

She didn't know if her mother was offering a veiled criticism or if this was her way of offering an olive branch of her own.

It didn't matter.

Watching her mother during her tour, Elizabeth felt the need for approval melt away. She no longer cared whether Minnie agreed with her life choices. She couldn't change her mother. Only Minnie could overcome her old-fashioned notions.

Chapter Thirty

Elizabeth was busy writing in her office when she heard voices in the corridor. The air shifted. A knock on the doorjamb jolted her out of deep concentration, and there stood George. She had been so involved with moving, she'd completely forgotten about him. By the time she remembered his itinerary, she assumed she had missed his show in town and had hoped he'd been and gone. George May was a temptation she didn't need.

"Hey, lady. I bet you're surprised to see me." George beamed at her, hands in his pockets like he belonged there. He leaned against the doorjamb while she studied him. He had cleaned himself up for his trip uptown. Black trousers and a clean white shirt made him look like a waiter. Though he wasn't perfectly handsome, southern charm oozed out of his pores, as usual. His smile was infectious.

Elizabeth heard Lillie and Matilda whispering, clearly ignoring their work to size him up. From the sound of it, her coworkers didn't find him wanting. He knew it too, as he tossed a glance into the corridor to make sure they were listening.

He was making her squirm, letting the office mates think she had a man on the side. They'd speculate about this interesting fellow who didn't fit in her Upper West Side persona. His mere presence made her feel something. Heat rushed into her scalp and her hair prickled. She stayed seated, not trusting herself to rise.

"I am surprised you found me. You must feel like you're in Egypt." She shouldn't be rude, she chided herself. Gran thought a lot of him, and he'd been considerate and helpful to them both.

"Nah," he drawled, refusing to be baited.

"So, to what do I owe this pleasure, George?"

"I have tickets to our show tomorrow night. I want you to come. We all do."

"That's very nice of you. Of your band, I mean. Where are you playing?"

"The Brisbane, on Forty-Fifth."

Her heart fluttered. That fateful place. She overrode her instant frown with a friendly smile.

"I know where it is. Tomorrow night, you say?" She was itching to go dancing. "I'll be there."

She walked around her desk to stand in front of him. He pulled tickets out of his right pocket and held them between his fingers. He studied her white blouse and gray skirt while she considered them. Her lips parted, eager to possess the tickets. She held out her hand, making him place them in her palm. The tips of his fingers rested on her palm, lingering ever so briefly, teasing her with the heat of his touch. A sharp intake of breath. She hated herself for responding.

"Promise me a dance?" A gasp came from down the corridor; the eavesdroppers apparently had no research to do.

"Um, perhaps."

George smirked.

"Just be there. Please. We'll give you a show." He wrapped his fingers around her hand holding the tickets. He leaned in and brushed his lips against her cheek.

Heart pounding against her chest, she stepped back and bumped into her desk. She perched her bottom on the edge as if she'd intended to all along.

"Oh, I… You don't mind if I bring a date?"

George didn't miss a beat. "Of course not."

He gave her a quick salute, his hand making his slick black hair move a little. "Until tomorrow night." He backed out of her doorway and left.

He'd barely turned out of the passageway when Matilda rushed to her office. Elizabeth sat still on the edge of her desk, stunned by what had just happened. George was in town and wanted to see her.

While Matilda peppered her with questions and commentary about his various selling points, Elizabeth slipped the tickets inside her purse. Her hands were shaking. She didn't know how many he'd given her. She'd worry about that later.

Waving off her coworker, she pleaded serious work responsibilities. She sounded like her supervisor. Matilda's face shimmered between curiosity and excitement. Who was that man and what did he mean to her friend? Indeed, the questions were valid.

And she had no idea.

****

Elizabeth, Anna, Jocelyn, and William walked directly up to The Brisbane's main door where they presented their tickets. A host dressed in a slightly shabby tuxedo and white shirt escorted them to a table positioned at the corners of both the stage and the parquet wood dance floor. A fresh coat of polish was visible between the early dancers' feet. Her guests suggested she choose her seat first, even though they'd all have a splendid view. The chairs upholstered in wine velvet instantly took her back to Gran's kitchen, where she'd shared that luscious wine with George.

Anna had been thrilled to get a ticket to The Brisbane when Elizabeth stopped by on her way home from work. They agreed they'd get ready together at the Alter home. Elizabeth hadn't moved her dance dresses to the apartment, while she searched secondhand shops for an additional wardrobe to store them. The sisters traded minutes in the hall bath, scouring their hangers and hangers of dresses until they found the perfect ones for each of them.

She'd chosen her favorite baby blue silk dress with its lush, full skirt, the one she wore the first time she and James went dancing. It made her feel beautiful and could be a full-skirted ballgown but for the hem ending mid-calf. The color offset her pale skin, dark hair, and brown eyes. It was sleeveless, perfect for a May evening, but she'd brought a wrap of diaphanous silver mesh in case they sat in a draft.

Anna was again her perfect foil. Her blonde hair waved closely around her scalp. She'd chosen Elizabeth's newest black sheath. It too was sleeveless, and the shoulders of the dress were a shimmery, sheer fabric. The same sheer fabric edged the dress hem with tiny pleats.

Jocelyn had also pulled out all the stops and dressed and styled herself like Clara Bow. Her blonde hair was thick and naturally curly, but she'd tamed a curl onto each cheek like a comma. Her black satin dress draped in the front and the back. Its straight skirt stopped below her knees. William looked smashing in a tuxedo he'd found at a secondhand store in SoHo.

Though Elizabeth was happy that everyone was

treating this as extra-special, she couldn't suppress a sense of dread. Her mind clouded with the memory of what happened the last time they were here and how it brought about the downfall of the James-and-Elizabeth dance partnership.

Elizabeth had an angled view of the stage. The band wouldn't be out for a while, so it was empty. Depending on where Serene stood, Elizabeth might have a bird's-eye view of George at the piano. And he'd see her too, if the stage lighting was subtle. Her insides did an unpleasant loopy loop at the idea of spending an evening under his constant gaze.

She'd crafted a friendship story about George, and no one, not a soul, was the wiser. To all and sundry, they'd never kissed, never touched, never stolen glances. They had danced once, the only minor detail she had willingly shared.

Serene appeared in front of her, and a surprised Elizabeth stood to greet her. The singer leaned forward to brush her cheek against Elizabeth's.

"I'm so glad Georgie found you yesterday," she said.

"Thank you to the band from all of us." Elizabeth swept her arm to include her three guests. Serene nodded her shiny blonde head at them all. Waving at Elizabeth, she swept through a curtain to go backstage.

They all talked at the same time about the lovely Serene.

The lights went down in the hall. Piano notes trilled over the room. The audience gasped. A few applauded and were shushed. A single beam brightened on the stage. George's straight black hair glittered like velvet as he swayed over the piano keys. Anna and Elizabeth grinned at each other. Both piano players, halting at best, the sisters recognized true talent.

Serene's voice started off stage, and as she entered, George only had eyes for the stunning singer. Her red fringe-covered dress shimmered as though lighted from within.

Anna leaned over and whispered, "Wow, he's got it bad for her." Elizabeth returned her gaze to the pair. She was glad the dim light hid her flush, and a flicker of jealousy jostled against her excitement. Couples moved slowly around the dance floor, pressing close together to match the mood of the ballad.

When it ended, the dancers clapped and whistled. Everyone was ecstatic about a grand night ahead with this high-caliber entertainment. The rest of the band members came on stage: Marty, Hank, Jelly, and Jimbo. Elizabeth pointed them out and announced their names. Her friends studied the five men and Serene until the next beat blasted out. William grabbed Jocelyn's hand, and they were off to dance. Anna and Elizabeth sat through a few more numbers before they succumbed to the beat and danced together.

When they returned to the table, four silver cups and a sweating silver pitcher sat on the table. Elizabeth surveyed the ballroom for a waiter to resolve the mistake. William had ordered nothing, Anna confirmed. She shook her head and joined her sister to find a waiter. The host who'd seated them came over, and when Elizabeth pointed to the pitcher, he pointed to the stage, saying, "Compliments of Mr. May."

Anna shrugged, poured two glasses of a foamy golden beverage. She sniffed it and wiggled her eyebrows. They clinked the metal cups, said, "Cheers," and took a sip. It was delicious.

Anna began nodding. "Sidecar." Her sister frowned at her.

"That's the name of the drink, silly. I don't remember what's in it." Anna tilted the cup against her lips again.

Trust Anna to know the name of an alcoholic drink. Suspicion about speakeasies and wild parties confirmed. Elizabeth surveyed the room for trouble. Would James be vindicated if the police came to The Brisbane on a raid tonight? She took a deep breath to quell her nerves. She was being skittish for nothing. Almost nothing. Except for breaking the law. Anna pulled her out of her trance and onto the dance floor.

During the first set break, the four enjoyed their drinks and hoped for more. They laughed and made jokes. Dance halls were perfect for people-watching, and they had some fun making up stories about couples. The girls, of course, made admiring remarks about the many dress styles swirling around the ballroom.

The Brisbane had excellent air circulation, which allowed dancers to keep dancing without falling out in puddles of perspiration. And though Elizabeth and her sister took a few breaks, they mostly stayed on the dance floor. William took them each for a spin, and a young man, probably Anna's age, asked her to dance. He stammered so nervously, she took pity on him and agreed. No one asked Elizabeth to dance, which was quite normal, and she was fine with it. She stayed on the dance floor as much as possible, but she didn't get maudlin over not having her own dance partner there.

Eventually, during a set break, George visited their table. William stood and shook his hand, thanking him for the drinks (which had been replenished) and praising the band. Jocelyn fluttered her eyelashes dramatically and put out a limp hand when she was introduced. George bent over to kiss it. She loved it even though she pretended not to, for William's sake. Elizabeth introduced Anna. He kissed the back of her hand, too. He held onto her hand a little longer and asked, "Do you mind if I borrow your sister for a bit?" She urged them off with a peal of laughter.

He walked beside her with his hand in the small of her back to guide her to the main lobby. He stopped there, ready to say something. "You know what? I could use some fresh air. Let's go out front."

People were milling about in front of the door under the marquee. He guided her down the sidewalk where they were alone under a canopy of black sky littered with winking stars. "Thank you for coming, Stick."

"Thank you for the tickets. Your show has been great. We're having a spectacular time. The band was wonderful before, but you're truly getting better. You must be happy about that."

The chill in the evening air settled over her, and she wished she'd brought her wrap. She fought off a shiver.

"So, your date is your sister?" He eyed her skeptically.

She waved off the question and feigned a look of boredom. She refused to meet his gaze. "Late notice, you know?"

"You are stunning." He stood back and made a production of assessing her. "He's missing out."

"Perhaps." The smile on her lips was a fraud. She needed to keep this conversation light. George made her anxious when he discussed her life.

He considered her, ever watchful. The poor little boy rushing headlong toward success. She reckoned he guarded his heart like she tried to protect hers. What was he thinking? She wanted to know.

"I almost forgot the reason I brought you out here." He smiled, relieved to change subjects. "Cora sent something for you." He began digging around in his jacket, finally finding the prize in the inside chest pocket. Between his thumb and forefinger, her garnet brooch glinted in the streetlamp's light above them. She had forgotten about it being missing and never asked Gran to search for it in her house.

"Oh! I'm so happy to have this back. Thank you and tell Gran thank you, too. No, never mind, I can write her myself." She leaned forward and gave him a quick hug. She held up the brooch in both hands as if she might lose it again. Overjoyed to be reconnected with this treasure and its many splendid memories, she kissed it. A giggle attached to tears escaped her lips. She studied the pavement.

A police car drove slowly by. Elizabeth licked her lips and shuddered. Please, no police tonight.

A breeze zipped around the corner, blowing her skirt around her legs. She shivered again. "Let's get you inside," George said as he took off his coat and settled it around her shoulders.

Inside, George slipped his jacket off her and dropped it in her chair. He held out a hand and bowed. "May I have this dance, *mademoiselle*? 'Tis the witching time of night.'"

She chuckled, surprised by his Shakespearean wisdom. "You're still practicing your French!"

"I am. You inspired me."

The band was playing the song they'd danced to in Philadelphia. She was ready for him this time when he dipped her back, her hair nearly brushing the floor. They spun around naturally, a couple to watch. Some dancers pulled back to give the two dazzling dancers space to show off. Others kept dancing, while more stood and clapped to the beat, an audience to the impromptu show of flying feet and the blur of blue silk swishing by. The song ended, and they stood panting, staring at one another, each daring the other to break the gaze. She brushed damp hair from her forehead.

He grabbed her hand and returned her to the table, where she dropped into her seat. The blue silk skirt billowed around her chair. He bowed his head over her hand and kissed it, his lips lingering long enough to send a tingle all the way to her navel. She was hopeless, she chided herself.

She'd engaged in a lot of self-reflection this year. While she had broken away from her parents' watchful care, she needed a break from the demon on her shoulder as well. The demon that told her lies about who she could be and what she could do. There were times she felt like she'd defeated those voices, but then events conspired against her. Like George showing up in New York. His touch had sent her spinning.

When George took leave of the group, everyone gushed their thanks to him for a wonderful night. They stayed through the band's last set, not wanting the night to end.

The foursome left the hall a little tipsy, fuzzy enough to blur the edges and brighten the tingling, celebratory glow.

****

The sisters slept until noon, woken together in Anna's room by their mother. She dropped their shoes in a tangle on the floor in the doorway. "You forgot these in the front hall last night. Or should I say, this morning?"

Anna stretched her arms above her head and arched her back, while Elizabeth rubbed the cobwebs from her eyes. Her mouth was dry. She swished her tongue over her fuzzy teeth.

"Ugh," she groaned and glanced in her mother's direction. But the doorway was empty. Mercifully, Minnie had nothing else to say at the moment. She promptly forgot about facing off with her mother when she tried to lift her head.

"Oh, no." The room spun; the ceiling became a swirling blur before she closed her eyes. Bile collected at the back of her throat. She crashed her head back into the pillow. "Anna. He-lll-p."

Her experienced sister, plainly no worse for wear, was already out of bed, but she crawled across the covers to her sister, full of giggles. The shaking bed didn't improve Elizabeth's queasiness.

"Hey," she whispered, "I'll bring you some coffee." Anna crawled off the end of the bed and left.

The thought of coffee made her feel positively nauseous, but she needed something to end the pain wreathing her head. A hundred elves were pounding her head with little wooden hammers.

Her first hangover.

During her first month at Mrs. Goldberg's, Elizabeth had still spent an occasional Saturday night with Anna. She'd stayed overnight with a purpose this time. Anna was helping Elizabeth move the last of her summer clothes that morning.

Anna's summer would be less exciting by a large measure. She had desired a summer of trips with friends and parties on weekends after classes finished. A flurry of fun to celebrate, no more exams, no more biology labs. Henry and Minnie had their own idea, however, and plotted to rein in their younger daughter's free spirit before the term even ended. So, in early May, her father had forced her into a job at his firm, running errands for executives, sorting and distributing mail—insulting tasks to thrust on someone of her station. Or so she believed until her furious father set her straight, behind the closed doors of his office.

Mortified, she'd confessed to Elizabeth how she had made herself invisible as she glided past his secretary, praying her father's raised voice hadn't passed through his door. She wasn't thrilled about being her father's slave all day, but she admitted to her sister that she was seeing a different side of Father, too. He was far more interesting to Anna now. Elizabeth told her she was growing up.

The apartment adventure gave the sisters an opportunity to bond as young adults on the cusp of making independent decisions. Anna's enthusiastic support solidified Elizabeth's decision that morning to confide in her about George. She prayed it wouldn't be a mistake.

Elizabeth struggled with how much detail to share.

"Okay, listen, promise me. Not a word."

"I'm all ears. And yes, I promise." Anna did a lip-locking motion on her mouth. Her fingers released the imaginary key over the side of the bed.

"I don't enjoy telling these stories, Anna. I don't

want to be hurt or to hurt anyone. Swear, please."

"I swear!"

"All right. Here goes."

"Get on with it!" Anna's blonde hair bounced with enthusiasm.

Elizabeth bit her bottom lip, then took a deep breath. "George is a big flirt. He can be quite irresistible. When he tries."

She told about the night she and Florence showed up at the Tangle Club. She and George danced, and it was more than a little thrilling. And he kissed her that night outside her room. Then he taught her to cook eggs the next morning. The end.

Anna's hand was palpitating over her chest, her typical dramatic response to a romantic story.

"It's not that romantic. Honestly, no romance there."

"All that charm, the piano playing, the wild dance moves… Oh, Elizabeth, he's quite perfect for you." Anna leaned in as if about to tell a secret, whispering, "You fit like hand-in-glove on the dance floor. It was a sight to behold."

Anna swooned and fell over on the bed.

Elizabeth dismissed the dramatics with a flutter of her hand. "No. No. No. He's got girls in every city. I'm sure of it."

"Well, look at him! No wonder."

She rolled her eyes, disbelieving that George was in any way the right man for her. Hand-in-glove?

"And then there was sweet little James." Anna looked pointedly at her.

"I used to wonder when James would kiss me. And then he walked away. We both walked away, I suppose."

"All I'm saying is…you've had two men…two!…

after you in the same year. You're lucky."

"Lucky!" Elizabeth snorted.

Chapter Thirty-One

A week had passed since George's appearance at
The Brisbane. Elizabeth still smiled like a Cheshire cat
when she thought about that night. Anna and Jocelyn had
mentioned again how impressive the quintet was.

Elizabeth could sense deep changes moving within
her. She had more clarity about her destiny. The renewed
excitement of attending university made her as giddy as
her eighteen-year-old self. Pouring over the university's
course offerings, she contemplated what she'd be
learning. August couldn't come soon enough.

Without an appointment, she hesitated outside Dr.
Sporian's partly closed office door. She might be eating
lunch. Elizabeth knocked once.

"Come in."

"Hello, Doctor…Clara."

"You came back!" Clara appeared delighted to see
her. She gestured to the chair beside her desk as she
slipped reading glasses into the pocket of her gray jacket.

Elizabeth smoothed her cream skirt under her as she
sat. She glanced around the office at the books,
certificates on the wall, small pieces of art nestled in the
shelves. She couldn't help but wish for an office like this
one day.

"I never really looked at all the fascinating things in
your office when I was a student. May I?" She pointed
to a bookcase, and Clara nodded. Elizabeth picked up a

small canvas of the seaside and asked, "This is beautiful. Who painted it?"

"It's a canvas by Donna Schuster. I was introduced to her in California. Long ago."

Elizabeth fingered it. "I guess this is the Pacific Ocean?"

"Possibly. You must have something to say, Elizabeth. I'm not rushing you, but…what's on your mind?"

Elizabeth sat down heavily.

"I've got all kinds of troubles. I know, hard to believe." She snorted.

Clara tilted her head, ready to listen.

Elizabeth poured out her heart and her head. James, George, the dance hall raids, Mrs. G, her mother, the basement apartment, the suffrage movement, the problem with men and society, all of it. It came out in a jumble, but Clara had no trouble keeping up. She was a woman, after all. At one point, she handed Elizabeth a pink handkerchief trimmed in thick white lace.

Elizabeth took a deep, heaving breath and looked at Clara, who smiled tenderly at her.

"Women like us…" She sighed. "The world's not ready. But, Elizabeth, here's my advice: don't make your dreams small."

Student stared at former professor. She blinked. Could she list all her dreams?

"What do you want? Do you know yet?"

Elizabeth looked down, still fearful that she wanted too much of the wrong things.

"I want a life. A life not bounded by a man's interests. I suppose one day I might want a family, too. Is that dream too big or too small?"

"You determine what's big and small. Whatever fits you. It's okay, though, to aim for something that may seem enormous or unattainable at any point in time. It's possible to grow into a big dream. Maybe you're the lucky generation, and society will catch up with you."

"I'm not sure my mother would agree."

"She's already made her choices. Now it's your turn to choose." Clara stood, and Elizabeth admired her black trousers, wishing she were brave enough to wear them.

Elizabeth sighed and walked over to the office window. The afternoon sun slanted through sycamore trees, a mosaic of greens and whites. She let the light burn into her eyes, waiting for an answer to be branded on her brain.

"Did you talk to anyone at Columbia yet?"

"I did. I've given it some thought; it feels so hurried to enter this coming August, but I'm eager to do it, anyway. Will you look at my application? It's due next week." Elizabeth pulled out the paper application from her bag.

"I'd be delighted to. Have you decided what you want to study? That may have some impact."

"English Literature."

"What made you pick that?"

Elizabeth leaned an elbow on the windowsill. "My father's in finance, business, but that doesn't interest me. Not much anyway."

"You selected literature by default, then?" Clara's voice possessed a touch of surprise.

"Not at all. Maybe I had to talk myself into it a little. I mean, I do read all the time, for work and in my free time. When I'm not out dancing. But when I reflect on my first years at Barnard, and the protests I got dragged to… I was a passive participant. I did nothing. Now, I have the right to vote, but did I earn it? When so many others gave so much. There's something I need to do. I just don't know what that is yet."

Clara leaned forward in her chair, not wanting to interrupt.

"I'm an observer. Most of the time, I have to be forced into action. Sometimes, it's because I'm not adequately informed. And with James, I used to tell him what I wanted, then feel guilty about not being aligned with his wants. I'm not being selfish. At least, I don't think so. But there are days when I feel uncommonly self-absorbed for a twenty-three-year-old."

Clara chuckled, and Elizabeth smiled shyly back at her.

"What do you need to do, then?"

"Combine my love of research with informing others. Become a writer, perhaps. Or a professor." Elizabeth bit her bottom lip, doubt etched in her eyes.

Clara tapped a finger on her lips, contemplating. "None of this has been easy for women. And it still isn't easy in many respects. Barnard was founded partly because Columbia refused to admit women. You'd be in a distinct minority in your classes. It could be quite lonely across the road."

She skimmed the application form, making an occasional comment about a response. She returned it to Elizabeth. "You'll get in with that short essay you wrote. It's fabulous."

Clara started making a list of things Elizabeth needed to consider. Elizabeth groaned internally about the most concerning detail. Class times would conflict with her job at the library.

Her mentor promised to research possible assistantships for her, one less thing for Elizabeth to figure out. She had a long list of quandaries to tackle. The list wasn't insurmountable, just complicated. But most things worth doing were infused with some difficulty or risk.

Was this really worth doing?

Elizabeth leaned against the cool glass. Through the window, she watched a young woman leave the building and raise her face to the sun. She was soaking up the heat and light so she could brighten the world. Elizabeth wanted to feel that way. Again. At the end of the war and the epidemic, she and her friends had spun through the quad, happy to be free from the envelope of sadness and fear that had sealed off the promised joy of young adulthood.

She had a path to that promise. Which meant leaping numerous hurdles. Was she ready? She was. Almost.

****

"I wonder what's going on with James. Do you know?" Lillie looked up from buffing her nails. Elizabeth had just finished quizzing her about a project that dovetailed with one of hers.

"Lillie, honestly." Elizabeth was tired of Lillie's constant prattle about James-this and James-that. Her crush was futile, Elizabeth was certain.

"What?"

Elizabeth now occupied Jean's old office and Lillie had inherited Elizabeth's old cubbyhole. She backed out of Lillie's office and as she began to turn away, she thought better of it.

"Perhaps you needn't worry about things that don't concern you," Elizabeth said sharply.

Lillie's head bounced up. Elizabeth caught Lillie's eye and raised an eyebrow. The young girl's cheeks turned as pink as her jacket and skirt ensemble. She realized she'd been found out, no doubt. Elizabeth had chosen not to exact revenge on Lillie for her little gossip caper with Mrs. Goldberg. That simple power over Lillie made Elizabeth feel old, no longer a carefree co-ed like Lillie.

"And by the way, about James. I saw a dark-haired woman meet him after work last week."

"You did? Why didn't you tell me?"

"I don't gossip."

"You are now," Lillie yelled, her voice pitched higher.

"He held her hand, too."

Elizabeth smirked as she entered her office. She wouldn't tell Lillie that she'd spoken with James just two days before.

Elizabeth had been standing on the library steps, contemplating whether to visit her family before heading to her apartment. Summer days were long, the sun burning the pavement even as it disappeared over a horizon blocked by skyscrapers. She'd welcome a day of rain. The pot of flowers by her door had looked a bit parched as she left for work that morning.

James stopped beside her, jolting her from her thoughts. They gazed together at the lines of cars, horns blaring.

"I can't imagine having to park or drive a car in the city every day. What a bugger that would be." James already had a trek on the subway between here and Brooklyn. It made for a long day.

"Hmm."

"Penny for your thoughts."

She cringed. Did every man employ this dull phrase? He'd asked it before, and George had dug the saying out of the grave, too. But that wasn't her real problem with the saying. She had many thoughts, too many of them. They should be worth more than was offered.

Of course, she didn't feel like saying any of that to James. It would require emotional energy she no longer wished to expend on him. She still liked James, though they'd done well to avoid being alone together in the library. They were merely cordial coworkers.

His businesslike tone tonight prevented her from asking him if he wanted her friendship. She suspected he'd merely say "yes" out of kindness. But he wouldn't mean it, leaving her disappointed when they'd never converse as easily as they once had. She'd always enjoyed his company.

So she smiled and answered his silly query. "I was thinking about dropping by to see my family before I go home."

"Home," James repeated. "I'm glad you've gotten settled. How is Mrs. Goldberg?"

"She and I are getting along swimmingly." She moved down one step and looked up at him over her shoulder. "Good night, James."

"Good night, Elizabeth. Be well."

****

"Hello, Father."

She found him in the back garden, sprawled in one of the blue Westport chairs they'd purchased on last summer's graduation trip to the Adirondack Mountains. Anna had just informed her that their mother was

274

attending some function with wives from her father's firm, so Elizabeth had him all to herself. She left her shoes on the back steps like when she was a little girl. Grass prickled her bare feet.

Henry patted the arm of the neighboring chair, an invitation to sit. The day's blistering sun had left behind an ombre sky, graduating from pale violet above the horizon to velvety navy blue above their heads. The stars were opening their heavenly dance hall. A blanket of warm sticky air encircled her arms and bare legs.

The night's warmth made her desire laziness over problem-solving work. They sat in the garden as fireflies enjoyed the feast offered by Minnie's pink and yellow snapdragons. The last time she remembered being this cozy in the garden was her last tea party. She might have been nine years old.

"Something on your mind?"

She smiled, keeping her gaze on the insects. "How'd you know?"

"Here you are. You've had a lot going on of late, haven't you?"

Elizabeth doubted he understood the emotional tumult that James and George had brought to her life this year. But she wouldn't repeat the soliloquy she'd delivered in Dr. Sporian's office earlier that day.

"I have, yes. I've been in my apartment for three weeks. And I love it."

"What are you worried about?" Henry gazed at her profile.

She bit her bottom lip, a sign of anxiety Henry recognized. His eldest daughter had been biting her lip since she was about four.

She leaned her head back and studied the stars,

searching for familiar dance moves. Taking a deep breath, she let the fresh scent of grass calm her.

"I visited Dr. Sporian at school a while back and again today. I'm considering a masters."

"Go back to school? Hmm. I didn't realize you were eager to turn your life upside down even more."

He chuckled and leaned back in his chair, mirroring her pose.

"What do you think?"

He put his hand gently over hers where it lay on the armrest.

"I want to hear what you think."

And so, she started talking about Clara Sporian.

"When I was a freshman in her British History class, she pulled me aside one day and asked if I wanted to conduct some research for a paper she wanted to publish."

"You've always been an impressive student, dear."

"Initially, I'd been ecstatic, but negative thoughts crept in once I gave it some thought. I lost more sleep over that invitation than any test I'd taken. And then, Jocelyn told me off." Elizabeth quoted her friend, "'You're lucky Sporian picked you for this. It's a real prize for someone as smart as you. Why are you being such a dolt?' That's what Jocelyn said, and I'm forever grateful for her bullying encouragement that day."

Staring up at the stars, Elizabeth reflected on how Dr. Sporian had provided the needed counterbalance to Elizabeth's harping mother. There at Barnard, alongside her favorite professor, Elizabeth blossomed into a confident young academic.

Elizabeth then haltingly listed the challenges Clara had spelled out, plus the excitement of studying something new. She watched him from the corner of her eye, but drew strength from the dancing stars overhead. He occasionally glanced over at her, so she knew he was listening. Keep going, his posture said.

When she finally ran out of words, they both quietly stared at the now-black sky, likely thinking about different things.

"I suppose…" Henry began.

She leaned forward to peer into his face. He smiled at her, and excited goosebumps prickled her arms. He would help her, somehow.

"Let's go into my study. Something to show you."

Henry was standing above her. Mystified by the invitation, she allowed him to pull her up, and they walked to the back stairs, arms linked.

In the study, Henry removed a large, thick envelope from the left desk drawer. He slipped on a pair of glasses. Light reflected off them and the shiny spots on his crown where he was losing his dark brown hair. The only place he'd gone gray were his sideburns, and they sparkled in the light too.

She pulled the same chair up to the side of his walnut desk like she'd done months ago.

"Before I tell you this, you must promise to keep it a secret from your sister. You didn't need this information in college, nor does she."

"I swear." Her promise reminded her of the one she'd extracted from her sister only a few nights ago.

"Thank you. You'll understand after I show you."

She nodded.

"My father, your Gramps, created a trust for you girls before his death. It's payable when you turn twenty-five."

"I won't be twenty-five for nearly two years. What does this mean?"

"It will be a small sum. It's invested in the stock market, so the amount may fluctuate each year. Not nearly enough to pay all your living expenses, but I think it could help you with your college dream, at least."

"You mean I must wait until January 1925 to start?" She'd finally declared a dream to Father, and it was already on hold for two more years. Her heart fluttered with disappointment. The spoiled little girl was stomping her feet inside her head.

"The dream is fine, Elizabeth. But what's wrong with waiting? Columbia's not going anywhere."

"I've already applied for the next term. My heart is so set on starting. I'm champing at the bit."

Henry slid off his glasses and polished them with a handkerchief.

"You'll have to manage on your own if you want to start now. You're that anxious to start studying again?"

Elizabeth nodded, mentally kicking the ground in a huff.

"More thinking to do. I'm so weary of running into walls. This past year has been nothing but." Tears pricked at the corner of her eyes, but she wouldn't cry in front of Father.

"Elizabeth, my dear, you've got a good head on those shoulders. You'll come to the right decision."

She flung her arms around him. "Thank you for listening to all my meandering dreams."

"Well, I suspect you have other dreams you've left unshared." He gave her a knowing glance as he returned the envelope to the drawer.

She had the good grace to blush about all her other

secrets. "I'll be all right, Father. Don't worry about me."

As she walked back to Mrs. G's house, Elizabeth hoped it would turn out she had told her father the truth, because right now she did not know how she was going to graduate school. She wasn't sure exactly what she'd expected to get from her father, but at least he'd listened. And he hadn't dissuaded her from the idea.

Suddenly, her experience of an independent life was less freedom and more constraints. Financial ones.

"Can I do all of this?" she asked out loud as she flopped onto the green brocade couch. She didn't see how.

Chapter Thirty-Two

"I've been accepted!"

Elizabeth nearly jumped out of her chair to hug the Columbia advisor, but she was certain he wouldn't like it. Merely looking at her appeared difficult for him.

The fellow described the program and its requirements. She had qualified to enter that fall term without additional prerequisites, so she could finish in two years. This was exciting and surprising news, but Elizabeth couldn't think of anyone to tell besides Clara Sporian.

Still, she left the Columbia campus with her shoulders bent in and her hands in her skirt's pockets. She was worried that she must complete two classes that met during the day on Monday and Wednesday mornings in the upcoming term. How was she to work at the library every day and complete her courses? This question kept erupting, and she hated having no answer.

Without options, Elizabeth feared her dream was melting away before it had even fully sunk in—the recurring theme of her life over the past weeks.

All the times she'd been called spoiled or felt the jealous glance of a coworker pummeled her. Suddenly, she found herself face to face with struggle.

Well…wasn't this what she wanted? To be an adult, to stand up to all life could dish up, and to win?

Later that evening, she cooked an egg in Mrs. G's

kitchen and sat at the kitchen table alone. Mrs. G was already upstairs getting ready for bed. While she ate, Elizabeth leaned over blank paper and listed everything she needed to say to Mr. Gerold in the morning. It seemed rather impossible. Such foolish dreams, she scolded herself.

Elizabeth slipped out of the apartment early the next morning, skipping breakfast. She prayed that Mr. Gerold would already be at his desk when she arrived. No time to meander through the shimmering park today. Huddled to herself on the subway, she let the swaying train bounce the thoughts in her brain, garbled and disorganized.

The lights were on in the research department. Elizabeth breathed a sigh of relief as she slipped her green cardigan over the back of her chair. Taking a deep breath, she stepped across the hall to Mr. Gerold's door, rapping her knuckles on the frame.

"Good morning, Miss Alter. To what do I owe this early visit?"

"May I come in and sit?"

He waved to the chair. "Certainly. Tell me what's on your mind."

Always to the point, she thought.

"Well, I…" She took a deep breath. "I want to take some courses at Columbia in the fall."

"Really?" Mr. Gerold rubbed a pale earlobe between thumb and finger. "You've been accepted?"

"Yes!" She nodded and grinned. "I can hardly believe it either."

"I suppose congratulations are in order."

"Thank you, Mr. Gerold. Um." She sat taller in the chair. "There is one slight problem."

"What is that, Miss Alter?"

"The two classes I must take this fall term are held two mornings. During my work hours, that is."

"Ah. That is a problem, isn't it? Do you have a proposal to solve your dilemma? I presume that's why you're here?"

Sneaky fellow, calling it her dilemma. Would he not help her at all?

She folded her hands together on her lap. "I do have one idea. Could I work longer hours the other three days?" She watched him considering it and hurried to reassure him. "I realize it's impossible to work forty hours over three days. I can come in after classes, but…"

He looked at her and cocked his head to one side, listening.

She continued, "But sometimes I might need to remain on campus after class to study or write. You know, do school things. I promise to tell you in advance."

Mr. Gerold touched his earlobe again. "I see."

"I know it's not ideal. Not with Jean gone and Lillie in training."

"You've given this a lot of thought."

"Yes, Mr. Gerold, I have. I love working here. I want to stay. Did you know in a few weeks I'll have been working here a year?"

"Indeed? That long?" He chuckled.

Elizabeth laughed along with him.

"Miss Alter, I will sign off on new work hours, but you need to visit Miss Chumley in the personnel department. She can discuss your new pay and such."

Elizabeth kept nodding while he talked, disbelieving she could have this problem resolved so easily and quickly. Was something finally going her way?

"Thank you, Miss Alter, you do fine work. I'm happy to be keeping you here."

"Thank you, Mr. Gerold. I'm happy to stay in this department—it's a good place to work. I will let you know what I find out from…um…Miss Chumley, was it?" Elizabeth stood.

"Yes, right. Very well." He seemed ready for her to leave, perhaps uncomfortable with all her gratitude.

****

"I mean, will I have to train everyone to do this work? Mr. Gerold is making me do it so he doesn't have to. When will I get my research projects finished?" Matilda stopped talking long enough to take two bites of a cookie. Elizabeth had been consoling Matilda for weeks now.

Lillie had proven to be difficult to work around. She was disorganized, distracted, and lazy. Matilda had threatened to poke Lillie's eye out with her nail file, yet Lillie persisted in her immature ways. She was only one year younger than Elizabeth, but their outlooks on life were starkly different.

June 1923 had roared into New York City, impersonating a hot and steamy dragon. The forks of the sun's fire in Central Park pierced the sturdiest city dwellers. Young people bared as much skin as possible to capture the sunshine. People moved slower, the subway air was more stagnant than ever, and taxis grabbed easy fares from the packed sidewalks.

"I got the impression that they hired Lillie to replace Jean. There's no new hiring to replace me, because I'm not leaving."

"I know. Tell me about the courses you'll be taking.

I will be living vicariously through you. My life's duller than dull. I still miss Dan."

Elizabeth patted Matilda's hand. Commiserating with Matilda about work was easy, but she had little to offer to help her friend get through the loss of her beau.

"They're classes about rhetoric and literary analysis."

"Sounds divine," Matilda snorted.

Elizabeth giggled. "And you can laugh at me when I'm complaining about writing my papers in my apartment's faint lamplight and dragging myself to bed in the wee hours. I may go blind."

Matilda laughed. Elizabeth smiled at the quick change in her friend's mood.

What she hadn't shared with Matilda, or anyone else, was the financial straitjacket in which she found herself. Elizabeth hadn't expected to be worrying about money a month after living on her own. And no way was she willing to hear the words "I told you so" from her parents.

A year ago, Elizabeth had been hired by the library at a monthly salary of ninety dollars. She thought she was rich the first time they paid her. Living at home, she'd been able to save at least half of it. Her savings had dropped precipitously in the past months as she prepared the apartment for her new life.

Her wardrobe held a few dresses and skirts she regretted buying earlier in the year. Their cost could have covered the price of the bedding and the bedroom curtains she'd purchased for the apartment. She gave herself a mental tongue-lashing every time she saw them hanging in the wardrobe.

Elizabeth had set aside two hundred dollars for her

upcoming college tuition and the required books, which devastated the remains of her nest egg. She struggled to conceive of a way to pay for her courses for the next year and a half. Gramp's trust money might take some pressure off, but she'd be nearly finished with school by the time those funds came her way.

She truly hated the idea of budgeting for clothes, rent, and food. None of her friends said anything about a budget, but now that she was facing a cut in her pay, every penny she spent pecked at her brain. *How does anyone live on sixty dollars a month?*

This was intolerable.

Elizabeth had to find a way to improve her income. Her conversation last week with Dr. Sporian about an assistantship at Barnard had been a tremendous disappointment. She'd relied on that hope after she learned how much her library salary would be reduced.

"Do you remember Dr. Campbell? He's in the Foreign Languages department."

"Yes, I had a Latin course with him in second year." Elizabeth smiled at the idea of working with that genteel man. His winter coat made of green plaid wool could be spotted across the campus quad.

"His last assistant graduated and moved to St. Louis. I think she was getting married." Clara didn't roll her eyes, but Elizabeth imagined her doing so on the inside. She nodded at her mentor, waiting to hear more.

"You'd have to be available the days his courses meet. At least most of them. He could best describe his preferences."

Elizabeth deflated and bit her bottom lip.

"I plan to keep my library research job. I've already adjusted my hours to accommodate my two courses that begin in August."

"Hmm. Assistantships are plum assignments."

"I agree, and I'd love to work with Dr. Campbell. I just don't think I could afford it."

Clara brushed fingers through the curly blonde tendrils on her forehead. She looked at Elizabeth sympathetically.

"Remember our recent conversation? The one about choices?"

"Yes, I've thought about little else since then." Elizabeth smoothed her hands over her green cotton dress and folded them on her lap.

"Assistantships open up nearly every year as students leave. Give it a year and see where you are then."

"All right. I can wait." Elizabeth smiled weakly at her mentor.

"It's not the end of the world, Elizabeth. I'm sure you'll land on your feet no matter what."

Elizabeth laughed. "That sounds like something my father would say."

Clara picked up a pen and pointed it at Elizabeth. "Well, you're fortunate to have someone like him in your corner."

"Yes, I suppose I am."

Looking back on that conversation, she didn't feel terribly fortunate. Not with her "fortunes" shrinking.

But that night in her apartment, she continued stewing over her budget quandary. While putting shoes and jewelry away, her fingers found the treasured garnet brooch Gramps had given her. As her fingers stroked the cut stones, she pondered how much money it would fetch. Back inside her jewelry box, it winked at her from the black velvet. For a moment, she experienced a pang of shame for thinking of selling it.

Elizabeth had dreamed the night before that she'd been trapped inside a piggybank. She had crawled out through the coin slot. She shook her head and slipped under the covers. She would not cry about this problem. Her bottom lip was already sore from biting it nervously morning, noon, and night. She didn't need blotchy cheeks and red eyes, too.

How could she make more money? Whatever could she do that someone would pay her for?

****

One Saturday night in late July, Elizabeth and Jocelyn ventured to Jasper Hall to see a new band. William had worked late that day and begged off, leaving Jocelyn without a dance partner. The two friends decided they would go anyway and dance together like they'd been doing for years.

Halfway into the evening, they were taking a breather when Mr. Bellamy walked by their seats and nodded a greeting.

"Jeepers! I just had a wonderful idea," Elizabeth exclaimed, clapping her hands in excitement.

Jocelyn raised her eyebrows, unaccustomed to this kind of outburst from her friend.

"Whatever's going on?"

"All right. So, I've been keeping a bit of a secret, and I may have found a way to fix my problem."

"Now you have my attention. Secret? Problem?" Jocelyn leaned forward.

"Let me ask you, do you ever worry about money?" Elizabeth bit her lip, concerned about asking such a personal question.

"All the time!"

"I'm so embarrassed, but I do too." Elizabeth looked straight at her friend.

"Really? I just thought you had Minnie and Henry around the corner."

"Absolutely not. The only real help I got when I moved was using Father's car to transport things, and a piece of furniture from the guest room."

"Well, what's this mystery idea about? I'm all ears." Jocelyn cupped her right hand around her ear and smiled encouragingly.

"I can teach dancing!"

"Teach…dancing." Jocelyn frowned. "I'm confused."

"To make money! I can give dance lessons."

"Oh. You want that manager to hire you for real pay this time?" She pointed toward Mr. Bellamy's departing back.

"No, no, no. But would a dance studio hire me?" Elizabeth's face filled with hope and expectation.

"They'd be crazy not to hire you! You're the best dancer I know!"

"But who would 'they' be? The dance studio where I took lessons as a young girl moved. My idea has fifty holes in it." Elizabeth frowned. She rested her chin on her hand and stared across the dance floor.

"Oh, come on. You will figure this out. I know you."

"If you see a place, you'll tell me immediately, right?" Elizabeth grabbed Jocelyn's hand.

"Naturally. And I will start paying attention when I'm out. I promise."

"Thank you for listening to my tale of woe. Let's dance." Elizabeth stood and held out her hand.

They glided to the edge of the dance floor and started moving to the music. They laughed and whooped along with the other dancers, but inside Elizabeth's head, ideas and worries were tumbling.

Chapter Thirty-Three

Several days a week, Elizabeth braved the August heat to search nearby blocks for dance studios. She ate her lunch while she wandered busy sidewalks looking for a second job. She'd begun doubting that teaching dance was in her future, and she'd have to regroup with a new money-making scheme.

Elizabeth searched newspaper advertisements for dance lessons with minimal success. She excitedly visited one such studio after work. The glass windows were filthy. A tattered sign hung over the door: FoxTrot Studios. Silly name, she thought. Wrinkling her nose, she muttered, "I'm not that desperate."

Jocelyn kept her promise to be on the lookout. Two weeks after their dance date at Jasper Hall, she told Elizabeth about a dance studio three blocks from her rooming house. Jocelyn had passed it nearly every day on the way between the house and her work. She had never noticed it before.

Elizabeth stood on the sidewalk and studied the painted windows. She couldn't see inside because they were solid black with blue-and-white lettering spelling out the name Pirouette Dance Studio in fanciful letters. The curlicues reminded her of George's truck lettering. A woman and a little girl dressed in a black leotard and white tights exited the building. The girl chattered while she skipped beside her mother. She bit her lip and turned away. She walked a block toward Jocelyn's place, thinking she'd drop by and surprise her this Saturday morning.

She was stalling. Doubt crowded her mind. Her heart raced with fears about teaching a class. Could she manage it? Did she have the patience to teach fidgety five-year-old girls? She hadn't taught dancing, not really, but a recent dream had been about her strutting around a mirrored room showing adult students the two-step.

Still chewing on her bottom lip, she spun around and walked up to the studio door. Music from an out-of-tune piano reached her ears. Taking a deep breath, Elizabeth pulled on the door handle and walked in.

She was greeted by the familiar smells from her childhood dance classes: the mingled scents of waxed wood floors, mothers' perfumes, and sweat. It made her smile, and her stomach stopped its clenching. However, the room she found herself in was empty. An old table a few feet from the door held a day-old newspaper.

The sound of the piano had stopped. Then she heard two female voices on the other side of the wall.

"Hello?" she called out, walking closer to the doorway across the room. She turned quickly and inspected herself in the wall of mirrors on the opposite wall. She'd dressed in a knee-length yellow cotton dress with white piping around its collar and belt.

The voices quieted, and footsteps sounded in the other room. The clicking of metal taps on wood floors brought another flood of memories. A tall, thin woman stopped in the opening, framed by the doorway like a Degas painting. Soft pink and gray tulle floated between her waist and her knees. She was not the tap dancer

Elizabeth had heard. This woman's feet were encased in pink satin shoes, the boxed toes lightly scuffed with dust.

"Yes?" she asked imperiously, as though visitors were rare.

"Hello. I…" Elizabeth stammered, having rehearsed nothing in the way of an introduction.

The woman's dark eyebrows soared up toward her hairline, a silky cap of dark hair ending in a bun at her crown. It was a youthful choice, rather than tucking hair in at the nape of her neck like Elizabeth's mother often did. She wasn't old, but she wasn't as young as Elizabeth. Maybe she was her mother's age?

"I'm Elizabeth Alter." She reached out to shake the woman's hand, who took it tentatively. "How do you do?"

"I am well. To what do I owe the pleasure?" She studied Elizabeth carefully.

"I'm looking for a teaching position. I have been dancing since I was four years old, so for almost twenty years!" Elizabeth smiled enthusiastically at the lady standing stiffly in the doorway.

"I see. What do you teach?"

"Oh, I haven't, I mean… Well, I taught a young man the foxtrot, the waltz, the shimmy, a few more."

"This was a boyfriend?" The woman's face filled with suspicion.

"Oh no. Actually, the owner of Jasper Hall asked me to do two dance demonstrations after he saw me giving my friend lessons on the dance floor. We did them for crowds of dancers."

Elizabeth couldn't look at the woman, who was still standing like a dance model. She glanced past the woman into the next room, which remained empty and silent.

"I see. Quite interesting," the woman said, but she didn't sound intrigued at all.

"I'm sorry, but I don't know your name." Elizabeth gave her a meek smile.

"Madame Moreau." She swiveled around and moved into the adjoining room. "Come."

Elizabeth took another deep breath and followed her through the doorway. She hadn't been tossed out yet.

"Adrienne?" Madame Moreau called out toward a folding screen painted with the same colors as the exterior windows.

"Yes, Mama?" A young girl, perhaps fifteen, came from around the screen, sandwich in hand.

"Put on your ballet slippers."

Madame Moreau looked Elizabeth up and down, even more slowly than the first time.

"You know barre routine?" Madame rolled her r's and Elizabeth wanted to hug herself with excitement.

"Yes. Um, I may have forgotten one or two." Elizabeth felt moisture forming under her arms.

Adrienne walked in and pointed at Elizabeth. "Who's she?"

"Maybe a new teacher. Do what she says."

Elizabeth's heart thudded. A wave of nausea coursed up to thicken her throat.

"*Bonjour, mademoiselle.* Shall we go to the barre?" Elizabeth walked stiffly to the wall-mounted barre.

Adrienne looked curiously at her would-be teacher as she stood at the barre.

"First position." Elizabeth mustered a confident tone.

The two dancers placed their heels together, toes pointing away from each other. They rounded their arms in front of their waists, fingers pointed.

"*Plié*." Elizabeth bent her knees and watched her young pupil. "Very nice, Adrienne."

Adrienne rolled her eyes.

Madame cleared her throat.

Elizabeth decided that was meant for Adrienne, so she continued.

"Second position."

"That's enough. Show me the foxtrot. Adrienne, you be the woman."

Adrienne giggled.

Moving away from the barre, the young girl held out her arms obediently.

Before beginning to dance, Elizabeth described the dance and its movements as if she were teaching a class. It was exactly how she'd taught James.

And then she led Madame's daughter through the steps.

After they stopped, Elizabeth looked expectantly at Madame Moreau.

"Not bad." Madame Moreau tilted her head, studying Elizabeth, who remained poised like a dancer in the middle of the room.

"Mama, may I go?" Adrienne whined.

"*Vas-y*," Madame said in French, waving her daughter to go. The girl ran back behind the screen where she'd come from. Adrienne hummed the tune Elizabeth had heard earlier on the piano.

"Come. Sit." Madame pulled two chairs away from the wall. The legs scraping across the floor echoed through the empty room.

"You want to teach in a room like this?" She waved dismissively at their surroundings.

Bravely, Elizabeth responded with a question of her own: "What kinds of classes and students would you consider for me?"

"That I must think about. I am the only teacher here. Another teacher could expand my offerings. It is a good time." Madame Moreau rested her chin on a hand, thoughtful. "You have not taught little ones, no?"

Elizabeth shook her head, feeling her chances fading.

"I have only one adult class. They are a bit hopeless." Madame pouted. "I should not say that. But I can let you have a try with them."

"All right. I'm willing to help with them. When is the class?"

"Tuesday night. Seven o'clock. It is one-hour lesson." Madame Moreau stood and walked over to a schedule stuck to the dividing screen. "They are learning waltz three days away. Will you be ready?"

"Yes!" Elizabeth stood quickly and walked over to the paper her new employer was examining. "It's not very full. Is this a slow time?"

"Summer is never good." Furrows appeared between her eyes. "This summer…terrible."

"Do you advertise your school?" Elizabeth kept her eyes on the paper, not daring to look at Madame Moreau.

"How? I do not know how. I depend on students to bring others."

"At the dance halls?"

"Interesting."

"What time shall I be here Tuesday evening, Madame Moreau?"

"Half hour early. We can discuss class then."

"I will see you Tuesday. I'm looking forward to it."

"Wait, we did not discuss money. I cannot pay much."

Elizabeth's heart sank. What had possessed her to agree to this without knowing the financial part?

"I will pay you one third of each student's payment. They pay ten cents per lesson. Your class on Tuesday has ten students, so thirty cents each week."

Elizabeth groaned inside. She'd added just over one dollar to her monthly income. A quick calculation told her that by avoiding the subway after work, she'd spend no money coming here, and two cents riding home.

"When can I add another class?"

Madame Moreau held up her hand and shepherded Elizabeth toward the door. "No rush. We will see how you do, first."

Elizabeth pulled open the door and stepped into the bright sunshine. Her stomach growled, a reminder she still had to eat every day, regardless of her scrimping and saving.

****

The opportunities to linger in her bed on the weekends or enjoy Mrs. Goldberg's cooking at dinner were fast disappearing. Mrs. Goldberg was sweet to her, and Elizabeth was grateful to her landlady. Mrs. G expected little from Elizabeth, which was the best part of her role as tenant.

Mrs. G didn't pry, give advice, or expect Elizabeth to dine with her every night. But Sunday night had become "their" night together almost immediately after she moved in. Elizabeth set the kitchen table while Mrs. G talked about gardening, family, and tried to explain how she cooked certain foods. Though bone-tired, Elizabeth behaved like a sponge, soaking it all in.

"Mrs. Goldberg—"

"I told you to call me Maggie."

"All right—Maggie, I must thank you for cooking dinner most nights. I'd starve otherwise."

Elizabeth didn't add that she'd kicked herself numerous times for not having an apartment with its own kitchen. Still, gratitude filled her heart that she'd found this basement apartment with the sweetest landlady in the world.

"I have to eat, too," Mrs. Goldberg replied every time.

"But…I should contribute more."

"My dear, I shall teach you to cook. Maybe one Saturday or Sunday each month? Real lessons, not you just watching me on Sunday nights."

"Um, I suppose."

"Don't you want to cook for a husband one day, dear?"

Elizabeth laughed.

"Do I need to add cooking to my dance card? Hmm…" Elizabeth grinned at Mrs. G, who had given up asking her about a prospective beau.

"Elizabeth, you buy butter, eggs, all the time. And then I don't have to. I appreciate you, too, you know." She pointed her knife for emphasis. "Now, make yourself useful and slice that bread you brought home yesterday."

****

Elizabeth stretched herself awake on the couch. The clock was ticking toward midnight. She'd been falling asleep here so many nights.

She worked late at the library on Tuesdays so she could get ahead on projects before classes began and her hours were reduced. Then she walked ten blocks to her evening adult dance class.

This week, Elizabeth had graduated her first set of adult students at Pirouette Dance Studio and started a new series of dance lessons. Though a few didn't sign up for more when summer ended, others brought friends and increased the class enrollment to fifteen. She had saved every penny of Madame's payment for that first class, since she was still putting in her full hours at the library.

Was she exhausted on Tuesday nights? Yes. Some evenings, it was all she could do to keep her eyes open long enough to hop off the train and walk the few blocks home. But she also found teaching dance invigorating. The smile on a student's face when they mastered a step was as intoxicating as that Sidecar drink she'd first tasted at George's band performance in May.

A new dance class started tomorrow. She was too nervous to eat breakfast. Meeting a dozen five- and six-year-olds would make the strongest man—or woman—quake in their boots.

When she'd wanted to move into an apartment, she had envisioned a life of quiet evenings, lone dinners, coming and going as she pleased. She hadn't expected to be exhausted most days. How much more tired would she be with two evening dance classes?

The demands of her graduate courses remained a mystery, but she'd know next week. How many nights would she be up reading and writing while the moon passed overhead?

She wouldn't have believed anyone who told her at the start of 1923 that she'd be living in an apartment, accepted to graduate school, and working two jobs. Now, with two-thirds of the year gone, she was astonished to see her independent life was working out fine.

Perhaps "fine" was an inaccurate assessment of her entire life. She was managing because she was organized enough to keep track of her daily life and the demands of her library projects. She loved teaching dancing, but it was more exhausting than she could ever have imagined.

Financially, she was barely getting by. On the days she couldn't afford to take the subway, she kicked herself for taking more than one class at Columbia.

She had nothing left to sell. She'd never purchased the second wardrobe she once needed, because with Jocelyn's help she'd sold some of her clothing to a secondhand shop. She'd gotten pennies against their real worth, but since Elizabeth had no room for them anyway, she had made the hard choice.

Chapter Thirty-Four

The Legacy Quintet played in Boston to ring in the new year 1924. Elizabeth hadn't seen George since his May visit to The Brisbane, but she kept up with his band's schedule, mostly through Gran. He'd surprised her with a note of thanks last June. He'd been so happy, he said, that she brought Anna and her friends to see the band perform.

The new year felt momentous for her. For the first time in her life, she began a year on her own. Elizabeth could see more clearly the path before her.

Her studies were going well, and the isolation that Clara had said she might experience at Columbia had not manifested itself. She made friends with classmates, both female and male.

"Friend, why won't you go out with any of your classmates? That Jonathan fellow is gorgeous. I wonder if he dances."

"First of all, I typically plead an obligation to my schoolwork."

Jocelyn guffawed. "Oh, I see."

"When's the last time we went dancing, Jocelyn?"

"Me? I went last weekend. You? I can't remember."

"Precisely. I am busy and bone-tired. And…the last time I went dancing with you and William was in November. I remember because—"

"It's February now. Lenin died last month, so don't

you think it's time to pull out your dancing shoes?"

"I don't know what that has to do with the price of tea in Chi—"

Elizabeth stopped herself, reminded of James using that expression. Had it really been more than a year since they braved the cold for lunch and dance practice?

Jocelyn snapped her fingers in Elizabeth's face. They were sitting across from each other at a deli near Jocelyn's rooming house. The clatter of dishes filled her ears while she gently swept the memories away.

"All right. Next Saturday? I don't have a ballet class to teach that morning. I won't feel so rushed and tired."

Jocelyn rubbed her hands together. "Hooray! Elizabeth returns to the land of the living. Or dancing, that is."

****

George and the band showed up in New York the following December.

Elizabeth hadn't seen him in over a year. The last note she'd received had come from New Orleans in August.

He found her at the library again. He didn't come bearing show tickets this time, but an invitation to dinner. Just the two of them. They had a lot of catching up to do.

"Last year, I saw this short film, *Running Wild*. And there's a dance. It's called the Charleston."

She hummed a few bars.

"Ah, yeah. 'Old Fashioned Love.' I know it."

"At the dance school where I work, we… I mean, Madame Moreau is overwhelmed by the demand to learn it. We barely know it ourselves."

"Hey."

"Hey," Elizabeth mimicked him.

"Let's go to Harlem tomorrow night."

"No. What? We cannot go there. It's just not…done."

George smiled and pointed a finger at her.

"I have connections."

Elizabeth reached for her glass of water, shaking her head.

"Yes, I do, Elizabeth. Let me see to it. You need to witness this dance there."

Elizabeth focused on her favorite crispy pork. She couldn't understand his bravado.

George left her on the sidewalk in front of Mrs. G's house. She pointed out the private entrance, though it was hard to see in the dark. He waited while she let herself inside and turned on a light. Returning to the doorway, she gave him a quick wave.

"Good night, Stick."

She giggled and shut the door.

True to his word, George turned up at Mrs. G's the next night to take Elizabeth dancing. And he had a magnificent surprise. Fortunately, she hadn't gotten rid of all her best clothes. She had chosen the wine dress that looked like a fluted column. Jet earrings dangled from her earlobes. Her headband was silver and black with a beaded flower just above her right eyebrow. George whistled when she opened her apartment door.

The Cotton Club had opened a year earlier in Harlem. It was a whites-only club with mostly black entertainment. Fletcher Henderson, the bandleader, was from the South, like George. He gave George a salute when they walked in. Elizabeth remained mute for the first hour in the club. Smitten by anything architectural, she took in the plantation-themed décor with open curiosity. George just grinned at her while she surreptitiously pointed at things on the wall.

George shook his head when she started taking notes about the Charleston as it was being performed. The program they'd been handed at the door was unreadable after she was finished scribbling on it.

"George, you've just raised my estimation with Madame Moreau beyond measure!"

He laughed and signaled to a waiter, who refilled their wineglasses.

"This is an amazing place."

"You've been here before?" Elizabeth's voice squeaked with surprise.

"Never been. And very happy to see it with you. Through your eyes." He raised his wineglass and clinked it against hers.

"Thank you, thank you for this. I'm… I don't know what I am! Over the moon!"

George adjusted his gray jacket and leaned closer to her. "This is real nice. Seeing you happy. You deserve it."

They sat close but not touching, facing the stage. She knew they made a handsome couple, tall and slim, both dark-haired. She watched him from beneath her eyelashes, enjoying the music. His foot kept rhythm.

"Let's dance."

George took her hand, and they spent the rest of the night on the dance floor. Elizabeth would never forget the music, the lights, the pulsing crowd. And George's face, smiling at her like it was the best night of his life.

Epilogue

August 1927, New York City

Her footsteps clicked across the familiar black-and-white tile floor in Barnard's Milbank Hall. She knocked softly on her colleague's doorjamb so as not to startle her. Clara looked up, pen poised above the research paper they'd discussed the day before. The next project would be a collaborative one, and they were excited about the chance to work together.

"How'd it go?" Clara pushed her glasses up into her frothy blonde hair. The silver frames were lost immediately amidst the new streaks of silver that caught light from the window behind her.

"It was fine. Well, at least I think so." Elizabeth smirked. She walked to the window and leaned her elbows on it. It had become a familiar debating spot for her over the past three years, first while she was a graduate student, and then when she began working at Barnard.

Barnard had just employed her as an English professor. Today, she taught her first composition class filled with freshman women. When she'd surveyed the room from an oversized podium, she saw children. So young, a little slouchy in their seats, not nearly as curious as they should be. She was momentarily disappointed until she found someone like her freshman self on the

304

second-to-last row.

Times were changing, but some things didn't change. She reminded herself not to be too hard on these students who had the same questions about life as she'd had. Her hope this year was to find a young woman like herself to challenge and encourage as Clara had done with her.

She turned her back to the window and smiled at Clara. "I saw a girl near the back who looked a bit like me. I hope I can be as good a guide to her as you've been to me. I mean that with all my heart."

"We danced a bit ourselves when you were a young student. You needed to grow. I also had to grow as a professor. We can never predict the future, but I'm sure you will have an impact. You have an inspiring story."

Elizabeth laughed. "I have much learning to do! My first class today taught me that."

She sat down in her usual chair, and they discussed teaching and students. Their conversation took them deep into the afternoon, until Elizabeth looked at the clock on Clara's wall and gasped, "Oh, I have to meet my sister for dinner!" As she gathered her bag and her books, one slipped to the floor. She resembled a scrambling freshman herself.

"That reminds me, I have something for you."

Elizabeth stood up, the errant book still on the floor.

Clara's hand came out from under her desk, holding an old leather satchel. "For your papers."

"Oh, it's lovely. But I couldn't—it's too much!" She blushed, moved by Clara's generosity.

Clara ran her hand over it and said, "It was my grandfather's. But he had several of these, and I already use one. I had this in a closet, and you need it. There's nothing else to say."

Elizabeth fiddled with the heavy leather straps that ran down each side of the brass clasp. "I can't believe it. It's so professional."

"You'll look like you've been doing this a while." Clara grinned at her. "Well, except for that youthful skin and trim figure."

"I can't wait to fill this with pencils and paper. And books!"

"Wait till you have several sets of papers to grade. You'll hate carrying that heavy thing then."

She smoothed her hand over the leather. "Thank you, Clara. This is a wonderful gift. It's perfect."

"I can't think of anyone else I'd rather give it to."

"My sister will be envious. Speaking of, I better get moving. I'm catching up with my sister and her fellow."

"You have a nice night, then. If I don't see you tomorrow, stop in before the week's over and report how your classes have gone. We can trade notes."

Elizabeth gave her a brief salute and stepped out into the corridor. She looked down at the satchel and sighed happily. Her steps down the main staircase felt nothing like her steps in the past. Pride and a sense of belonging welled inside her.

Had she arrived? It felt like it, just a little.

****

Because she'd left campus later than planned, she arrived at her favorite Chinese restaurant, Wung Lu's, a bit damp with perspiration. As August ended, it was finally cooling off, but the city air was still thick with steamy humidity. Elizabeth was thankful to be first to arrive so she could apply a hanky to her face.

She was perusing the menu when Anna and Charles

arrived. They burst through the door, bringing with them the sound of the traffic outside. Anna was laughing up at her beau of four years. Charles was the funny one; he loved telling jokes. He still loved dancing, too. They tried to get out into the city with the group at least once a month.

Jocelyn had finally quit playing the field and dated only William these days, though marriage didn't appear on the horizon yet. They still came along for the dancing.

Anna had finally graduated from Barnard, though it took her an extra year. Their parents and the college were quite ready for her to figure it out and move on. She had a job in an insurance office. Charles had been employed by Lord and Taylor for over six years.

"Dinner's on me tonight," Charles announced.

The sisters stared at him. Elizabeth murmured dissent as Charles kept talking.

"I got a promotion today."

"Charles, that's marvelous!" squealed Anna. "Do tell."

"I'm now manager of the shoe department. And handbags and all those other accessories." He waved it off as if he didn't understand a woman's need for such things.

"That's quite a coup, Charles!" Elizabeth raised her glass of water to him and said, "Cheers." They all clinked their glasses together and tossed offers of congratulations and cheers to more good luck across the table.

"How was your first day?" Anna put down her menu and leaned toward her sister.

"Oh, just fine, I guess. I was nervous. All those faces staring at me, depending on me and all my wisdom." She rolled her eyes.

"But look at this." She lifted the slim leather satchel onto her lap. "Dr. Sporian gave me a gift. It was her grandfather's. Isn't it wonderful?" She stroked the leather while she talked.

"That's a lovely gift. Very professional," Anna said, reaching across to lift the strap and run her fingers down the soft, tan leather.

"Exactly what I thought, Anna. I'll look like I belong, at the very least." She smiled at her sister.

Charles frowned at her. "Of course you belong."

Her eyes got wet. So much kindness today.

The waitress showed up to take their orders, the same things they always requested. Some ruts were delicious ones.

As soon as the tiny waitress turned to leave, Anna licked her lips, ready to ask something. Something embarrassing or personal, Elizabeth thought.

"So…have you heard from George?" Anna wiggled her eyebrows.

Charles pointed at Anna and looked helplessly at Elizabeth. "I told her to leave you alone."

"What? She's my sister!" Anna bumped against Charles's side, grinning.

"I can ask you anything, right?" Anna looked at Elizabeth for confirmation.

"Anything? As we get older, the limits grow, you know. Some things are none of the other's business. But—"

Anna sighed loudly and fell back against the seat. She cast a glance at Charles for help. He was focused on turning his water glass in circles on the table.

Elizabeth took a sip of water and set the glass down.

"Yes, I've heard from George. I received a letter two days ago. He's fine."

"Saturday? You got it Saturday and didn't tell me when we were out dancing?" Anna whined.

"And there's that limit you just bumped up against. Honestly, Anna. Can't a grown woman have a secret or two?" Elizabeth gave her sister a stern look, then smiled.

"All right, but you told me an awful lot when he was here in April! Like the walk in Central Park, the kiss under—"

Elizabeth cleared her throat.

Charles laughed out loud and put his arm around Anna, pulling her in close. "Hey, she already told me. Your secrets are front page news, didn't you know?"

Elizabeth shook out a white cloth napkin and put it on her lap as the waitress headed their way with a loaded tray. "Oh, I understand my sister." She pointed a fork in her sister's direction and said, "I'm just hoping she learns as she grows older. Ha! A hopeless dream."

Anna scooped rice and crispy pork onto her plate, all the while peppering Elizabeth with questions. "What did George say? When's he coming back to New York? Think he'll stay longer to romance you?"

"Anna!" Elizabeth nearly choked on a mouthful of rice.

"Just give up, Elizabeth." Charles chuckled.

"All right, all right. New subject." Anna took a sip of water.

"Sounds good to me." Elizabeth smirked at the couple sitting across from her.

"Madame Moreau."

"What about her?" Elizabeth's eyebrows rose in curiosity.

"When're you going to tell her you're quitting? After your present classes end?"

"Why would I leave?" Elizabeth's voice pitched higher.

"You're a professor now! You can't—"

Elizabeth put down her fork and glared at Anna. "Can't what?"

Anna chuckled and held up a hand in surrender. "You're right, you're right. No one should tell you, Elizabeth, that you can't do something!"

"Don't forget it."

"Do you really need the money?"

"You really are nosey, young lady. Hm, the money. Perhaps I should finally tell you that there's very little money in the dance world." Elizabeth shook her head and rolled her eyes.

Anna's mouth opened and snapped shut.

"Perhaps you've noticed that I haven't worn a new dress in years." Elizabeth held out her left arm and lifted the sleeve. "Look at this cuff. See that? Mrs. G taught me how to repair the tear."

"But I thought you took the job four years ago for more money!" Anna looked at her sister in disbelief.

"I did. I knew the more students I had, the more money I'd make. But I learned something." She chuckled. "There are only so many hours in a day, and nights in the week."

Anna and Charles glanced at each other.

"I *need* to teach dancing, and that's the truth. I love doing it." Elizabeth's eyes prickled again with unbidden tears.

Anna placed a hand over her sister's. "I understand. Honestly, I do."

Elizabeth nodded. She didn't mention the money from Gramps' trust fund because that was a secret until Anna turned twenty-five next year.

Though barely fifty dollars a year, Elizabeth had set it aside for a true rainy day, not for paying for college, taxicab rides, or dinners out.

She'd become so disciplined about money, she didn't recognize herself. And her independence was tepid, at best. She lived in a basement and didn't have a kitchen or bathtub of her own. She found herself buried in compromise. Still, she was on her own, out from her mother's eye.

The trio parted on the sidewalk after a long dinner, notable for its camaraderie, joy, and laughter. The sisters could always share a "do you remember" story from their childhoods, which Charles always found amusing. Minnie stories were everyone's favorites.

As they started up the street together, Elizabeth announced, "I'm catching a taxi tonight. I'm exhausted." Her fortunes may have improved slightly since Barnard hired her, but hopping in a taxicab was still a splurge.

A dozen eggs cost nearly a dollar! When Elizabeth was in college, that had equated to half a day's wages. She ate a lot of them, even though Mrs. G had introduced her to baking and given her many lessons in roasting vegetables and carving a chicken. Elizabeth couldn't imagine when she'd ever roast anything.

Elizabeth was a disastrous baker, burning at least one pan of cookies every time she tried. For now, she baked on the rare occasions George and his band came through town, insisting they all needed to eat something homecooked.

A taxicab pulled up beside her. She pulled open the

door and slid in. "Twenty-Three West Eighty-Seventh Street, please."

She brushed back her hair and closed her eyes. It had been a good first day as a college professor. Telling George about it would have been icing on the cake.

George's most recent letter, postmarked Chicago, had been brief, as usual. He'd taken to sending her a note when the quintet arrived in a new city. His notes usually filled her in on any band member news. Sometimes he included descriptions of the clubs that hired them; he knew how much she loved building interiors.

But George had surprised her with his closing. Quoting Dickinson, he wrote, "So we must keep apart, you there, I here, with just the door ajar."

She did so love Dickinson, but whatever did he mean?

At dinner, Elizabeth had shared nothing about his recent note. Keeping mum might help her sister to mind her own business sooner rather than later. Besides, even though George's notes were mostly impersonal, she enjoyed the delicious secrets she found in the words he meant only for her. Often he signed off, "See ya, Stick," and she'd shake her head with a smile. Such impertinence!

Mrs. G still had no telephone, so Elizabeth's communication back to George was rare. She had invested in telegrams to him, just one after the very first letter he mailed her back in 1923 and another one after she finished her degree at Columbia in May of 1925.

For a brief time, she sent him notes in care of Gran, but George stopped visiting Gran when the quintet began a lengthy tour along the East Coast. As it was, Elizabeth rarely saw George more than three times a year. His band was doing very well, and she didn't begrudge him his terrific success.

Did she love George? Did he love her? When he looked at her, she saw admiration in his dark eyes. She hadn't forgotten his little speech in Gran's dining room. Elizabeth didn't believe, though, that he wasn't right for her.

"I'm not your man," he'd said. Quite possibly, she thought, he could be. They had deep feelings for each other, she was certain. Their one passionate kiss had become a distant pleasant memory. It never shaded their time together. Not for her anyway.

Elizabeth looked forward to his visits, when she had advance notice he was coming. If he showed up unannounced, she happily tossed off all other plans to be with him. Time with George always ended too soon.

Perhaps she was successfully developing a lifelong friendship with a man? She wasn't sure. They still had much to learn about each other, with only scattered moments together for such lessons.

Right now, she loved her independent life more than a man.

Whenever Jocelyn asked about their relationship, Elizabeth answered honestly, "Time will tell."

A word about the author…

Julie is a teacher at heart. She spent most of her career in higher education. But all the while, she read lots of books and dreamed.

She lives in Virginia with her dogs and near her three adult children.

Website: juliejranson.com

Thank you for purchasing
this publication of The Wild Rose Press, Inc.

For questions or more information
contact us at
info@thewildrosepress.com.

The Wild Rose Press, Inc.

Printed in the USA
CPSIA information can be obtained
at www.ICGtesting.com
LVHW020538120624
782946LV00011B/790